Beyond Ragnarok

Carl Alves

End of Days Publishing
Copyright © 2021 Carl Alves
ISBN: 9798412663951

Cover art and design by Kealan Patrick Burke

Created in the United States of America
Worldwide Rights

All rights reserved. No part of this book may be reproduced, scanned, or distributed in any form, including digital, electronic, or mechanical, to include photocopying, recording, or by any information storage and retrieval system, without the prior written consent of the author, except for brief quotes used in reviews.

This book is a work of fiction. All characters, names, places, and incidents are products of the author's imagination or are used fictitiously. Any resemblance to any actual persons, living or dead, events or locales, is entirely coincidental.

DEDICATION

I would like to dedicate *Beyond Ragnarok* to my wife, Michelle, and my two boys, Max and Alex, who always strive to make me a better person.

ACKNOWLEDGEMENT

Thank you to my readers, who continue to support my writing career. A special thanks to Kealan Patrick Burke for the great job he did on the cover, and Erin Zarro, for her help in shaping this novel. An extra special thanks to the Nordic people, who created a rich mythology that still resonates with us today.

Chapter I

John Madison, the CEO of BioInception, scanned the auditorium at his company's headquarters. He addressed the crowd from a podium. "Welcome, my friends. Many of you have travelled a great distance to join me in the eve of our triumph. I want to thank each and every one of you because you believed. You have kept true to the teachings of your forefathers and their forefathers before them. As the world entered the modern era of high technology, it would have been easy for you to give up the old ways, but you have stayed true despite society's temptations. Look around the room. You will be the leaders of our brave new world."

For a moment, the audience took their eyes away from him. Some clapped. Others greeted their fellow followers. People from over thirty countries and six continents had gathered here. They were the chosen, the ones who would carry out his mission. He would share control of the planet with them, but he would leave no doubt who was in charge.

After all, they were mere mortals.

John moved around the room, making eye contact with his followers. "The planet has fallen to imperialists, terrorists, and those who loathe the principles we hold dear. It is time we take it back. I will reshape this world in my image, and you will be my vessels to bring about this change. There will be no need for war since the survivors will follow me alone. There will be no starvation since we will rid the planet of its gross overpopulation in one sweeping effort."

The audience chanted his name. Not his given name of John Madison, but his ancient one that he had been known by for centuries. Their rapture was intoxicating. He could tell them to commit suicide now, and they would obey.

At the moment of his greatest triumph, he had to remain the forceful leader of his fervent and devoted followers. He struggled to control the boyish exuberance he felt, wanting to gloat in vindication before those who had tried to thwart him. For they would soon be dead, and he would rule what was left of this world.

The auditorium was filled with the eager faces of his followers, who had come from every corner of the globe to enact his plan of mass destruction. They looked like junkies needing a fix, and their drug was power. Pure, unabated, and eternal. He would give it to them. His foes had so woefully underestimated him. While they were about to wage a battle for the ages, he would bring this world to its knees.

John opened a briefcase and removed a vial containing clear liquid. He held it up for all to see. "What I hold in my hands is the lifesaving vaccine. While others around you perish in a most gruesome fashion, while society crumbles, you will be immune. Tonight, we will administer it to each of you. In two days, you will count your blessings that you received it."

John pulled back his long blond hair, which had been tied into a ponytail. He wore an Armani suit for this festive occasion. He sat back and watched as they assembled into four lines at the corners of the auditorium that led to four stations where his people administered the vaccine. His followers rolled up their sleeves and spoke in low, eager tones.

After receiving the vaccine, they would get a briefcase containing additional vaccine to bring back with them. They would provide it within the next twenty-four hours to a list of people who had already been informed of their privileged status. Each briefcase included a doomsday device, an engineered mix of the Ebola virus and the avian flu.

John's team of scientists had been working on the deadly compound for the past decade. They had tested and perfected it to the point that it was ready to be unleashed on the planet's population. Its effects on test subjects exceeded his wildest expectations. Everyone who contracted the virus would die violently and painfully, just the way he wanted it. This was his coming out party, and he wanted to make it unforgettable. An airborne virus would have been more effective than Ebola, but the beauty of Ebola was that the deaths it caused would be so horrific that it would create widespread fear and panic. The masterstroke of his team of scientists was to engineer it with the avian flu, combining the deadly properties of both viruses.

Within seventy-two hours, after the necessary people had been vaccinated, the third phase of his plan would commence. For the last two years he had been scouting locations around the globe to unleash his doomsday device. He had chosen spots that would maximize the most damage: airports, stadiums, places of commerce, and popular tourist venues. Within two weeks the virus would reduce the Earth's population to a fraction of what it was now. Within a month, people would become sparse. Within a year, the population would drop to levels it had not seen in a few thousand years. And most importantly, it would be his to rule with an iron hand.

For the last few centuries, the world had eroded to its current abysmal state. It needed to be cleansed. It needed a leader that would restore it and bring about fundamental change that would endure.

The prophecies foretold that the world would be destroyed after the great battle. He was determined to change fate. The survivors would be his chosen ones and those resistant to the virus, which his scientists estimated to be less than one percent of the population.

John stared at the faces of his followers. Oh how the gods had underestimated him.

Chapter II

Magni gritted his teeth as he backed up against the wall of the courtyard. Each time his brother thrust his sword at him, he went into a defensive posture to parry it. On the few occasions when he mounted his own attack, Modi easily deflected the blows. This was about technique, not strength. If it was about strength, then nobody could beat him.

Magni focused on his form, and turned the tide of the duel, making Modi back up.

The brothers had been dueling since dawn. Besides the ongoing threat from the frost and fire giants, Magni had heard disturbing rumors lately that chilled his immortal blood.

The clang of swords echoed loudly. They continued to battle as the momentum shifted between them. Magni practiced different stances and techniques, knowing a real battle would be far more chaotic. Still, the better his skill, the greater chance he would prevail in a life and death struggle.

He took his eyes off Modi when a vision of blonde loveliness blinded him. She was like the sun, holding the world together. Her eyes were a shade of violet blue that mesmerized him. She smiled at him. He never had to question the sincerity of that smile since truth was deeply rooted into her being. It was Freya, his beloved. No matter how often he saw her, she still had the same spellbinding effect on him.

His distraction allowed Modi to knock him down, who stood over Magni and glared. "She'll be your undoing. You can't take your eyes off your opponent in combat."

Magni dusted himself off. He rubbed the bruise on his chin from Modi's latest blow. "If this were a real fight, I assure you I wouldn't."

"It's time to get serious, brother. The end of days is coming. I can feel it in my bones."

Magni sighed. This was all anyone spoke of lately. How could they be so sure after all this time?

He forgot about his conversation with Modi when Freya sauntered toward him. No being in any of the nine worlds could touch her beauty.

Freya put her arms around his neck and kissed him. "If that had been a real fight, you would have been killed."

Modi threw off his gloves. "My point exactly."

"We've been dueling all morning. It was fatigue."

"You can't afford to have fatigue against a fire giant," Freya said. "They won't allow you to recover from a mistake. What good would you do me if you were dead?"

"Very little, I suppose."

"Perhaps you could teach my brother some sorcery," Modi suggested.

"The way I perform magic, I'm just as likely to hurt a friend as a foe," Magni said.

"You perform that little illusion spell where you project another person's image fairly well," Modi said.

"Which is great as a practical joke," Magni said. "Little good it would do me in battle."

Modi stretched his powerful muscles. "To what do we owe this visit? I assume you have a good reason to interrupt."

Magni rolled his eyes. Besides being a great warrior, his brother was also a brilliant poet, writing poems that enchanted the Aesir, yet he lacked tact and could be blunt to the point of being rude.

Freya remained unaffected by his gruff manner. "I come with a message from the Allfather."

Magni's brows rose. Why would Odin send Freya to deliver a message when a valkyrie would have been sufficient for the task?

"And what does Odin want?" Modi asked.

Freya shrugged. "You'll find out when I do. It's important. I could see it in his eyes. He wants the Aesir to meet tonight in Valhalla. No exceptions."

"We will be there," Magni said.

"Good. I'll see you then."

Magni knelt on the ground, staring at Freya as she left, admiring her curves. When she was gone, he turned to Modi. His entire body was tense, just like a feline ready to strike.

"It could only be one thing," Modi said.

"And what's that?"

Modi scowled. "Don't play the fool. The battle."

"Why are you so fixated on Ragnarok?"

Modi frowned. "What a foolish question. Ask Heimdall, or Odin, or father. They've been preparing for this for centuries."

"Odin has been trying to stop this for centuries."

"You know how much I respect Odin, but his best efforts won't stop it from happening." Modi stared into the distance. "The Battle of Ragnarok will define us. And we will be a monumental part of it. That's why we must be ready. We can't lose. If we do, then Loki and the giants will rule not only Asgard, but all of the worlds. We can't let that happen. That's why I've been tough with you."

Magni put his hand on his brother's shoulder. "When the final battle comes, I will fight with the spirit of a thousand warriors. And we will prevail."

***

As Magni and Modi approached Valhalla, they encountered Tyr, who wore his usual surly expression. "This had better be good. I was about to embark on a great hunt."

"I'm sure you won't be disappointed," Modi said.

Tyr was the bravest of the Asgardians, sacrificing his hand when they had bound Fenris, the giant wolf that terrorized the Aesir. He could do no wrong in Magni's viewpoint even if he wasn't the friendliest person Magni knew.

Once inside Valhalla, Magni sought out Freya, who stood next to her brother, Frey. Her eyes appeared troubled as she avoided his gaze. Perhaps she knew more of what Odin intended to say than she had let on.

Magni wore a broad smile when his father appeared. He walked across the room and hugged Thor. Thor patted him in the back, nearly knocked Magni over. They often had tests of strength. Although Thor was reputed to be the strongest of the Asgardians, Magni often bested him in these contests.

"It's good to see you, father." It had been many months since he had last seen Thor, which was not unusual since he was often away on one quest or another.

Thor nodded. "How have you been?"

"Good."

"And your brother?"

"Fretting as usual."

"Understandable given the circumstances. And Freya?"

Magni smiled. "Doing well."

Thor ruffled Magni's hair. "Take care of her."

"I will. So, why have you been away for so long? You never even told me you were leaving."

Thor took a deep breath. "I'll explain later. First, we must listen to Odin."

"So much mystery." Magni meant that to be humorous, but Thor did not smile. Usually, his father was a jovial sort, always being in on the joke.

Other Aesir entered the room. The gatherings at Valhalla were gallant feasts with gourmet food and lavish entertainment. Today, the mood was grim as evidenced by the dour expressions on the faces of his brethren.

After the Aesir entered the great hall, Odin closed the doors. All eyes fell upon the Allfather. He took his usual seat at the head of the table next to his wife, Frigga. Magni was struck by how old they looked.

The others sat at their normal places around the table. Some valkyries were also in attendance. When the time came, they would be called on to fight, and Freya would lead them. They would be a valuable asset against their enemies.

All conversations came to a halt when Odin called for silence. "Thank you for joining me in Valhalla tonight. As you know, or have heard, or speculated, dark times are upon us. For many years I have fought against this. I have done everything I could to prevent it from happening."

Magni's heart ached. Odin had tried so hard to avoid this conflict, but it was impossible to fight fate. What was destined to happen was going to happen, and not even Odin could prevent it.

The Allfather shook his head. "I have tried to make peace. I have made concessions, even though it would have been politic not to, all in an effort to defy the prophecies. Thor and I have been monitoring this for some time, and the signs are undeniable."

Magni glanced at his father, who had a stony face. Unlike Odin, his father welcomed the battle ahead. He was Asgard's greatest warrior, and this would be the ultimate test of his prowess in battle.

Odin looked around the room and made eye-contact with his brethren. "The Battle of Ragnarok is upon us, and I can no longer stop it. This is a battle we can't lose. We can't let Loki gain control of Midgard and the other eight worlds. I shudder to think what kind of darkness Loki and his ilk will create if we fail.

"I ask that each of you remain near Valhalla in the upcoming days and weeks. Prepare yourself for battle. Join in devising strategy to destroy the enemy."

Odin took a deep breath. "I love all of you. My children, my friends, my comrades. Few seated among us will survive this battle. I have lived a long and fruitful life. I cherish the time I've spent with you."

There were nods and somber expressions throughout the room. Even the unflappable Thor wiped tears from his eyes.

"The Battle of Ragnarok will test the strongest and heartiest to their limits. When I look around this room and see your fortitude, I know we will prevail."

The Aesir raised their fists and shouted. Even Magni, who was not prone to such outbursts, joined in. Before long, echoes filled Valhalla with chanting and singing.

Odin waited until the great hall quieted. "It will be time to fight soon enough. Now we will feast."

Magni searched out Freya. If their time was limited, then he wanted to spend as much time as possible with her.

Chapter III

The feast at Valhalla lasted until the morning. Magni held back during the debauchery. Unlike most of the others, he was not in a celebratory mood. He toasted and broke bread with his brethren, but Odin's words remained in his head. This was the last time he would feast with many of his friends and family.

When it was over, he started to return to the hall he shared with Modi, but his father stood before him wearing a melancholy expression. Behind him stood Odin, tall and imposing with his one eye. He had gained eternal wisdom after sacrificing his eye in order to drink from the spring of Mimer. His eye patch was an example of how much Odin had sacrificed for the Aesir. Magni, in turn, would sacrifice anything for Odin.

"We must talk, son. Get your brother. This is important."

"I'll find him." If this was so important, then why hadn't they spoken about it earlier?

He walked through the hall. It did not take him long to find Modi. He often knew where his brother was even when they were miles apart. When Modi wounded himself in battle, Magni felt it. When his brother experienced great joy, Magni's spirits also lifted.

Modi's favorite valkyrie was sitting on his lap. She whispered something in his ear, and he laughed.

When they made eye contact, Magni motioned with his head. He did not need words to communicate with his brother.

"I hope you have good reason to ruin my revelry."

"Father and Odin want to speak to us now."

"Very well." Modi kissed the Valkyrie and strode toward him. "I shall return."

The brothers walked in silence. In the main hall, Odin and Thor waited for them. They then went into Odin's private quarters within Valhalla.

Odin instructed the brothers to sit. He folded his hands. "As you both know, we have been preoccupied with the battle that lies ahead of us. For many of us it will be the final battle. I'm certain that I will not make it out of Ragnarok alive."

Thor nodded. "Nor will I."

Magni felt a twinge in his heart. What they said was true if the prophecies were to be believed, but he had a hard time accepting it.

Odin continued, "I fear we may have been short sighted, an inexcusable mistake. We have only seen Ragnarok, but what lies beyond is of greater importance than the battle itself."

Thor leaned into the table. "Over the last several months, I've been trying to learn what Loki and the giants are scheming. They will stop at nothing to ensure that there are no survivors on our side. They do not merely want to defeat us. They want complete annihilation."

Modi's eyes narrowed. "Then they intend to take Asgard?" One of the nine worlds united by the tree, Ygdrassil, Asgard was the home of the Aesir.

"No," Thor said. "They intend on seizing control of Midgard."

Magni gasped. The Aesir were the guardians of Midgard, a sacred pact made many centuries ago. Throughout the ages, they had intervened to defend Midgard from outside threats, but he had never thought Loki would be one of those threats. Magni could only imagine the havoc Loki could wreak in the world of mortals.

Odin closed his eye. He appeared to be in slumber. When he opened his eye, his face held tight concentration. "As you well know, you two are to survive Ragnarok."

Magni had always wondered if that was a blessing or a curse. He and Modi would survive the battle, but their loved ones would die. Was that worth it?

"But fate isn't a constant thing," Odin said. "It is like the shore of an ocean. The tide rises and falls. Erosion changes the landscape. What you see one day may be different the next. We need more information. That's why we will journey to Yggdrasil."

Yggdrasil was the tree of life. The guardians of Yggdrasil were the Norns, three maidens who were as old as creation. The Norns could see into the future and had decreed many prophecies. Although prophecies were destined to happen, they could be influenced by external factors. Still, whatever the Norns said almost always came to pass. Magni and his brother had only been to Yggdrasil once. It was on that occasion they learned of their special role at Ragnarok.

Thor stood. "We have to go at once. I have already arranged for provisions for the journey."

"What if Loki and the giants attack while we are gone?" Modi asked. "Without us, the Aesir will have no chance. You decreed that we remain in Asgard."

Odin shook his head. "This is too important. We must see the Norns. Tyr will lead in my absence. As for your concern,

Heimdall has assured me that our enemies are not ready to attack. They will be soon, however."

Magni glanced at his brother. "Then let's not waste time."

They left Valhalla, leaving Magni to wonder if the great hall would still stand after Ragnarok. If it did, would there be anyone left to fill it?

They entered a massive chariot pulled by stallions. In the lead was Odin's powerful, eight-legged steed Sleipnir. The stallion was one of Loki's offspring and had made the journey numerous times in the past.

During their travels, Thor told them about his activities for the past several months. Magni was stunned to learn he had journeyed to Niflheim, the underworld, the dominion of Loki's daughter, Hel. To journey there and back must have been a harrowing experience, especially in this time of high tension.

"How did you make it out of there?" Modi asked.

"With great stealth." Thor clutched his mighty hammer, Mjolnir. "And I had to smash a few heads."

Magni stared at his father's deep brown eyes. They looked as if they held all of the world's secrets. "Is it true then? Is Loki in Niflheim?"

Thor shook his head. "However, Hel is preparing the monsters of the underworld. They were in full battle mode."

Modi folded his arms. "Then where's Loki?"

"It bothers me to no end," Odin said. "He's supposed to lead the forces of the underworld against us. I can't imagine he would let others determine the outcome of the battle. He may be my blood-brother, but I know he wants our doom."

For a time, no one spoke. Odin's relationship with Loki had long been a sore spot among the Aesir. They had tolerated him because long ago he had aided Odin, and they had become blood-brothers, a bond even stronger than kin. Loki had always been mischievous, looking to create mayhem, but he had usually been harmless. That all changed when his actions led to the death of Odin's beloved son, Balder. Since then, his behavior had become increasingly treacherous and sinister. He was no longer welcome in Asgard, although his reach was far and wide, and he still managed to create havoc. Magni would give anything to know what Loki was planning.

Sleipnir never tired during the journey. Unfortunately, the rest of the stallions waned, and they had to stop for the evening. While the others pitched a tent and prepared a fire, Modi rode off on Sleipnir. By the time they had pitched the tent and grew a large fire, Modi and the stallion returned with a large boar.

They roasted and ate the bore. Afterward, they drank fine wine, and Modi entertained them with poetry. Magni had always envied his brother's ability with words. Even their father, who was not one for poetry, seemed to be moved tonight. Perhaps he was sentimental because the end was near.

They left early the following morning. The stallions were rested and traveled with blazing speed. By mid-day, they neared Yggdrasil, the separating point from which the first humans had spawned thousands of years ago to populate Midgard.

Dusk was beginning to settle when they reached the giant tree. Magni looked in awe. He could hardly see the top of it, which was thin and wispy. The trunk was thick and course, about fifteen meters wide. Woven into its bark were depictions of great warriors and battle scenes. Magni smiled at the sight of his father striking down a frost giant with Mjolnir. Another had Odin leading the Great Hunt. He glanced at Modi, who appeared to be staring in equal fascination. Under different circumstances, Magni could have spent hours studying the tree's carvings.

As if to remind them of what they came here for, the three Norn sisters, Fate, Being, and Necessity, emerged. Although they were not beautiful by normal standards, each had her own attractiveness. Their faces were serene and eternal. They were older than Odin, as old as time. Regardless of what transpired in the days to come, they would still be there, retaining the memory of what had once been and harboring knowledge of things to come.

Odin and Thor bowed and placed their fists above their hearts. Magni and his brother replicated the gesture. The Norns, in return, curtsied.

Necessity, taller and thinner than the other sisters, was the first to speak. "Allfather Odin, thank you for coming in this time of great distress."

Fate, short and plump, stepped forward. "And, Thor, thank you for bringing your sons. They must know their part in what is to come."

Magni shifted uncomfortably. This attention was new to him. He was one of the least important among the Aesir. Things were taking a dramatic turn, and he and his brother would be front and center on this new stage.

Being grabbed Odin's hand. "Please rest."

Odin shook his head. "We appreciate your kind gesture, but we must do what we came here for and be on our way."

Necessity bowed. "Of course, what you say is true. The Battle of Ragnarok will start in ten days."

Magni took a deep breath. Ten days. That was too soon. He stared at Thor and Odin, and realized they had been preparing for this their whole lives.

Chapter IV

With his feet up on his mahogany desk, John Madison let out a loud laugh. He pressed the intercom button. "Klaus, you have to see this." He chuckled as Klaus walked into his office.

"Yes," Klaus said.

John motioned with his fingers. "Come here. Look at the television screen."

The big German folded his arms. His eyes remained expressionless and his face impassive. It was hard to faze Klaus. He had been a clandestine operative in the German intelligence organization, taking high risk operations around the globe. All along, he had been one of the faithful, one of the silent people who had followed John before his rebirth into this world. He would do anything John asked of him, having already killed dozens of enemies upon his order.

A middle-aged woman appeared on the television screen coughing out blood and bleeding through her orifices. The cameraman kept his distance from her. As her fits became more violent, the cameraman backed further away from her. Four others were dead, lying in a pool of their own blood, on the steps of the state building in Albany, New York. They had been staging a protest to demand an audience with the governor. While waiting, a few of their members had died from the hideous disease that plagued humanity, the one John had unleashed.

"This is beautiful." He glanced at Klaus, who remained expressionless. "Don't you find anything humorous? She was demanding that the governor do something about this disease, and while waiting for him, she bled out and died. Don't you see the delicious irony?"

Klaus shrugged. "The governor of New York is already dead."

He patted Klaus on the back. "Exactly. The whole thing is futile. I still haven't figured out why the governments are pretending some of their more prominent politicians are alive. They can't hide it forever. Can't these people just die with dignity?"

"They're weak and stupid. I would put a bullet in my head before letting the disease take me."

"I know you would." John pointed at the woman on the television screen. "Look at her. She looks like a slaughtered pig." John kept laughing, but Klaus's expression didn't change. He waved the German away. He was a valuable asset, but the man had no sense of humor.

John flipped the channels on his remote control. Many stations had gone off the air. He put on the BBC, which was still broadcasting.

Things were not faring better in Europe. The death, destruction, and chaos was exhilarating to watch. They estimated the death count to be four million in Great Britain alone, surely a conservative estimate. There was mass death in Germany, Spain, and Russia. Martial law had been declared in most countries, something that was hard to enforce since law enforcement officers in those countries were dying as well. Lawlessness plagued major cities. Hamburg was burning to the ground. He had seen footage of the nasty conflagrations.

Human nature was a beautiful thing. As if it was not bad enough that he had unleashed this doomsday virus on the populace, they were destroying themselves. All the better. He wanted the Earth's population to be reduced to a manageable number. There would no longer be vast overcrowding.

The BBC showed the spreading of the disease in Asia, Africa, the Americas, and Australia. There was footage of Antarctica. He made a note in his tablet to send a team to investigate the frozen continent. Although there were no permanent residents in Antarctica, scientists and researchers stayed there. Because of the continent's isolation, they probably had not been infected. They would be a welcome addition to his new society—if they met his demands and accepted him as their leader. He would give them the option of falling in line with him and receiving the vaccine or be exposed to the virus.

He flipped through the channels and frowned after discovering Fox News was no longer broadcasting. What a shame. Although he enjoyed the footage from all of these valiant reporters, Fox News had provided the goriest and most revolting coverage. They had been instrumental in spreading terror and fear. He poured Scotch in his glass and offered a toast to the departed network. May they rest in peace.

Before long, all of the television stations would be off the air with nobody left to operate them. The survivors were desperately hanging on to survival in this disease ravaged world. After a few days with no communication from any television broadcasters, his people would commandeer the current broadcasting networks, and he would address the survivors, a monumental address that would live in the annals of history.

He turned off the television. As tempting as it was to watch this footage, he had work to do.

He took out his laptop. A few days after the pandemonium had ensued, he introduced himself to various world leaders and begun negotiations. He reviewed the detailed notes he made of conversations with them.

His phone rang. There were constant interruptions, making it hard to get any work done. It was his personal assistant, Inga. Besides being efficient at her job, she was a beautiful blonde who was more than eager to please him in whatever way he desired.

He answered the phone. "Yes, Inga."

"It's the president of the United States. He said it's urgent that he speak to you."

John rolled his eyes. "Of course, it's urgent. His country, or what's left of it, is falling apart. His once mighty power base is slipping from his hands. These are dark days for the president. Have some sympathy."

Inga giggled as she transferred the call to him.

"William, to what do I owe the pleasure?" John refused to acknowledge the man's title. As far as he was concerned, there was no longer a United States of America, just as there was no Great Britain, Saudi Arabia, Japan, or any of the old countries. The old world was dead. The new world belonged to him.

"You have to stop this, Madison. You're a madman."

"I'm a madman who holds all the cards."

"People are dying by the thousands."

John sighed. What a silly little man. How had he become the leader of the most powerful nation in Midgard? "Of course people are dying. That was my intent."

"How can you let this happen, you heartless bastard?"

John smiled. "With ease. Actually, I've enjoyed watching the coverage. Haven't you?"

"This is insane."

"Let's get to the heart of the matter. I've given you time to consider my proposal. When will you hand over control of your military weaponry?"

The former president breathed heavily on the other end. John smiled, picturing the man squirming. He had no option, really. The US military had virtually disbanded. There were still skeleton crews of troops in a handful of military bases, but they were struggling just to survive and maintain the peace. They were certainly in no position to strike against him.

"What you're asking for is impossible," the president said.

"Is that so? The way I see it, you have little choice. If you had met my demands earlier, your wife and oldest son would still be alive. I could have given them the life-saving vaccine before they died so horrifically. You still have a chance to save your own hide as well as that of your daughter and youngest son. Can you live with yourself—for however long that lasts—if you let them die in such a gruesome manner? I don't think so. Now give up control of your weapons. It's not like you have any power left. Your military forces have been virtually disbanded."

There was a long pause on the other end of the line. "I need time to think about this."

John laughed. "Time is a luxury you don't have. You're tucked away in a bunker, yet your people are still getting infected. How long will it be before the virus spreads to the remainder of your family? Tick Tock. Time is running out. If you want to live, then you must agree to my demands. Willie, face it. Your country no longer exists. You're the president of nothing. You're the commander in chief but have no one to command. Save yourself while you can. You may think it was noble that the captain of the *Titanic* sunk with his ship, but I think the man was an idiot. If you get infected and die, I'll still get what I want. Your vice-president is dead. The Speaker of the House has gone into hiding. Most of your cabinet is dead."

"How do you know that?"

"I know all. I'm a god. Now, Willie, make the right decision. This is my final offer."

John rolled his eyes. He was already bored with the conversation. He began typing. He had too much to do to get bogged down with this silly little man.

The president said something, but John was no longer paying attention.

"What did you say?"

The president sighed. "I'll do it. I'll give you what you want."

"A wise decision. I'll transfer you to my assistant, Klaus. He'll work out the details of the exchange."

Without a further word, John transferred the president to Klaus. He couldn't bother himself with this negotiation. That's why he surrounded himself with good people. They handled the details. John was a big picture thinker. He had an entire world to run, after all. Fortunately, his intelligence and capabilities far exceeded that of ordinary mortals.

This president was beyond a fool if he thought he would survive. John wanted to remove any symbols of the old power structure. The last thing he wanted was for somebody to rally the survivors.

He walked over to a large map of the old world and put a pin on the United States. One more country down. They would join France, China, Saudi Arabia, and more than a dozen other nations who had surrendered their military infrastructure to him. He rubbed his palms together and smiled. The world was crumbling faster than he thought it would.

His plans were in place. He had people ready to take over the legacy governments after their leaders surrendered power. His team was armed and organized. The survivors would look for guidance in the weeks and months ahead, and he would provide it.

Soon, all broadcasting outlets would be off the air. Then he would address the world and proclaim himself as their savior, the new messiah. He would lead them through this tragedy. His rules would be strict and his penalties harsh, but after all the people had been through, they would more than welcome his firm hand.

John's vision was coming to fruition, and there was nothing that could stop him.

Chapter V

Magni's feet trudged the damp earth. As their small party walked past Yggdrasil, a million thoughts flooded his mind. *Only ten days until the start of Ragnarok.* That left little time to prepare. Time, which normally held little consequence to an immortal, was now a precious and fleeting thing. If Odin was willing to leave Asgard at this time of crisis, then the Norns' message had to be of vital importance.

The dense forest they traveled through changed in color and intensity. The dark, matted woods became light and flowery. Large blossoms appeared out of nowhere. Not only did the sky brighten, but so did the ground. Magni became disoriented. He had to close his eyes to gain his bearings.

Ahead lay the Norns' sanctuary, a large wooden structure carved into the woods surrounding it. It was perfectly camouflaged. If he didn't know what to look for, he would not have seen it.

The three maidens were an extension of nature. Their essence existed in the forests and trees, in fountains and streams, in the dirt and rocks. The nine worlds flowed through them. They were its passive caretakers. As such, they were closely aligned with the Aesir, who ruled the heavens and were the guardians of Midgard, the realm of mortals. Although Odin let the people of Midgard decide their own matters, from time to time he intervened. On those occasions, he usually sent Thor to do his bidding.

Magni stopped suddenly and gasped as Midgard came into view. Modi stared at it wide-eyed. It stood beyond the tall, wooden sanctuary of the Norns, so close that he could reach it by throwing a stone.

He had not been there in centuries. Midgard looked drastically different than it had when he had last seen it. Vast, heavily populated cities sprawled across the landscape. Massive buildings towered to the heavens. Vehicles running in land, air, and sea crowded his view. It was a dizzying sight as the world flashed by in panoramic view in front of him.

"Midgard is so different," Modi muttered.

Magni nodded.

Modi frowned. "Why has it changed so drastically?"

"Progress," Odin replied.

"I'm not sure that's a good thing," Modi said.

"You might be right, but there's little we can do about it. Once, ages ago, we molded Midgard in our image. Now the mortals have molded it into theirs." Thor motioned to the wooden fortress belonging to the Norns. "We have to go."

Fate stood at the entrance and opened a door. It was a peculiar dwelling place. The interior of the fortress matched the exterior. Trees and bushes grew wildly. Plants and flowers sprouted from all corners. The furniture that adorned the rooms was an extension of the flora and shrubbery growing inside.

"Please sit," Necessity said.

Magni sat in front of a large table on a chair that was part of the same wildly grown oak tree that made up the table. He raised his brows as a fox scampered past his feet.

Being placed dark cups in front of them and poured steaming blue tea.

Magni took a swallow of the strange brew. He recoiled at its sweet and spicy taste. He did not find the beverage the least bit appealing but drank because he was thirsty and did not want to offend his hosts.

Fate, who was nearly three heads shorter than Magni, looked up at the brothers. "The fate of the world rests on your capable shoulders."

Magni swallowed hard.

Modi folded his arms and glanced at his brother. "Wonderful."

Fate stepped toward the rear of the room with her two sisters.

"It's time for the prophecy to begin," Being said.

The Norns held hands. They appeared to fall into a trance. Their eyes changed colors. Fate's turned red, Necessity's blue, and Being's black. They hovered off the ground. The air around them turned thin and cool.

Magni felt he had to brace himself or he would float. He waited in quiet anticipation, knowing the next words spoken would alter the course of his life. He glanced at his brother, whose hands were folded tightly.

Necessity was the first to speak, her long, angular jaw jutting forward. Her voice was deep and harsh. "Magni. Modi."

He and his brother snapped to attention.

"Ragnarok will commence in ten days, but it will not be your concern."

A deep frown formed on Magni's face. *Ragnarok is not our concern.* He glanced at Modi, whose face was taught.

This time Being spoke. Her voice was softer than her sister's. "The ultimate victor at Ragnarok has been decided. Much that had been prophesied will not come to pass. The players and their motivations in this ever evolving game have changed."

Magni felt a strong urge to shout questions at the Norns, but Odin gripped his hand and gave him a sharp stare.

Fate's plump face looked motherly as she smiled at them. She folded her thick arms underneath her chest. "The battle is not your concern. What matters is the aftermath. Loki has long seen Ragnarok as a losing proposition. He has made alternate plans."

This was absurd. Magni needed to focus on the Battle of Ragnarok. His father, his people needed him. The Norns had to be wrong. The Battle was the only thing that mattered.

Necessity's serene face darkened. "Loki will survive the Battle of Ragnarok and bring about humanity's darkest days."

Modi's jaw dropped. "What? But how…"

Magni's head throbbed. This did not make any sense. "But Loki is supposed to die at Heimdall's hands. That is what the prophecy revealed all those centuries ago. Loki and Heimdall will fight to the death and each die at the other's hands. That will turn the tide of the battle."

"Fate is not set in stone," Fate said. "It can be molded like a vase. That is what you must come to understand. What has been foretold can change. It was never meant to be static, but more like a river that flows. It is a mistake many have made, but one you must not make."

Modi rubbed his eyes. "We need to know more. How will he bring about humanity's darkest days?"

"He will unleash a plague upon them unlike anything they have ever seen," Being answered. "Perhaps he already has. Time is an amorphous thing to us and is not always linear. Regardless, billions will die."

Magni asked, "What kind of plague will he unleash?"

"That is not known," Being replied.

"How can he possibly unleash a plague?" Modi asked.

Fate patted Modi's shoulder. "You must understand that we don't know the details. We can only see things that are to come, not the mechanism that will put them in place."

Magni leaned back. This was a nightmare. With the Battle of Ragnarok imminent, now they had to worry about this? Thor and Odin remained silent. They would not be around to stop Loki.

"That is why we requested you brothers be brought here," Necessity said. "Magni, Modi, you will survive Ragnarok. You two must stop Loki."

Magni closed his eyes. He had been fully prepared to fight in the battle. Like the rest of the Aesir, he had been preparing for it for centuries, but this new task left him perplexed.

Modi asked a litany of questions. "When will this take place? What can we do to stop Loki? Where can we find him?"

But the Norns could provide no answers, just this vague pronouncement of a nightmarish future which he and his brother had to stop. The Aesir were Midgard's guardians, a vow they swore solemnly several millennia ago.

"We can't help you in your journey," Being said. "Nor can we tell you how to go about it, but after the Battle has completed, you must stop Loki. It may even be too late by then."

Destiny could be a cruel thing. Not only would all of their friends and loved ones die, but they would be saddled with this grim task that they would have to blindly accomplish. But perhaps they could change destiny at the Battle also.

Magni interrupted his brother's stream of questions. "There's no point. If they could help us any further, they would."

Modi had an anguished look. "But we need more information."

"Your skill, talent, intelligence, and resourcefulness will be your guide," Odin said. "This will be a difficult task, but you must finish it."

Thor nodded. "If I could do it myself I would, but my days are numbered. However, if I could pick anyone else to do this, it would be my two sons whom I love and cherish. You may doubt yourselves, but I don't. I know that you are more than equal to this task."

Magni could not be sure if it was the strange light in this darkened room, but he thought there were tears in Thor's eyes. His father never cried.

Thor continued, "You have made me proud to be your father. You are the future. Odin and I are the past. You must guide humanity through these dark days. We will be gone, but we will be with you in spirit always."

Modi hugged his father, and Magni joined them.

Modi pulled back. His face radiated with fierce intensity. "We won't let you down. We're going to stop Loki."

Magni nodded. "But first we're going to win the Battle of Ragnarok. And when I find Loki, I'll kill the bastard."

Chapter VI

Magni had never been so anxious to return to Asgard. The meeting with the Norns created a sense of urgency within him, and the upcoming battle had never felt more real, especially knowing what was to come.

Although he should be concentrating on the battle's aftermath, he seemed incapable of it. He sought council from Odin and Thor, but neither had any suggestions as to what he and his brother would have to do since they knew as little about the situation as he did.

Once they arrived in Asgard, he and Modi decided they would worry about it later and focus on Ragnarok first.

In their absence, Tyr had formulated a war council. They would be meeting later that evening. Although he lacked the combat experience of Tyr and some the other Aesir, he had ideas on what would be effective against their enemy.

He and Modi traveled to Tyr's council located in his hall in the hills west of Valhalla. There were a dozen Aesir and several valkyries present, but his eyes immediately found Freya, who was deep in conversation with her brother, Frey.

Magni waited until they finished speaking before he approached. He gave her a chaste kiss on the lips.

Freya's face was creased with worry. "How was the journey to Yggdrasil?"

Magni shrugged. "What I learned has muddled my thought process."

Freya frowned. "Why?"

Tyr stepped into the room.

There was so much Magni wanted to say, but it would have to wait. He shook his head. "Not now. Meet me tonight."

Freya nodded and then stood by Tyr.

Tyr's physical stature was not overly impressive but his intense demeanor was. He wore a perpetual scowl. He had long, dirty blond hair and a bushy beard. His eyes were a piercing blue, and his lean body was covered with muscle. His most obvious feature was that he only had one arm, something that he never tried to hide. It was that feat of bravery, when he lost his arm to the Fenris Wolf, that had once saved the Aesir. Despite his abnormality, he was the most talented sword fighter Magni had ever seen. When he spoke, Magni felt compelled to listen.

"When the battle starts, we will be significantly outnumbered," Tyr said.

Freya waved her hand. In front of them appeared the flat plains of Asgard. Magni stared closely. It looked remarkably similar to the real thing. Freya had an amazing command of magic, greater than any other in Asgard. She could perform intricate illusions with little effort.

Magni seldom used magic other than a few tricks Freya had taught him. He was a warrior who preferred to use might over finesse. More often than not, his use of magic led to trouble instead of any benefit, so he had learned to distrust it. Although some Aesir like Freya and Odin had skillful use of magic, others, such as his father, completely disdained its use.

"We will be attacked on three fronts," Tyr continued.

With a quick movement of her hands, Freya conjured images of the enemy throughout the battlefield.

"Thrym will be leading his frost giants by sail from the north. Surter will lead the fire giants out of Muspell from the south traveling by land, and Loki will lead the monsters of the underworld by ships from the sea. They will converge near the entrance of Asgard.

"They will attack as one unified force because that is their only chance of defeating us. There's little we can do about the difference in numbers. Each of us will be called upon to perform extraordinary feats of prowess in the battlefield."

Tyr paused while Freya conjured some familiar images that hovered in the air in front of them.

Tyr continued, "The key to winning the battle will be to slay a few prominent members of the opposition."

Introductions were not necessary. All were familiar with them. They included Thrym, the leader of the frost giants. Then there was Garm, the hound of hell, a ferocious beast who guarded the entrance to Niflheim, the underworld. Garm only allowed the wicked to enter and did not allow any to leave unless authorized by Hel, the ruler of the underworld.

In the sea was the Midgard serpent, Jormangandr. The serpent was there most powerful and deadly foe. Jormangandr was so enormous that his body stretched for miles. In Midgard, they once believed that the serpent's body spanned their entire world. Attacking Jormangandr's body was useless. The only way to defeat the serpent was to attack his head, not an easy feat because of the beast's size. Although Magni had full confidence in his fighting skills, he knew the only one capable of killing the serpent was Thor.

Growling in the background was the image of Fenris Wolf. One of Loki's offspring, Fenris Wolf was so immense and dangerous that he made Garm look like a puppy in comparison. Tyr had learned just how dangerous Fenris Wolf was when he had lost his hand when the Aesir had bound the beast. Unfortunately, Fenris Wolf would eventually break free of the chains that bound him, as decreed by prophecy.

Magni scowled at the sight of Surter, the leader of the fire giants. He felt a burning hatred whenever he saw him. After Freya had turned back his advances, Surter had vowed to kill her. He would make it a point to meet Surter in the battlefield. Although it would be important to eliminate Surter for strategic reasons, for Magni it was personal.

Next to Surter was Loki's daughter, Hel. Her face was half dark, half pale. She reigned over the underworld and commanded its monsters. She was a vicious opponent, one not to be underestimated.

Then there was Loki. In the image Freya had conjured of him, he wore his long, blond hair in a ponytail, and had his customary sly grin. Although not physically imposing or renowned for his skill in combat, Loki was the key to victory. He was the mastermind behind the forces opposing the Aesir. Without him there would be no Ragnarok. He had set everything in motion. It all started when his treachery led to the death of Odin's son, Balder. Without Loki, the giants and monsters would be rudderless and would never oppose the Aesir. Apparently, Asgard wasn't enough for him. He wanted to rule Midgard as well.

Tyr folded his arms. "If we kill these seven, the others will fall or flee. You may have heard how things will transpire at the Battle of Ragnarok. Forget about everything you've heard."

Magni frowned. He wondered if Odin had told Tyr about their visit to the Norns.

Tyr continued, "If you find an opportunity, do whatever you can to incapacitate or kill our principle targets. That will turn the battle in our favor. We are fewer, but we are stronger."

Tyr nodded at Freya, who stepped forward. The image of the battlefield and the main participants faded. "I will be leading the valkyries into battle."

Magni glanced at the two valkyries in the back of the room. They were female warriors who had lived their lives in Midgard. After death, they entered Asgard to serve the Aesir and harness their fighting skills for this moment. Their entire existence had been leading to this fight. The way Freya trained them, he had no doubt they would shine.

Freya had a determined look as she resumed speaking. "I will be dividing the valkyries into two groups. One will fight the frost giants coming from the north and the other will engage the fire giants coming from Muspell. Frey will be leading the elves in battle against the giants as well. The Aesir will fight the monsters of the underworld and the principle targets Tyr has named."

Magni listened closely to Freya and Tyr. They had devised a sound strategy. The only problem was that when it came to the actual fighting, it would get chaotic. He had been in skirmishes against giants and monsters before. Nothing ever went as anticipated. A collision as vast as this one would be unwieldy.

When he left the war council, he made up his mind. He would find Surter first and kill the bastard. Then he would set his sights on Loki, and he would slaughter every foe in his path to Surter and Loki.

***

Late that evening, Freya arrived at Magni's home. Magni had stayed up because of his burning desire to see her once more, but he didn't think she would show. Not that he could fault her. Only six days away from the battle, she had her hands full in preparation.

When he took Freya into his arms, he felt her weariness. He took her inside and lowered her onto his bed. She closed her eyes and leaned her head against his massive shoulders.

"It's been a long day," Freya said.

"It has." Magni kissed her. "I'm glad you're here."

"So, tell me what happened when you spoke to the Norns."

Magni took a deep breath and relayed the details of his journey. "This task we have been given bothers me. I don't want to think about it now. Neither does Modi."

Freya stared at him. "You'll have to before long. If the Norns are right, the battle will start in six days."

"If I kill Loki at Ragnarok, I can put an end to whatever he's planning."

"Don't you think others plan on doing the same thing?" Freya asked. "For ages, Heimdall has wanted nothing more than to kill Loki at the final battle. The Norns' prophecy can only mean that Loki will survive."

Everything she said was true. A sense of despair overwhelmed him, and he turned away.

Freya grabbed his hand. "What is it?"

Magni took a deep breath. "The fact that Modi and I have been given the task of stopping Loki tells me that everyone else is going to die."

He looked up at Freya, who wore a deep frown. Magni stood, folded his arms, and paced around the room. "I'm not going to fool myself into believing that they would choose us if there were better options."

"You underestimate yourself."

Magni shook his head. "This task is of monumental importance. This means that Odin and Thor will die at the Battle of Ragnarok. It also means that Tyr and Heimdall will not survive." He choked on the next few words, hardly able to bring himself to say it. "It also means you won't live, for if you survived, you would be given this task instead of Modi and me."

Freya held his hands and looked deep into his eyes. "I don't know what's going to happen at the final battle. I'm fully prepared to die."

"As am I."

"We need to vanquish our enemies. Losing is not an option. Whatever sacrifices need to be made, we'll make them. If I die, then I will die. But your road will not end at Ragnarok. You can't afford to lose focus in the upcoming days. If you have been called upon to stop Loki, then you have been chosen for a reason."

Magni shook his head. He was to stay strong but was fighting a losing battle to stop tears from flowing. "I can't bear to lose you. You mean so much to me. I don't even have the words to express it."

Freya put a finger to his lips. "I already know."

"I love you."

"And I love you."

Magni sighed. "I can't imagine life without you."

Freya held him close and whispered in his ear. "My time is coming to an end. I wish it were not so, but it is. Nothing can change that. Your time isn't. Don't lose yourself to despair. Whatever Loki is plotting must be inconceivably treacherous. You and your brother must be vigilant. Don't worry about me. When it's all over, you can shed your tears. In the meantime, be strong. You're too important to the Aesir and humanity."

Magni shook his head. "I can't lose you."

Freya kissed him. "Until the final battle comes, let's enjoy what little time we have together."

Chapter VII

John Madison walked thought the entrance of the underground bunker. He imagined that once upon a time this was one of the most heavily fortified places on the planet—the location the president of the United States would flee to when all hell broke loose. Yet, he walked in here with the no problem. Of course, it helped that he had one of his followers in the inside—a member of the president's cabinet and a senior adviser—who disabled the bunker's security including any motion sensors and alarms.

Oh, there were still several secret service agents left who had not deserted or fallen victim to the virus, but old Willie's protection now was nothing like it had been back when he had been the president of the country formerly known as the United States of America.

To John's right was Klaus, carrying a Gochler and Koch G36 assault rifle. He and six additional members of his elite guard accompanied John. He could have come by himself if he wanted to, but a show of force might be enough to convince Willie of what was already obvious—this his country was no more and there was no reason to desperately attempt to hang on to power. It was unbecoming, and the man should have more dignity. *Mortals*.

John strode forward, his head held high.

"Identify yourself," a man in a blue suit shouted. Given that he was pointing a firearm, he was most likely one of the remaining secret service agents.

John held his arms outstretched. "I'm the king of the world. Haven't you heard? Or have you been tucked in this bunker for so long that you don't know what's going on in the outside world?"

"Don't move any further or I'll shoot," the brave man in the blue suit said.

John chuckled. "Do your worst."

The man opened fire on him, and his partner in the blue jeans and black polo shirt opened fire on the others in John's party.

John created a shield of air around himself to deflect the bullets coming in his direction. While the bullets harmlessly careened away from him, he conjured a ball of fire, which he held in his hand. He waited until the pesky secret service agent stopped firing before he lowered the air shield. He threw the ball of flame, which enlarged in size and heat as it made contact with the open air, travelling to the agent. By the time it reached him, it was a massive streak of fire that engulfed the man's entire body. The air was a little chilly, so John moved forward with his palms out to warm his hands as the man screamed in agony.

The other agent, who was dressed so shabbily wearing jeans, did not last long as John's men opened fire and put the poor fool out of his misery. They continued walking down the corridor, which led to the conference room where Willie spent much of his time these days.

Before they could reach it, three more Secret Service agents or bodyguards emerged from the room he intended to enter. This time they did not waste any time with banter and just opened fire. *How rude.* He at least wanted to have a chance to speak with his foes before he killed them.

Instead of creating a shield of air, this time he shot bursts of air to change the trajectory of the bullets so that they veered away from him. Before he could incinerate the president's last line of defense, his men opened fire and killed the three bodyguards. He glanced back and found that one of his elite guardsmen had also fallen. A pity. He had hoped to make it through this escapade unscathed, but it was not to be.

When the proverbial dust settled, he opened the door to the conference room and found the old president standing behind the long table, his face ashen, sweating profusely, his hair unkempt. The man was a mess. It was hard to believe that at one point this man had been the most powerful man on the planet. John glanced up at the screens in the room and realized it was showing live footage of the corridor from which they had just emerged. All the better. That meant he had just seen that display of power outside. The negotiations would undoubtedly go easier now.

John crossed his arms. "Willie, is that how you greet the leader of this new world? You're making it increasingly difficult for me to show mercy on you."

Klaus moved forward and put his assault rifle to the head of the former president.

"Now, we had negotiated a deal in good faith, and then I come to find out that you had no intention of following through on your end. Not only that, but you have been conspiring with other world leaders to resist my demands." John laughed. "Do you know how utterly foolish that is? You have no government any longer. Your congress has disbanded. Your vice president is dead. Your Speaker of the House has gone into hiding. What's left of your military is hardly worthy of calling them a fighting force. Your secret service no longer exists. You have nothing. Face it, Willie. It's over. I know that it's a harsh reality, but you must accept it.

"Now, I will give you one final chance to make things right." John produced a vial from his jacket pocket. "This is the vaccine. The one that will allow your two children, your remaining family members, and those who you have surrounded yourself with to survive. You have only kept yourself alive by sealing yourself in this bunker, but you can't stay here forever. I won't allow that. With this vaccine, you can resurface and join our new world—albeit one in which you will no longer be president, but it's better than the alternative."

"You're a madman, Madison," the former president said.

John laughed out loud. "You are such a silly, little man. When will you learn that is of no consequence to you? The only thing that is relevant is that you no longer have a country. Law enforcement has disbanded, as has your government. Now, you will give me everything I want—the codes for the nukes, the locations of all your weapons, military infrastructure, the means to use it, all of your satellite data and capabilities, or, very simply, you and those you hold dear will die. What will it be, Willie?"

The response was obvious. After all, Willie had no leverage. John spent the bulk of the day in the bunker with the former president learning all he needed to know. When he was satisfied that he indeed had all that he came for and there was nothing of value Willie could provide him, he motioned to Klaus.

"Very well. Administer the vaccine to them." John gave a dramatic pause. "Did I say give them the vaccine? I meant eliminate them." He waved his hand and walked out of the room to the sound of gunfire erupting behind him.

***

John Madison sat on the plush leather sofa with his head tilted back as Monique, a gorgeous dark-skinned woman, applied makeup to his face. As the world sat on the brink of destruction, as pandemonium in the streets was the order of the day, as lawlessness seeped through the fabric of society, he sat in quiet luxury.

Klaus approached him stone-faced. The man seemed incapable of displaying emotion. "You have five minutes before you are supposed to go on."

John waved his hand. "I'll be there when I'm ready."

"The world is waiting for you," Klaus said. "I'm sure you don't wish to disappoint your subjects."

"And what exactly are they going to do if I'm a few minutes late? The survivors have been waiting for days with bated-breath to hear me speak. A few more minutes isn't going to drive them away."

Klaus stared at him with cold, gray eyes. "Would you like me to tell the producers to post a message that there will be a delay?"

"No need. I'll be ready. Monique, can you wrap this up, my darling."

"As you wish." Monique brushed his long, blond locks. She then put up a mirror so he could look at himself.

"How do I look, my darling?" John asked.

"Like a god," Monique answered.

John chuckled. "I suppose you're right. It's not easy being this beautiful, but somehow, I manage. What do you think, Klaus?"

Klaus stood with a blank expression on his face.

John giggled. "How silly of me. I shouldn't expect you to answer. You're so loaded with testosterone. So, do you think the world's ready for me?"

"I would assess that they are."

"They have been through so much suffering over the past month since I first unleashed the virus. Now, their savior is going to speak to them. How exciting!"

This was the culmination of John's plans. He would stamp himself as the rightful ruler of the world. The leaders of every country that mattered had already surrendered power to him. Some were reluctant and had to be coerced, but in the end, their power bases had so thoroughly eroded that they had no choice. For those that were particularly stubborn, he had staged about a half dozen coups around the globe to seize power.

After John had rested control of the former United States of America, the other countries fell in line. The prime minister of the country formerly known as Great Britain could not relinquish power quickly enough after his friend from the United States abandoned ship. The prime minister of France, a pathetic little man who had been indignant when John had first asked him to surrender his military assets, now could not stop kissing John's posterior in an effort to gain leniency. When it came to Russia, John had been very impressed while negotiating with the president. The man was a tough bastard, and John had been so impressed with his hard nose style in the negotiations that he offered him a position of power and influence in the new world's social structure. When the Russian agreed, John authorized the use of the actual vaccine and not a placebo for him and thirty people of his choosing. John needed men like that on his side.

Of course, not all of the world's leaders were smart enough to take his offer. Some of these fools actually defied him.

As he tried to explain to these people, it was pointless to resist. He had organized soldiers under his command, numerous military assets throughout the world, and most importantly, his men were healthy. What was left of the resistance was flimsy at best, and often times pathetic. Many of the resisting armies were ragtag groups of people who managed to survive the virus, were often underfed, lacking in supplies, and any kind of real leadership.

Canada tried to resist, but his forces crushed them in two days. His coup of Saudi Arabia lasted five hours. The Chinese were stubborn, but after consulting with John's new friend, the Russian dictator, and giving them favorable terms to give them some level of status in this new world, they also surrendered power. Israel provided the most difficult resistance. It took his forces a week and the loss of quite a few lives to subdue them.

He had dispatched his people throughout the globe to run these areas using extreme force to ensure rule. He received daily reports from his lieutenants. They struggled coping with the general lawlessness of the survivors, so he allowed them to kill at their discretion to maintain order.

John had persevered, and now this was his moment, his shining, glorious moment where he would reveal himself to the world. They would fear him initially, but, in time, they would revere and adore him. He had been preparing this address for weeks. After all, first impressions were vital. This would dwarf any address given by any leader in the history of this world, even the one given in Gettysburg by Abraham Lincoln.

Klaus appeared at the door as Monique applied finishing touches to John's makeup.

John planted a kiss on Monique's soft lips. "Thank you for beautifying me. I'll reward you later. It will be an experience you'll never forget."

As Klaus led him out the door, John asked, "Do you think I should stick to the script or ad-lib?"

Klaus stopped to straighten John's tie. "You should stick to the script. It's an excellent speech."

John believed the German, since the man was not one to give high praise. "I'm glad you approve. Let's be done with this."

Klaus led him to the studio, which had been owned by a major American network before they went off the air. When John was selecting his chosen for this post-apocalyptic world, he included highly intelligent people with skills that would help him achieve his goals. Naturally, this included military and intelligence personnel. This also included people at high levels of finance, science, and technology, and, pertinent to the moment, broadcasting. His people had commandeered the studio and would be using it to send John's message around the world.

In another time, he probably would have held a press conference where he would field carefully selected questions from reporters, but there were no reporters anymore. They had joined the huddled masses fighting for survival. Instead, he stood in his comfortable studio surrounded by production personnel.

He set up the studio so that it resembled an old-fashioned fireside chat. He wanted to radiate an image that he was in charge, that there was no reason to panic, that he had everything under control.

The production manager had insisted his speech be transcribed on a teleprompter. He agreed, even though it was unnecessary. He had the speech memorized. Unfortunately, even his followers could not always grasp that he was no ordinary mortal and not subject to their limitations.

He would be speaking in English, but his broadcast would be translated into dozens of languages so that people around the world could hear his message. He was fluent in many languages, but it wasn't practical for him to conduct so many different broadcasts.

The producer gave him a one minute warning. John did some light stretches as he waited. The producer counted down from ten and signaled for him to start.

John did not speak at first. He wanted the viewers to take in all of his regal majesty. No doubt they expected someone tall and beautiful, larger than life. He was all of that and more. When he started speaking, he used a calm and assuring tone. "My friends, we have all been through difficult times. In the last two months, each and every person viewing this telecast has lost many close family members and friends. Many of you have lost your parents, your spouse, your children. Some may feel completely alone. I assure you that you are not. My name is John Madison. I feel your pain. I know the horror and devastation you have felt, not just from the virus that has killed so many, but the inhuman violence and destruction brought about by those who have survived this dreadful disease only to hurt other survivors."

John narrowed his eyes and raised his voice. "My friends, I am here to tell you the worst is over. Those of you who are listening to me have persevered through a lifetime of misery in the past two months. I salute you for your courage in these trying times. You have survived this virus that has killed so many. Due to the pattern of spread of this virus, most likely you have natural immunity to this insidious disease.

"I am here to offer you hope in this time of darkness. The source of this virus is unknown and will likely never be discovered." John paused a moment to prevent himself from chuckling.

"Although we may never know about its origin, my team of researchers has created a vaccine. We have tested it and have complete confidence that it will immunize those who are not naturally protected against the virus. Therefore, you need not worry that any children being born into the world will be subject to its dreadful clutches.

"Society as we knew it has experienced a complete and utter collapse. Therefore, by necessity, I have assumed the role as the leader of this new world. To survive, you will need a strong and steady hand. You will need tough rules and strict enforcement. I will provide this. You need to put complete and absolute trust in me. I will guide you through these difficult times, and together we will forge a new and better world."

John slowly walked around the stage as he spoke, not looking at the teleprompter. He was a gifted orator, and this was his finest speech.

"That is not to say there won't be trying times. In order to survive and even thrive, I have taken tough measures. First, everyone will be required to register at the following locations." Dozens of locations in cities across the world scrawled at the bottom of the screens on the monitor. "We will centralize the survivors in these cities. For your own safety, it will be illegal to live anywhere other than these cities unless your new job function requires it."

He had to keep close tabs on his subjects in order to prevent the formation of renegade groups. He would send out military squads to collect anybody who had not heeded his call and registered in the chosen locations.

"In order to create a productive society, everyone will have jobs assigned to them. This will vary depending on the current needs and the skills you offer. The first and most daunting task will be clearing the dead. The streets are littered with them. We will properly dispose of the bodies to prevent the spread of disease. We will clean the cities and rebuild what has been destroyed. Since the world's population has been considerably reduced, we will also tear down buildings and structures that are no longer necessary.

"I have created laws that everyone must comply without fail and without question. Everyone who registers will receive a handbook with these laws. Failure to follow the laws will result in severe punishment, up to and including death. Do not disobey me. The best course is to follow my commands religiously."

He had a number of other restrictions he would be imposing, but he did not want to unveil them just yet. At the top of the list was banning all organized religion. He was the only god to be worshipped, and, in time, when the people could fully grasp his greatness, they would worship him just as his chosen had for centuries. Until then, he did not want competition. After all, what did their gods do for them anyway?

He was getting to the tricky part of his speech. He thought the people could accept most of what he said. The next part would be delicate.

John brought his palms together in front of his face. "We are entering a bold new world. Things will be different. You will encounter beings you have never seen before. They are giants. Some are slightly larger than a very tall human, around three meters tall, and others are as tall as five meters. You need not be afraid of these giants, for they are under my control. They are a race that has spawned forth as a result of recent mutations due to the virus. They will help me enforce law and order, and respond only to me. As long as you follow the rules I have set forth, you need not worry about the giants.

"Change is often difficult, and many are resistant to it, but in these trying times, it's necessary. To restore order, I will implement curfews. Registration at my designated centers is mandatory. Anyone who does not register will be brought in and will be punished harshly. You have one week to register. I suggest you find your way to the closest registration center immediately."

John gave a winning smile. "We can get through this together, but I need cooperation from everybody. I am the guiding light that you have been seeking and I will restore our world to its former glory. I will be providing transmissions in the upcoming days. This broadcast and the ones that follow will be repeated so that all will be able to hear."

When the telecast ended, John pumped his fist in the air, and clasped hands with Klaus, who was standing nearby. He could only imagine how exciting it had to be for people to witness his greatness after what they had been through. He looked forward to being the supreme leader of the world. It was a role he had always desired but had been denied to him by those who thought they were superior to him. Well, they were dead now, and he was the one left standing.

Chapter VIII

On the eve of the Battle of Ragnarok, there was nothing left for Magni to do. He had spent the previous week in rigorous combat training with Modi. He had assisted Tyr and Odin in strategizing for battle. The Aesir had their defenses ready. Freya had the valkyries in full battle mode.

So, Magni spent the evening with Freya. They had a late picnic with fresh fruit and roasted meat. After the meal, they sat by the fire holding each other.

Freya snuggled close to him. "I wish tomorrow would never come."

"As do I. But it will all the same."

Earlier that morning, Heimdall, who guarded the Bifrost Bridge, a marvelous rainbow structure that stood at the entrance to Asgard, confirmed that the fire and frost giants were near. Tomorrow he would sound his great horn, which would signify the start of the battle.

Freya filled her wine glass. "At least we have tonight."

Despite himself, Magni could not prevent tears from forming in his eyes. "I still can't believe that tonight will be our last together."

"You can't fight fate."

Magni turned away. He was crying while Freya remained strong, even though she was facing her impending doom. She had accepted her death with dignity, but Magni could not.

"I'm going to do whatever I can to keep you alive tomorrow."

Freya shook her head. "You'll do no such thing. Don't even think about me when the battle starts. You must do your part in ensuring victory for the Aesir. That's your only concern."

"How can you say that?"

"Because my time has come to an end." Freya closed her eyes. "I can feel it deep in my bones. One world ends while another begins. You and your brother will be the stewards of that world, just as Odin and Thor have been the stewards of this one. I willingly accept my fate, just as you must accept yours. You can't run and hide. You have to be strong."

Of course, she was right. He was being weak and sentimental. Perhaps it was because he doubted his own abilities. "If only tonight could last forever."

Freya grabbed his hands and met his gaze. "If only."

There was so much he wanted to say to her. If he had Modi's poetic eloquence, he could relay his feelings. The best he could do was hold her close.

Freya pulled away. "Are we going to spend this evening mourning, or are we going to have one last great night that will burn in your memories for as long as you live?"

Magni tilted his head and grinned. "The latter."

"Good. I was hoping you would say that."

Freya leaned in and kissed him deeply.

***

Magni awoke before the break of dawn, the place next to him in his bed empty. Freya had bidden her good-bye last night. No doubt, she was preparing her Valkyries for battle. Today was a day for extreme violence, bloodshed, and death. There would be carnage on a scale to make the heavens shudder.

Magni stretched his arms. With the sunlight barely peaking above the horizon on this calm and clear morning, he walked the short distance across the damp plain to his brother's hall. He could hardly remember ever seeing this much activity along the plains of Asgard. All around him, the Aesir were preparing for battle, putting on armor, preparing their weaponry. Valkyries were on the march, as were their allies among the dwarves and elves.

It was so hectic that Magni hardly had the opportunity to greet his friends on the way to his brother's hall. When he arrived, he found Modi in his parlor sharpening his axe on a sharpening stone while wearing an intense gaze.

Modi rested the axe against the wall and looked up at his brother. "There will be much going on today on the battlefield, much that we want to accomplish, but above all we have to look after each other."

Magni looked down, a cast of guilt falling upon him. He had been so intent on killing Loki and Surter as well as protecting Freya, that he had not put much thought into Modi's wellbeing. He couldn't lose Modi. That would be like losing part of himself.

Magni and his brother had been fighting together from the time they were just boys in the plains of Asgard. Magni knew how to anticipate his brother's moves, probably even before Modi realized he was going to make them. Modi also had the uncanny ability to anticipate what Magni was doing and react to it without communicating. It was as instinctual as breathing.

Modi folded his arms. "Of course, we always look after each other, but it's especially crucial because of our mission. If what the Norns said it true, and I have no reason to doubt them, then we must both survive Ragnarok. I can't imagine being able to accomplish this mission without you by my side."

"I have no intention of seeking my own safety," Magni said.

"Nor do I. I will fight with reckless abandon, but we need to make it a priority to protect each other. We must stay close."

Magni stared off into the distance. If he had a choice to save his brother or Freya, who would he choose? It would have to be Modi. It was his duty to serve as a guardian of Midgard, a promise made long before his birth. His duty superseded his personal concerns.

"You're right. We have to look after each other today." Magni grinned. "Plus, we do our best fighting together."

"How true. If father fails in killing Jormangandr, then we must finish the job. The same holds true if Odin doesn't kill the Fenris Wolf. They will be our deadliest foes."

"Father *must* kill Jormangandr," Magni said. "If he is incapable of doing it, then how will we?"

"We'll find a way." Modi's voice held no conviction.

Magni didn't want to consider battling the Midgard Serpent. From his earliest childhood, he had heard terrifying stories of the beast's power.

During breakfast, Magni took no pleasure in the food, but ate to restore his strength. They hardly spoke. His brother appeared tightly wound, while Magni felt hollow inside. Why did it have to come to this? It was Loki's fault. Odin should never have let him into the halls of Valhalla.

They were sitting in silence when Heimdall's horn sounded.

Modi stared into his eyes. "Are you ready?"

"As ready as I can be."

Modi clutched his brother's arm. "Victory must be ours. Defeat is not an option. We must protect each other."

Magni nodded. "We will."

"Then let's fight as we never have before."

Chapter IX

Magni felt a sense of awe as Odin led the Aesir onto the battlefield. The Aesir army had a collective intensity to their gazes, a sense of purpose he found reassuring. Victory would be theirs. There could be no other way.

Magni stared across the battlefield at the frost giants disembarking off massive ships. The earth shook as fire giants marched toward the Aesir from their homes in Muspell to the south. Hideous, misshapen creatures from the underworld that should never have seen the light of day emerged from other ships.

Magni's gaze focused on Surter, the leader of the fire giants. He was massive, over five meters in height, with legs as thick as tree trunks. Fire leaped from his red hair. His entire body bristled with flames. He held a flaming sword that was longer than Magni was tall and carried himself with total arrogance, looking upon the Aesir with disdain, no doubt searching for Freya.

He glanced to his left and caught sight of Freya. She somehow managed to look both stunning and formidable, decked out in bronze plate armor covering her forearms and shoulders. A massive procession of valkyries, the female warriors whose entire existence had been geared toward this day, followed her.

Her twin brother, Frey, led the elves and dwarves onto the battlefield. They had long been allies to the Aesir and had agreed without hesitation to join this fight. Magni was glad to have them on his side.

Odin strode forward on Sleipnir, his eight-legged stallion. He abruptly stopped and turned. "Today is the day that legends will be made. All that we have worked for, all that we represent, will be decided on this battlefield. We will fight until there is no breath in our lungs. We will fight until there is none left standing on the other side. We will show no mercy, give no quarter, and we will not lose. Death to our enemies. We fight for more than ourselves. We fight for humanity." He raised his spear. "And we will prevail."

Thor raised his hammer, Mjolnir, over his head and gave a war cry that made Magni shiver. "Let's kill every last one of the vermin."

Tyr and other Aesir shouted until they collectively worked themselves into a frenzy.

Odin turned around, pointed his spear forward, and led the charge.

Magni glanced at his brother. His face was serene. Knowing how Modi fought, that would soon change.

The frost giants were the first to meet their charge. The plan was to let the valkyries engage the frost giants in battle to free the Aesir to fight other more dangerous foes. Magni did his best to work past them but could not stop himself from slashing at the knees of a frost giant in his path. The giant fell. Moments later, Valkyrie arrows found their mark in his chest.

Surter was too far away to engage in combat, so he sought out Loki, who was supposed to be leading the creatures of the underworld, but Loki was nowhere to be found. Instead, his daughter, Hel, with her staff raised high and her half black, half pale face, led the charge.

Before he could think too long on the matter, a long serpent with big, black eyes and rows of jagged teeth slithered toward him. He braced himself, his sword held high, his feet spread apart to meet the charge. It whipped its long tail at him. Unprepared for the blow, it smashed him in the back, knocking him forward.

The serpent extended its long, lean body before rushing at him. This time he was ready. Just before it reached him, he grabbed the serpent's throat with both hands. He squeezed hard and flipped the serpent over. He landed on top of it, still squeezing its throat. It fought hard and snapped its jaws at him, biting him on the bridge of the nose, but he would not let go of his grip.

He released his left hand from its throat and reached for the dagger clipped on his belt. He freed the dagger, slid it into the beast's belly, and tore its abdomen. The serpent thrashed violently but could not break free from his grip. Eventually, the serpent went limp. Magni let go, got to his feet, and wiped blood from his face. He would undoubtedly shed much of his immortal blood today, but he had been hoping to avoid his first wound so early.

Magni turned to look for another foe. His eyes went wide at the sight of a massive ripple coming from the sea. The ripple soon became a tidal wave that crashed onto the battlefield. Jormangandr's head rose from the sea as his body writhed.

Magni dove for cover as the first tidal wave approached. The waves swept away many combatants, friend and foe alike.

The onrushing water knocked Magni over. He grabbed hold of a large rock until the wave passed, then wiped salt water from his eyes, waiting to see if Jormangandr was going to unleash more tidal waves, but the serpent had stopped, his keen, red eyes set on the lone figure that approached it. Magni felt a sense of dread as his father closed in on Jormangandr. This was Thor's last stand, the greatest warrior among the Aesir, the greatest warrior who had ever lived. He could only hope that his skill in combat would be enough to send the serpent to the bottom of the sea.

***

Thor strode toward the beast. They locked eyes, and he smiled. He had dreamed for centuries of smashing the Midgard Serpent's thick skull with Mjolnir.

Jormangandr had an impossibly big torso, deadly venom in his bite, and could sustain an unlimited amount of damage. Many thought the serpent could not be killed. He would prove them wrong today.

Thor glanced back at Modi, who was severing the head of a creature with the body of a jackal and the head of a lion. He could not find Magni. He sighed. He wanted to see his sons one last time in case this fight with Jormangandr would be his last.

The Midgard Serpent roared as Thor's feet touched the shore.

"It's time to meet your master." Thor raised his war hammer and sent a bolt of lightning at the beast.

Jormangandr dove under the water as waves knocked Thor over.

When he rose to the surface again, Thor shouted, "Don't be so timid. I only want to kill you." He shot another bolt of lightning at the beast's neck. The Midgard Serpent staggered backward. Thor continued sending bolts of lightning at it, electrifying the water around them.

Jormangandr went down and remained there for a couple of minutes. Thor stood guard. There was no way he could have finished the beast that easily.

Jormangandr emerged close to the shoreline and let out a loud roar.

Filled with false bravado, Thor said. "So, you decided to come and play." He braced himself for Jormangandr's attack.

***

Modi pulled his spear from a creature with skin so dark that it appeared to have been charred. His spear tip was covered with dark soot. What manner of beast was this?

He glanced at his brother, just a short distance away. Magni did not need his help right now. He was fighting well. More than well. He was fighting with skill that few could match.

A long moan captured his attention. He turned and felt a sickening chill as he spotted Garm, the hound that guarded the entrance to the underworld, on top of Tyr. The hound was mauling the one-armed Aesir warrior.

"No!" Modi shouted.

He hurled his spear at Garm. It flew through the air with incredible velocity and pierced the hound's side. Garm turned and snarled, as if offended that someone would interrupt his meal.

Garm charged after Modi with impossible speed for such a large creature, green blood flowing out of its side, the spear flapping in the wind.

Modi pulled out his sword and prepared for Garm to jump at him since it had been in full stride, but the hound tricked him by feinting a jump. Instead, it went for Modi's legs. He grunted in agony as Garm tore into his left knee.

He dropped his sword, which would be useless in this close combat situation. He grabbed Garm's jaws and pried them off his knee. Garm snarled and tried to attack, but Modi held off the beast. He got to his feet and landed a vicious kick to the hound's side, causing Garm to squeal.

This only seemed to enrage the hound. It bull-rushed Modi and knocked him down. Garm attacked with ferocious intensity. Every time the hound tried to bite him, he gripped its jaws, keeping it at bay, but each time it became more difficult. Before long, he would suffer the same fate as Tyr.

He got separation from the hound and had a sudden jolt of inspiration. When Garm charged, instead of trying to fight it off, he grabbed its front legs and used its momentum to flip it forward. Garm flew through the air and landed on its back with a crashing thud.

Not wanting to lose his advantage, Modi picked up his sword and lunged at the hound, burying his blade deep into its side. Garm gave a low moan as Modi removed his weapon. He brought it overhead, and with all his might, slashed down. The blade cut through fur and bone. Moments later, Garm's severed head rolled on the floor.

Modi grinned despite himself, amazed at the blow that had cleaved Garm's neck. That may have been the most perfect strike he had ever landed.

His elation was short lived as he glanced at Tyr, who looked in terrible shape.

Modi trudged over and dropped to one knee. Tyr, who had always been a magnificent warrior with incomparable courage, had been reduced to a ragged, mutilated version of his former self. Garm had torn apart his abdomen, shredded his chest cavity, and left him a bloody mess. Tyr's breaths were rasping flickers, those of a dying god.

Modi had been filled with unusual serenity thus far. He had fought with calm and skill, but seeing Tyr in this state caused his anger to rise, threatening to overtake him.

Tyr attempted to speak, so Modi lowered himself to hear him. "Loki…must kill…Loki."

Modi nodded. "I will." But where was the bastard? He had not seen Loki yet. He grabbed Tyr's hand.

Tyr spat blood. "Be strong." Then he died.

Blind hatred filled Modi as he prepared to take his next victim.

***

Magni had been working his way toward Surter, but it seemed as if a wall of fire giants blocked his path, each uglier than the previous one.

To his right, a valkyrie fought in hand-to-hand combat against a giant with a thick beard and scars lining his chest. The valkyrie fought with tenacity, but her opponent's size and strength was too much for her to overcome. Freya had instructed them to fight the giants at a distance, but in the chaos of battle, anything could happen.

The fire giant struck her twice with his sword and was about to go in for the kill.

Magni temporarily abandoned his quest to find Surter. Just as the giant was about to cut the valkyrie in half, Magni ran from his position and deflected the giant's sword with his own. With the giant off balance, Magni tackled him, knocking him off his feet with a resounding thud on the wet grass. With both hands, Magni raised his sword and held it like a dagger. He brought it down and plunged it into the giant's chest, creating a popping sound as it pierced the giant, green blood shooting up at him. Within moments, the green blood covered him. It had a vile taste. He tried to spit it out, but the taste remained in his mouth.

He helped the fallen valkyrie to her feet. His eyes narrowed at the sight of Surter shooting blasts of fire from his flaming sword. Frey was fighting off two fire giants who were blocking his path to Surter. If Freya's brother could not reach Surter first, Magni was going to destroy the leader of the fire giants.

This thought only lasted a moment as a winged tiger with massive fangs approached him from the air. He braced himself for his next fight as he kept Surter in his sights.

***

Frey fought two fire giants simultaneously with fierce determination. He knew the conditions of the battle. He knew the disparity in numbers between the two sides and what was expected of him, but this knowledge did not make the fight any easier. Just when he thought he had an advantage over one giant, the next pressed the attack and put him in the defensive.

He felt onrushing heat before the blast of fire struck him. Searing pain ripped through his shoulder and face. He gritted his teeth, his eyes locked on a grinning Surter. The leader of the fire giants was shooting balls of flames at the Aesir and valkyries. He had to get to Surter, but every time he tried, a giant or some unspeakable monster blocked his path. If he could only get Surter in a one-on-one battle, he was certain he could bring the leader of the fire giants down.

Frey turned, ducked low, and swung his sword, connecting with the knees of a giant. When the giant fell, he brought his broad sword up and jammed it into its throat, a killing blow.

Frey fell forward, his world momentarily blackening. Without having seen it, he knew the second fire giant had just smashed the back of his head with his mace. Frey stumbled forward, trying to regain his senses. He lost his sword in the attack. To make matters worse, the giant who had just struck him was blocking his path to his weapon.

The giant struck at him, but even in his dazed condition, Frey was too quick. He evaded the blow by stepping to the side. He waited until the giant attempted to strike again. As her mace descended toward him, he ducked, and lunged at the giant. His foe's skin was red and charred, typical of her race. Her breath was rank and her gaze intense.

Frey could not reach the dagger on his belt, so he rained down punches and elbows at the giant. After the first few blows, the giant attempted to cover up, and when that did not work, she turned her back on Frey. He took advantage of this poor defensive posture by wrapping one arm around the giant's neck and used his free arm to tighten the grip.

The giant got to her feet, leaving Frey dangling in the air as he held on to his grip. He squeezed harder as the giant tried to grab at him, but Frey kicked her leg, knocking her down. Eventually the giant stopped fighting, and Frey let go.

Surter's massive frame stepped in front of him. Frey looked up at the fire giant's cruel eyes, which glinted with pure satisfaction.

Frey took a deep breath. Without his sword, he was no match for Surter. He had wanted to kill Surter for centuries, just as the leader of the fire giants wanted to dispose of him and his sister. It was a long running feud, and now it would come to its conclusion, but he would not prevail.

***

"No!" Freya cried. She watched in horror as her brother stood in front of Surter, defenseless.

The leader of the fire giants slashed Frey in the neck and shoulder with his flaming sword. Then he ran his blade through Frey's abdomen. Frey sunk to the blood-soaked ground as Surter pulled his sword out of him.

Freya abandoned her duties in commanding the valkyries. Her twin had just died, and with him, part of her had died. Using her magic, she conjured icy blasts and shot them at Surter.

The first two caught him by surprise and knocked him off his feet. Before long he rose to his full height. He snarled and charged after her, flaming sword in hand.

He shot fire at her from his flaming sword. She managed to avoid the fire, but the ground around her lit up, its heat radiating and amplifying the coppery scent of blood that had been shed.

Freya focused on her next round of attack. She had to stop Surter with her magic before he reached her, where he could use his overwhelming size and strength advantage. She held up her hands and twirled her fingers. Moments later, large metal spikes generated in the air. She thrust them with the force of her mind at the onrushing fire giant.

Surter stopped in his tracks. His eyes went wide. He swung his flaming sword in front of him, trying to deflect the metal spikes. He knocked a number of spikes aside. However, a few found their mark and pierced him.

He howled, his eyes bulging, flame leaping out of his hair and beard. He pulled out a metal spike that had jutted into his thigh. As he was reaching for another, Freya bombarded him with icy blasts, knocking him down.

She ran forward, going in for the kill, preparing to crush him with a giant wave of energy.

With amazing agility that belied his size, Surter leapt to his feet. She gasped, sure she had dealt him a more severe blow. He spun, holding his sword with both hands. On the back end of his spin, he fully connected with his sword, slicing her abdomen from end to end.

Freya felt her insides burning. She looked down at her belly and stared at a mess of blood, intestines, and fire. She looked up long enough to see Surter's sword coming at her neck.

Chapter X

When Frey fell to Surter's flaming sword, an unreal sense of dread gnawed away at Magni. Having dispatched the winged tiger, who fought with a raging fury and kept coming back even after Magni had thought he had dealt her killing blows, he could only stare as Surter left his friend lifeless. Frey had been defenseless without his broad sword. It was a cowardly way to kill a noble and valorous warrior. Magni wished Frey could have died with dignity, but the Battle of Ragnarok was not about honor. It was about victory by any means.

He should have felt remorse about his friend's death. Instead, cold panic seized him. He found himself struggling to breathe. He wanted to jump out of his skin. Surter had wanted Frey's head, but his ultimate prize was Freya. She had rejected the leader of the fire giants, and he had vowed to kill her at the Battle of Ragnarok.

Magni locked eyes with Surter just before Freya came at him shooting off icy blasts after her twin brother fell. Magni charged after him, trying to join Freya in the fight against him, but was intercepted by a wall of fire giants. Magni gritted his teeth. Even outnumbered, he could defeat these giants, but he had to get to Surter before he could harm Freya. He could not face the prospect of losing her. *Damn the prophecies.* He had to save her.

Just as he was about to counter the attacking fire giants, Modi joined him at his side, a snarl on his face, a burning intensity in his eyes. They did not need to communicate. He was so familiar with Modi's fighting style that he could anticipate his brother's movements.

The brothers fought side-by-side and back-to-back with remarkable efficiency. Modi charged at a red-faced fire giant with his battle axe. The giant brought his sword down in an attempt to fend off Modi's charge, but Magni parried the blow with his own sword, allowing Modi to cleave the giant's legs with one brutal shot.

They then turned their attention to the other fire giants. The brothers met their attack, Magni with his sword, Modi with his shield. They simultaneously repelled blows from the giants and unleashed their own strikes.

There was no time to think. Magni operated out of instinct. He ducked to avoid the attacking blade of a fire giant, sidestepped an enemy spear, spun, and swung low with his sword. At the same time, Modi swung high with his battle axe on the same giant. The giant collapsed as Magni took out his knees and Modi cleaved his neck.

They fought as a lethal unit. Each defended blows aimed at their brother, and used the opening created by one to finish off an opponent. They killed the five fire giants in their path, but the skirmish took too long.

Nearby, Freya rained icy blasts at a fallen Surter. Magni shook his head. From his vantage point, he could tell Surter was not as hurt as he pretended to be.

"Freya!" Magni screamed.

It was too late. Surter sprung to his feet and ran his flaming sword through her abdomen.

"No!" Magni trembled as Freya dropped to her knees. He ran hard, but before he reached her, Surter's long sword extinguished the burning flame that had been Freya's existence.

Magni tackled Surter off his feet. He pounded the giant with his fists, relishing the pain in his hands as the flame surrounding Surter's face singed them. It didn't matter how much he hurt. It could not possibly match the utter devastation of Freya's death. All that mattered was making Surter pay for what he had done.

Surter flung Magni off of him with his forearm. Magni would not be deterred. He charged after the giant. Before Surter could grab his fallen sword, Magni picked him up by the waist and squeezed as hard as he could. Although Surter was more than twice his size, Magni was far stronger. Surter's face turned from red to green as Magni squeezed, only releasing his grip when Surter scratched Magni's eyes.

Before the giant could regroup, Magni lifted him off his feet and flung him to the hard dirt. He pounced on Surter and clubbed the back of his thick skull with his fists. Magni's hands throbbed, but he did not care. Undoubtedly, the giant felt worse.

Surter wedged his knees in between himself and Magni. With his thick legs, he thrust Magni off of him. He lunged for his sword, but Magni landed a roundhouse kick to the giant's head just as he bent to reach for it. Surter's head shot back, and he fell to his knees.

Magni pulled out his sword, lifted it overhead, and plunged the sword into Surter's chest. He took a deep breath and thrust his weapon deeper into the giant's heart. When he pulled out the sword, Surter gasped for breath and clutched his wound.

Magni trembled with rage and loss. He brought his sword to the giant's throat. "You bastard! You took Freya away from me."

He sliced Surter's throat. The giant choked on his own blood. He raised the sword and slashed at the fallen giant's neck. The first few blows did not do their intended task, but Magni did not stop until he decapitated Surter.

Magni stumbled toward Freya's body. Even in death, she looked radiant. He had known it would happen, but that did nothing to diminish the blow. He reached out and gently touched her face. The future he had hoped for was destroyed. Even if the Aesir were victorious today, what would it mean without Freya by his side?

Tears streamed down his cheek as he leaned closer to her. "I love you more than anything."

Someone grabbed his shoulder and pulled him to his feet. It took him a few moments to realize it was Modi. His brother looked like a savage, his nostrils flared, blood covering much of his face. His eyes glowered. He spoke through gritted teeth. "Now's not the time for grieving. Now's the time for killing. Take your sword, and let's crush the enemy."

Magni nodded. Freya had sacrificed her life. He had to make this sacrifice mean something. He would take his revenge on anyone foolish enough to cross his path.

***

Odin grunted with exhaustion. He had been chasing Fenris Wolf all over the battlefield. He watched the wolf devour dwarves, elves, and his Aesir brethren. The gigantic wolf was a terror in the battlefield. Odin continued to pursue him, trying to engage Fenris Wolf in a one-on-one battle, but the wolf had managed to elude him thus far. Every time he got close, some giant or monster blocked his path.

Fenris Wolf was no more than fifty meters away. Nothing stood in between them.

The breaking of the chain that had once fettered Fenris Wolf had signaled that Ragnarok was imminent. After learning that Fenris Wolf had been unbound, Odin pushed to stave off the battle, which proved to be futile. Ragnarok had come no matter how hard he tried to prevent it.

Odin took a deep breath. He had never felt this weary. He was old, as old as time itself, but he had never felt ancient until now. He had led many great hunts, voyages to the ends of the nine worlds, had been in countless adventures. He had hoped his experience would prove to be the difference in the final battle, but that experience could not overcome how slow and weak he felt. In his younger days, he would have crushed these beasts of the underworld with little effort. Now, his entire body was nicked with wounds, and every step he took felt labored.

Fenris Wolf smiled at him, all jagged teeth. Perhaps this had been his strategy from the beginning—to tire Odin out and weaken him for their confrontation.

Odin clutched his trusty spear, Gungnir, which had saved him in countless battles. He needed his spear to come through again. Crafted by the dwarves, it had magical powers. It was light weight and compact, and could pierce through anything, including Fenris Wolf's thick hide.

Fenris Wolf charged at him. The beast had thick, dark fur, and hollow eyes. His face exhibited intelligence. He was capable of forming facial features and could speak in Aldska, the language of the Aesir. He was more than three meters in height and five meters in length. His powerful jaws could snap someone in half. Fenris Wolf had shown his destructive capabilities over and over today.

Odin braced himself for Fenris Wolf's attack. When the wolf jumped at him, he thrust Gungnir at it. Although his spear pierced the wolf's side, the blow did little to stop his momentum. He fell on top of Odin, growling, saliva dripping on Odin's face. Despite the beast's immense size, Odin lifted it off his body and removed his spear. He would not give in to Fenris Wolf so easily.

Fenris Wolf snarled and circled back. "This is your last dance, ancient one." The wolf's voice was harsh and jagged.

Odin hefted his spear. "If so, I will take you with me. There's no place in this world for a monster like you."

Fenris Wolf sniffed the air. "You call me monster? You offend me. I am a royal creature of splendid majesty. The Aesir have never recognized my greatness."

Odin spoke softly. "I tried to bring out the good in you, but you have too much of your father inside. Like Loki, you are evil and rotten to the core."

Fenris Wolf produced a sound that could only be described as a chuckle. "You realize, ancient one, what will happen when we defeat you. Midgard will be ours." Fenris Wolf lifted his head and howled. "Can you imagine those foolish mortals dealing with the likes of me?"

Odin nodded soberly. "That's why I must kill you. I never wanted this to happen. I wanted to live harmoniously. Your father and I had once been the best of friends. Loki and I were blood brothers."

Fenris Wolf circled toward him. "Ancient history. We intend on forging a new history, one without the Aesir. The plan is in motion. The world is ours. The only thing left is to get rid of your dying bones."

Odin hesitated. What was the wolf talking about? He had been so busy preparing for Ragnarok that he had ignored all else. Had he made some fatal flaw? "What do you speak of?"

Fenris Wolf feinted at him but did not charge. "Did we come here to talk, or did we come here to fight?"

Odin clutched Gungnir. "We'll fight to the death."

He ran toward Fenris Wolf. The wolf bounded to the side, his sharp teeth visible. Fenris Wolf tried to flank him, but Odin flipped his spear from one hand to the other and slashed his hind legs. Fenris Wolf yelped but did not stop moving. His massive jaws clamped onto Odin's right arm.

Odin used his free hand to pry apart the wolf's teeth, his immortal blood dripping from his battered arm. After freeing himself, he gritted his teeth, biting down on the pain. Before the wolf could attack again, he used Gungnir to stab Fenris Wolf. This time the wolf issued a loud yelp and backed away.

Odin's eyes locked in on Fenris Wolf as the battle raged around them. He and his nemesis circled each other. Odin could no longer pay attention to the overall battle. Right now, he could only concern himself with Fenris Wolf.

***

As Magni surveyed the battlefield, he was astounded at how many had died. The ground was littered with giants, valkyries, monsters, elves, dwarves, and Aesir alike. With so many dead, who could even determine a victor?

Ever since Freya's death, he had been numb to the killing around him. He no longer felt fatigue as he and Modi went from one skirmish to another.

He spotted Modi engaged in a fight with two frost giants and bounded down the hill after them. Modi had his back to one frost giant as he fended off the axe of a second frost giant. His brother was in a vulnerable spot, so Magni launched himself at the larger frost giant and tackled him to the ground.

Modi glanced back at him. "What took you so long?"

The frost giant still standing swung his axe at Modi, who ducked low to avoid the blow. Magni rose to his feet and ran his sword through the giant's abdomen.

Modi turned his attention to the frost giant Magni had tackled. He used a two-handed grip on his axe to decapitate the fallen giant.

Modi's eyes went wide. "Odin's in trouble."

Magni followed his brother's gaze. Odin and Fenris Wolf had been fighting for some time now, and Odin was clearly getting the worst of it. Blood covered his face and body. His arms and chest had been mangled. His breathing was labored, and his movements slow.

"He needs our help," Modi said.

Magni nodded.

By the time they reached the Allfather, it was too late.

Chapter XI

John Madison looked up from the massage table where a scantily clad female with strong hands was giving him a heavenly massage. Klaus walked into the room. As usual, the tall, powerfully built former Stasi officer was all business. Klaus was incapable of appreciating a massage given by a beautiful woman. Still, he could be useful.

"Yes, Klaus. Why don't you sit down and stay a while?"

Klaus looked down. "I prefer to stand."

"Of course you do." The guy needed to relax. If not for his vicious streak and complete lack of inhibition to kill, John would not care to have him around. His indispensable skills made up for the fact that he was clearly not the life of the party.

"Would you like a status report?" Klaus asked.

"Why not?"

Klaus folded his arms. "There are no more official governments opposing you. With the falling of South Africa, Israel, and Australia, the last of the functioning governments of the old world are no more."

John smiled. "Excellent news. That happened far quicker than anticipated."

"It happened quickly once they learned the United States had fallen." Klaus frowned.

"The news is not all good," Klaus said.

John arched an eyebrow. "Oh?"

"We are seeing pockets of resistance in various corners of the globe, most notably in Philadelphia, northern Japan, Brazil near the Amazon basin, and Manchester. Groups have banded together to resist your rule. They have disregarded your handbook, so we have made arrests."

John raised himself from the massage table. He waved off the gorgeous masseuse. "Enough." Without a word, she left. "I don't understand why anyone would resist my rule. I am giving them a chance to avoid chaos, destruction, and certain death. I am rescuing them from a world on the brink of ruin and giving them a chance for salvation. I am providing a firm hand to guide through these dark times. What is wrong with these people?"

"Apparently not everyone agrees."

John Madison threw up his hands. "This is preposterous. I expected the existing governments to try to hold onto power, but after disposing of them, it should be smooth sailing."

Klaus's face remained impassive. "It is natural that they would resist new rulers. This is human nature."

"It's rubbish if you ask me."

"Regardless of the merits of their motivation, something must be done."

"That's what I like about you. Straight to the point. No messing around." John put his shirt on and began pacing. "What to do? What to do?"

"Yes, that is the question."

"How Shakespearean of you, Klaus. WWOD."

"What's that?"

"What would Odin do?'

"Why do you care?" Klaus asked.

"Now, now. He once was a dear friend."

"And now he's a dead old fool."

"All the same, the Allfather had a knack for dealing with these situations. He did not give up his eye to drink in the well of Mimer and gain eternal wisdom for nothing."

Klaus narrowed his gaze. "If he was so wise, then why did he die at Ragnarok while you still live?"

John raised his glass of wine to Klaus and took a swallow. "I can drink to that. Now back to these idiots resisting my glorious rule. I need an elegant solution."

John did not bother consulting the German. His method would result in mass casualties among his new citizens. John wanted to establish his rule as absolute but would rather avoid killing too many people. After all, he needed people to rule.

John closed his eyes and raised his index finger. "We can use the giants to demolish the resistance movements. We'll identify who they are and where they're located and unleash the giants on them. Then I'll call off the giants. This way I won't have to take responsibility for these attacks, yet I can establish my benevolence by making the giants stop, showing my omnipotence. If I can control giants, well then, I must be all-powerful. And we'll televise it all. It's brilliant."

Klaus nodded. "Your idea has merit. The giants will crush these weak-minded fools. Since I was a child, I have always wanted to see them in action."

John put his hand on the big man's shoulder. "Well, my friend, you will have your chance. Coordinate with Hrugnir, the new leader of the frost giants. Since they are unfamiliar with this world, it will require much instruction. Start with Japan."

Klaus grinned. "I look forward to it."

"What else do we have on the agenda?"

Klaus was all business again. "Your new friend, the Russian dictator, would like to set up a face-to-face meeting."

"Very well, set it up. Tell him I look forward to meeting him. He was a formidable opponent, and he will be a valuable ally. He had a great deal of experience in the old KGB. That kind of expertise will be valuable. Anything else?"

"Many of the survivors of our new world are finding religion. They have been opening churches, synagogues, and mosques worldwide."

"No, no, no. That won't do. As is clearly stated in the handbook, there will be no worship of any deities other than yours truly. I will not dispute the existence of these other beings, however, they have proven to be insignificant. After all, where were they when the disease spread, and people started dying? Nowhere. Therefore, they do not matter. I have persevered and now I reign supreme."

"What would you like me to do?" Klaus asked.

"Destroy any churches or places of worship. We will set up centers where people can pray to me. And perhaps, if they are lucky, I will listen to what they have to say. Anything else?"

Klaus shook his head.

"Good, good."

After Klaus left, John picked up his phone and speed dialed his personal assistant. "Yes, Inga, send one of my concubines to my office. Running the world is stressful business, and I need to unwind. A red-headed, voluptuous one would be preferable. No, make that two. It's been that kind of day." John hung up the phone and pondered what Odin would do.

Chapter XII

Thor shuddered as the Midgard Serpent rose in front of him. Its head was hundreds of meters above him, far from its full height. To destroy Jormangandr, he would have to attack the beast's head, its smallest and most vulnerable point.

He raised Mjolnir, and his war hammer launched him into the air. Among its many powers, it gave him the ability to fly. Against an adversary this big, flying was essential.

Jormangandr opened his wide maw and spit acid. Thor stopped in mid-flight and waved his hammer, creating a blast of air that repelled the acid. He pointed his hammer outward and flew toward the serpent. As he drew closer, the Midgard Serpent opened his jaws in an attempt to swallow Thor whole.

He swung Mjolnir and connected with the top of the serpent's mouth. Jormangandr recoiled, sending massive waves to the shore. Thor had struck a mild blow. It would take far more to do serious damage to the serpent.

He lunged forward and clung onto his scaly neck as Jormangandr thrashed about. Putting his hammer in its sheath strapped across his back, Thor climbed up its neck. The ride was rough as Jormangandr thrashed, causing hellacious waves to drench the blood-soaked battlefield.

Thor smashed the back of the serpent's neck with Mjolnir. Jormangandr bucked violently, throwing him into the air. He flipped end over end before crashing into the icy water. In the process, Mjolnir flew from his hand. Jormangandr dove under water, whether by choice or because he had been injured, Thor could not tell.

Despite his pain and the threat the Midgard Serpent would pose when it reemerged from the water, he had to regain Mjolnir. Whenever he threw Mjolnir, it would return to his hands due to the magical properties of the war hammer and the gloves he wore. However, this was not the case in water.

He dove after Mjolnir when it splashed into the water. He swam deep and intercepted his hammer before it reached the bottom of the ocean.

With Mjolnir in hand, he swam back to the surface. Jormangandr's massive frame loomed in front of him. He silently cursed. He was defenseless under water even with the aid of his war hammer. He tried to swim away but did not go far when Jormangandr enwrapped Thor within its body and lifted him out of the water.

Thor gasped for breath as the serpent constricted the life out of him. The serpent had wrapped itself around his arms, legs, and waist. Thor tried to use his heavily muscled arms to pull away from Jormangandr, but he could not gain any leverage. He tried to smash the serpent's hide with his hammer, but Jormangandr did not seem phased. He was losing breath quickly. He had to do something before it choked him to death.

Using both arms, he shimmied upward. The serpent still maintained a tight grip, but he now had room to maneuver. He took his war hammer, swung it in the air, and hurled it at the beast's head. It flipped end over end through the air and found its mark under the serpent's left eye.

Nearly out of breath, Thor let out a smile as Jormangandr loosened its grip enough to pull himself free. He took a deep breath as he stood on top of the serpent. He felt like putting his hands on his thighs and resting, but instead extended his arm, and his trusted war hammer found its way to his outstretched hand.

Moments later, Jormangandr flung Thor off him. He landed in the water again. His eyes went wide as the serpent stretched its long neck toward him. He attempted to swim away but before he could, Jormangandr sunk its fangs into him. Thor screamed in agony. He had hoped to avoid that for as long as possible. He had felt the effects of Jormangandr's poison in the past. In large doses, it was lethal. Even in smaller doses, it could debilitate him.

He wanted to use Mjolnir's power of flight to get him out of the water, but before he could, Jormangandr's massive fangs bit him again. Thor screamed once more. He had to turn the tide of the battle, or it would all be over for him.

***

Modi fell to his knees and screamed. "No!"

Magni gritted his teeth. Just as with Freya, he was too late to do anything. No matter how well he fought today, he could not save the ones he loved most.

The look of Fenris Wolf after he tore apart Odin's throat was one of triumphant glee. Blood dripped from the wolf's sharp teeth. His eyes glistened in the high morning sun. He lifted his head and howled. This seemed to give the giants and monsters renewed energy as they attacked with added fury. With the leader of the Aesir dead, this was their opportunity for victory.

Odin's son, Vidar, charged after Fenris Wolf. He opened his mouth wide and tried to clamp those powerful jaws around Vidar's throat, but the son of Odin held those jaws apart with his powerful arms. He reached for his sword, and, for a moment, Magni thought Vidar would succeed in slaying the beast, but he could not hold Fenris Wolf's jaws opened for long. The wolf leapt on top of Vidar and tore his throat, leaving behind a mess of bloody gore. Copious amounts of blood flowed from Vidar as he choked and died, another victim of Fenris Wolf.

Magni grabbed Modi by the shoulder. "Get up! Now is not the time for weakness."

Just as his brother had awoken him from his haze following Freya's death, now it was Magni's turn to rouse his brother after the Allfather's brutal massacre.

Magni stared at his brother, an animalistic snarl forming on his face. Modi trembled as he rose to his feet. Magni had never seen his brother in this type of fury. It was just as well because Modi did his best fighting when he was in a full berserker rage.

He and Modi spaced themselves apart as they approached Fenris Wolf.

The wolf continued to chew big chunks of Vidar's flesh, seemingly unperturbed at their arrival. It sniffed the air. "What do we have here? More Aesir ready to die. Ah, Thor's boys. The chosen ones. You two will die all the same." Fenris Wolf howled.

Magni wanted to come back with a retort but could not think of anything that would not sound trite. It did not matter. It would come down to a test of will and skill, not words.

Modi twirled his axe before charging after Fenris Wolf. Magni hesitated, waiting for the wolf to fend off his brother's charge. When Fenris Wolf committed to its defense, Magni sprung at him with his sword.

With cat-like agility that belied his size, Fenris Wolf ducked beneath Modi's axe and knocked him to the ground with his front paws. Instead of attacking, he turned toward Magni and dove for his legs. Magni reacted in time to hurtle over the wolf. He slashed downward with his sword and sliced the wolf's hide.

Fenris Wolf grunted but otherwise gave no indication of pain as he circled back. It would take far more than that to stop this monster.

Modi sprung to his feet. He and Magni stalked Fenris Wolf from either side, closing in around the beast. Fenris Wolf jumped at Magni. He held his sword upward, but the wolf pinned him, knocking the sword from his hand. It was as if a mountain had crashed on top of him. The creature's combined size and strength was unlike anything he had ever dealt with.

Modi came from the other side and slashed Fenris Wolf's hind legs. Magni could not see the result of the blow from his vantage point, but it must have made an impact, since the wolf backed off of him. Without his sword and with only small or long range weapons that would prove useless against this foe, Magni got to his feet and charged at the wolf. When they collided, it felt like he hit a solid wall, but the wall toppled.

Fenris Wolf snarled at him, his eyes showing the first signs of trepidation.

Modi wasted no time attacking Fenris Wolf with his axe, landing a few solid blows. The wolf bled profusely but did not seem to lose any strength. He turned on Modi and clamped his teeth onto his arm.

Modi screamed, blood gushing from his shoulder. Magni felt his brother's agony. He grabbed his sword and slashed at the wolf, ripping his face and belly.

Fenris Wolf mercifully stopped biting Modi and turned his wrath on Magni. He growled and jumped on Magni, his full weight slamming him.

Magni desperately tried to fight off the wolf. Breathing became a laborious task. He gripped Fenris Wolf's front legs. The wolf bit his face, so Magni let go of his front paws and grabbed his jaws. Blood and sweat streamed down his face. The wolf's saliva dripped onto him. His massive teeth tore through Magni's gloves and ripped his hands. His hands bled as the wolf's sharp teeth dug into them. He tried to ignore the pain but that was like trying to ignore the sun on a bright day.

Magni cursed under his breath. He was fighting hard to hold off Fenris Wolf but could not maintain this grip forever. "A little help would be nice!"

"Right with you, brother." Modi took a wide swing at Fenris Wolf with his axe, but it had no apparent effect.

Meanwhile, holding onto Fenris Wolf's jaws became an increasingly difficult task. He kept whipping his head, trying to bite Magni. The wolf dug his legs into Magni's chest and abdomen. The pressure was so intense, he could hardly breathe.

Modi swiped at the wolf's snout, a blow that was dangerously close to Magni, but his brother was precise with his swing. The blow clipped the top of Fenris Wolf's nose. He snarled, jumped off Magni, and knocked Modi off his feet. His brother's eyes rolled to the back of his head.

Before Fenris Wolf could attack a badly dazed Modi, Magni reached for two daggers in his vest and threw them at Fenris Wolf. The first landed in his thick hide, doing minimal damage, but the second caught him in his neck. Blood dripped from the wound.

Fenris Wolf's eyes went wide, his nostrils flared. "You will die, son of Thor."

He may have enraged the wolf, but the attack had its desired effect as Modi was back on his feet. Fenris Wolf leaped on top of Magni once more and pinned him to the ground.

From the corner of his eye, he saw Modi throw down his axe.

Magni's eyes went wide. "What are you doing?"

Through gritted teeth, Modi replied, "I'm going to kill this monster."

It was a good thought, but what was Modi going to do, will the wolf to die?

Modi ran to Odin's corpse and took Gungnir from the Allfather's hands.

Magni renewed his efforts at holding back Fenris Wolf.

Modi leapt onto the wolf's back. Fenris Wolf ignored him, apparently not thinking him to be a sufficient threat, and continued to try to mangle Magni. Modi plunged Odin's spear into Fenris Wolf's back. The wolf's eyes went wide, and he let out a choking gasp.

Instead of trying to fight off Fenris Wolf, Magni brought him closer. Modi removed Gungnir from his back and stabbed him again with the spear. The wolf yelped. He tried to pull away, but Magni held onto his jaws.

Modi continued to plunge the spear into Fenris Wolf. Magni felt the wolf's strength ebb as his blood poured onto Magni's face. His eyes were covered with the wolf's blood, and he had to spit it out of his mouth. Through this, he held on as Modi stabbed the wolf with maniacal glee.

Eventually, Fenris Wolf collapsed on top of Magni.

Magni spat out blood. "The job is done."

"We can't be too sure." Modi continued to plunge Gungnir into the wolf's neck.

"I am quite certain," Magni said from below.

"Very well." Modi jumped off the wolf's back.

Magni slid out from underneath the giant carcass and reached for Modi's outstretched hand.

Modi smiled. "We killed Fenris Wolf. *We* did it."

Magni nodded. He felt utterly exhausted. "We did, but the battle's not over yet."

"Not hardly."

They turned their attention to the sea, where their father continued to battle Jormangandr, a fight that had been going on for the duration of the Battle of Ragnarok.

Modi's smile faded. "Father's in trouble."

That was an understatement. Although Jormangandr had sustained some heavy damage, Thor looked to be near death.

***

Magni and Modi fought their way to the shoreline. Despite the thousands dead, there were many left. As a result, it took longer than they would have liked.

They boarded a boat near the shore, Modi carrying Odin's spear, Gungnir. With Odin's death, it was only right that he held the spear. It would serve him well in their fight against Jormangandr.

As they rowed out to sea, the prospect of fighting the Midgard Serpent terrified Magni. If anybody could kill Jormangandr, it would be his father, but Thor had failed. Killing the serpent seemed an impossibility, but he and Modi had just defeated Fenris Wolf. Perhaps they could defy the odds once more.

Although he appeared lifeless, Thor was still in the water using his war hammer to shoot bolts of lightning at the serpent. When Jormangandr was not dodging lightning bolts, he was attempting to bite Thor or smash him with its body.

The waves nearly capsized their boat. They held steady and rowed until they reached their father. Magni leaned out, grabbed Thor by his shoulders, and hauled him into the boat.

Thor tilted his head back and slowly opened his eyes. "I wanted to see you two…before it was…too late."

Magni held onto his father's hand.

Thor gave a weak half smile. "I did my best…but I failed. You must…finish the serpent. Take Mjolnir…and my gloves, Magni." Thor closed his eyes for the final time.

Magni nodded, tears streaming down his face.

Modi had a look of grim determination. "Do as father says. Don the gloves and attack the beast. I will do what I can to distract him."

"But Mjolnir is father's hammer."

Modi shook his head. "He's dead. You're the only one beside him who could even lift it. Mjolnir is yours. Now go."

Magni felt numb as he slid the gloves off his dead father's hands. If he were to wield Mjolnir, he needed these gloves, which had magical properties linked to the hammer. He hefted the dense hammer. Modi was right. With their father dead, he was the only one who could use it.

As soon as he put on the gloves, he felt a surge of power and strength unlike anything he had ever experienced. His exhaustion was lifted like a fog over the horizon. It had come as an incredible surprise to the Aesir when Magni had first hefted the hammer since Thor had been the only one capable of it. And that was without the gloves. As much as he hated to admit it, Mjolnir felt right in his hands.

Magni raised Mjolnir with one hand and lifted himself in the air. Jormangandr's head was coming straight at him, his mouth open wide. Magni did not change course and went straight for the Midgard Serpent. He wound up the hammer and smashed his snout, causing the serpent's head to rock back.

Jormangandr shot out a heavy viscous fluid that Magni wanted no part of, so he lowered Mjolnir and plunged into the cold water near the base of the serpent's neck. Jormangandr craned his neck and bit him. Magni screamed in pain. He could not let that happen again. The same poison that killed his father would put an end to him as well.

Jormangandr thrust his body outward and coiled Magni within his grip. Air escaped Magni's lungs. His ribs cracked. He stiffened his entire body in order to fight against the constriction, but it felt as if he was in the world's most powerful vice. The serpent went to bite him again, but as he dipped his head, Gungnir sailed past Magni and pierced the Midgard Serpent's eye.

Jormangandr recoiled and shrieked. He loosened his grip, giving Magni a chance to escape.

He grabbed the serpent's scaly skin and climbed on top of it. The serpent continued to attempt to bite him, despite being blind in one eye. Magni had a hard time keeping his balance and staying away from his gaping maw. Fortunately, help came in the form of arrows sinking into the serpent's neck. Magni looked over and found his brother stringing more arrows into his bow while standing in the boat. If not for Modi's help, he would be dead by now.

This was Magni's opportunity. The serpent had been badly wounded during his fight with Thor. He had seen from his vantage point Thor giving Jormangandr numerous heavy blows. Now, the serpent was partially blind. Yet he still stood. Magni was going to change that.

Magni climbed up his neck while Modi fired arrows at the Midgard Serpent. There was little Jormangandr could do to stop Magni other than try to buck him off, but he held on.

The serpent's skin was slick, and its scales were sharp. It took a while for Magni to reach the top of his head, and he nearly fell off several times. He hefted Mjolnir overhead and slammed it onto the serpent's skull. The thud of the hammer reverberated in the air. The serpent shook and shuddered. He let out a massive hiss, and Magni once more smashed its head with Mjolnir.

The Midgard Serpent swayed violently, so Magni flattened himself against his skull.

"Keep at it," Modi yelled from below.

Gingerly, Magni got to his feet. He took a wide stance and once more slammed Mjolnir into the serpent, whose body writhed, forming giant waves.

"Hit him again," Modi shouted from below.

Magni nodded and continued to bash the Midgard Serpent's massive cranium with Mjolnir. With each blow, the serpent lowered into the sea. He tried to throw Magni off, but his movements became labored. Magni stopped counting how many blows he had dealt the beast. He was numb with grief, crazed with revenge, and sick of the utter destruction of this battle, yet he still smashed the serpent, only stopping when the beast finally sank lifeless into the sea.

Magni pulled Gungnir out of the serpent's eye before the spear became submerged and irretrievable. It was far too valuable a weapon to lose.

When he reached the surface of the water, Modi was waiting for him in the boat. He lifted Magni into the boat and clasped his shoulder. "You did it, brother. I knew you would."

Magni sighed and slumped back in the boat in utter exhaustion. He looked at the shoreline where the fighting was coming to an end because there were so few left to fight. "We have won the battle, but at what price?"

Chapter XIII

The magnitude of the battle hit Magni as his brother rowed their boat to the shoreline. He had experienced a wide array of emotions from the incredible elation of defeating the invincible Fenris Wolf and Jormangandr to losing his father and the love of his life. Now he just felt numb.

He gazed aimlessly at the sporadic fighting still taking place while Modi remained stoic. He wished he had his brother's inner strength to endure this emotional turmoil. Modi was the ultimate warrior. No matter what he was feeling inside, he would keep fighting regardless of the odds or the circumstances of the battle. Even after their father had died, he remained singularly focused on the task at hand. Magni could not have made it through today without leaning on his brother's strength.

They reached the shoreline and walked onto the blood-soaked field. The opposition seemed to have no more stomach left to fight as the remaining giants retreated.

"It's over," Modi said.

Magni nodded.

"We have won. It was not pretty, but we did what needed to be done."

Magni buried his head. "What have we actually won? Everyone I have ever truly cared for except you is dead. Freya, Thor, Odin, Tyr, Frey, all of them. This victory is hollow."

Modi put his hand on his shoulder. "We fought for more than ourselves. This battle was to protect humankind. It was important enough for them to sacrifice themselves."

Magni folded his arms. "Once more, I say for what? Long gone are the days when the mortals held us in veneration. Long gone are the days when they had temples dedicated to us, or sang songs of our glories, or spoke reverently about our adventures. They have forgotten us. We are but a myth to them."

Modi stopped walking and stared into his brother's eyes. "I share your pain. No one should have to experience the loss we have today. So much has been taken from us, but you know as well as I that we are caretakers of Midgard. They are our responsibility. Whether they worship or revere us is irrelevant. Do you think that Odin would have engaged in this war if it was not absolutely necessary?"

"Odin did not want to fight them; he did all he could to avoid this confrontation."

Modi nodded. "Very true, but in the end, he realized the Battle of Ragnarok was both necessary and unavoidable. With Loki and his minions plotting our demise, there was no other course we could take."

Magni continued walking. "Maybe so, but it still bothers me that this was done for a people who do not even acknowledge our existence. They died for nothing."

Modi glared at him. "Don't soil their memories by suggesting such a thing. They died for the very thing you and I were willing to sacrifice our lives for."

Magni grew silent. He knew his brother was right, but it did not change the bitterness that grew in his heart.

They continued walking toward the battlefield. The fighting stopped. The remaining giants and monsters were now boarding the vessels that had carried them to this hallowed site.

"I just wish it did not have to be like this," Magni said.

"Wishing will change nothing. What's done is done. We must pick up the pieces and move on."

Modi was not being heartless. He was also hurting inside. He was just being practical.

"There is only one thing that truly bothers me about this whole affair. Where was Loki?"

Magni shook his head. "I fully expected him to lead the charge. I wanted to take his head off. I kept searching for him during the battle, but he was nowhere to be found."

"The Fates foretold that he would lead the monsters of the underworld against us, that he and Heimdall would fight to the death, but he was conspicuously absent."

Magni folded his hands and brought them to his lips. "Perhaps he's a coward, and despite his bluster, he did not have the courage to fight."

Modi shook his head. "Loki is many things. He is a scoundrel, an evil bastard, a trickster of the highest caliber, but he is not a coward. Also, why would his forces fight us without their leader? This was his fight. Why would the others fight us to the death if he was not willing to do so?"

"I don't know." Magni had those same thoughts when it became apparent Loki would not be joining the fray. "I have a dreadful feeling about this. We're not seeing the full picture. There will be many things we must do in the aftermath of Ragnarok, but above all we must answer those questions."

"What good is it to destroy the giants if Loki lives? There will never be peace as long as he exists. We must find and kill him."

The valkyries, dwarves and remaining Aesir—the few that were left—gathered around Magni and Modi.

Magni let his brother address the gathering crowd of weary warriors. He did not have the energy to speak.

"You have all fought hard today and have done yourselves proud. You will be the legends that will be remembered for centuries. The physical scars you retain today will pale in comparison to the ones in your heart. Thank you for giving all you have to give.

"The Battle of Ragnarok is over. We are victorious."

Cheers came from the crowd, but it was far more subdued than it would have been in other circumstances. Those left were undoubtedly weary to the bone, and it was hard to muster any jubilation after so many had died.

Modi continued, "Although victory is ours, our losses are innumerable. We will honor the valiant warriors who died by entombing the fallen Aesir in their rightful places in Valhalla and giving proper burials to the others. Then we will determine what needs to be done to move forward in this new world after Ragnarok."

Magni looked up to the sky. For the first time in this otherwise dreary day, the sun broke through the clouds. It would be a new beginning. Modi spoke of moving forward, but he had no desire to do so. His heart had shattered today. What was the point of rebuilding? It would never be the same.

Modi continued. He spoke eloquently, and the survivors seemed to be listening intently, but the words held no meaning to him. He wished the battle was still raging. He wanted to rush into a line of giants and slaughter every last one of them. If they killed him in the process, then so be it. Perhaps he would have been better off if Jormangandr had dragged him to the bottom of the sea.

Lost in his contemplations and ruminations, he did not realize that Modi had stopped speaking until his brother put a hand on his shoulder.

"Let's go, Magni."

Magni raised his brows. "And where exactly are we going?"

"We are going to help gather the dead."

Magni nodded. At least that would keep his mind occupied. It was the least he could do for his fallen brethren.

The Aesir who had been slain would be put into tombs in Valhalla. Before long, their bodies would vanish. Where they disappeared to, Magni did not know. It was a mystery among the Aesir. They would bury the fallen dwarves and valkyries since their corpses would decompose. They had already designated an area near the battlefield that would be the final resting place for the fallen warriors. They would build a monument to honor those who had died for this noble cause.

Although the work was tedious, Magni was glad to do it. He and Modi took special care of the bodies of Odin, Thor, Tyr, and the other leaders of the Aesir. He told Modi that he could not bear the grief of disposing of Freya's corpse, so his brother handled that himself.

By nightfall, it became evident that the burial process would take some time. After they put Frey into his tomb, Modi said, "We have done enough for today. Let's retire to my hall. I have a bottle of wine that I'd like to open so that we can drink to our fallen comrades."

Magni nodded. "I would like that."

"Tonight, we will celebrate those who have fallen." Modi gave him a hard stare. "For tomorrow we have much work to do, and it will not be easy."

Magni was certain that his brother did not mean the burial of dead. That would be left to others. His brother was referring to Loki and the mission the Norns left for them.

Chapter XIV

Magni and Modi spent the morning speaking with survivors of the battle. Not surprisingly, nobody had seen Loki. Had Loki been present, he would have made his presence felt.

Loki's absence was a mystery, one they had to solve. The only interesting piece of information the morning yielded was that the only significant member of the opposition to survive was Hel, the ruler of Niflheim, the underworld. Despite her resourcefulness, Magni figured she would have died like the rest. Undoubtedly, she was back in Niflheim, licking her wounds.

Thyrm and Surter, the leaders of the frost and fire giants respectively, had met their demise. The giants had been thoroughly decimated and would not be a threat in the near future. Magni had anticipated far more giants on the battlefield. Every last one of them should have been fighting. Yet another mystery they needed to solve.

Modi bit into an apple. "Hel will be the key to finding Loki. Besides being his daughter, she has always been his close confidant. Not to mention, he entrusted her to lead the monsters of the underworld."

Magni nodded. "Fortunately, she still lives. I never thought I would be thankful to know that she's alive. Hel makes me shiver. Anyone so focused on death is not someone I'd like to spend time with."

Losing so many he loved tore Magni up inside, but the only way to have their deaths mean something was to follow through on the Norns' prophecy. Otherwise, he would lose his sanity.

He and his brother consumed entirely too much ale the previous evening. After sleeping for a few hours, his body was sore and his head foggy, but he was ready for action.

Modi grinned. "I think we will be spending some quality time with Hel. She has pertinent information we need. Fortunately, it will be easier to reach her now. After I killed Garm, she no longer has her pet to protect her."

Going to the underworld would be an arduous task, something very few had ever attempted and survived. Thor and Odin had travelled to Niflheim on several occasions, but they were no longer around for council. To make matters worse, with Heimdall dead, there was nobody to operate the Bifrost Bridge to get to Niflheim.

Modi frowned. "I'm not thrilled with the prospect of going to Niflheim, but if we're to find answers, then we have no choice. I suggest we make haste."

Magni folded his arms and looked out the large window at the front of Modi's hall. One day ago, the battle raged just beyond the hill in the distance. "What about all the burials and the ceremonies for the dead? The others will look to us for leadership during these times."

Modi was stone-faced. "The dead will stay dead. This can't wait."

"As much as I dread it, I agree that we have to deal with this now. I have a feeling we've already lost too much time. Loki is a schemer of the highest magnitude. Whatever he has concocted will have major ramifications."

"Then we are agreed. We will take Sleipnir and leave this afternoon. She has made the journey before and will be able to get us to Niflheim."

Magni turned away. He wondered how Odin's magnificent stallion would react to his passing. He could not imagine life in Asgard without Odin. His steady hand and infinite wisdom had always steered the Aesir. Magni and his brother were a poor substitute.

His brother put a hand on Magni's shoulder. "I know this isn't easy. It would be difficult enough if we just had to mourn the loss of those we love, but we must blindly stop Loki without knowing his plans. Nor do we have the advice and countenance of Thor and Odin to guide us. Of those who survived the battle, we are the strongest, smartest, and most courageous. That is why the Norns gave us this task."

When Magni did not respond, Modi turned him around and brought their faces close together. "You need to get out of this malaise. I can't do this alone. The truth is, you're stronger than me, both mentally and physically. I don't stand a chance without you. Are you with me, brother?"

"Of course I'm with you. Just give me the rest of this morning to sort out my feelings and pack a few things for this journey. Then we will go to Niflheim."

***

Before he could move on, Magni had to visit Freya's tomb. The deaths of the others were terrible, but losing Freya felt like someone had ripped out his soul.

He travelled alone to Valhalla. Once inside, he glanced at the trophies and stuffed game lining the walls. They were the trophies of hunts from jollier days. Would those days ever return?

He took a deep breath before entering the room that housed Freya's tomb. Somehow, he had to find a way to live without her. They had been lovers for over a century, and the intensity of his feelings for her never waned for a moment.

He knelt in front of her tomb. Her body lay still inside. In a few short days, it would vanish to the great unknown. He lowered his head, not knowing what to say.

"I killed Surter and avenged your death. And we won the battle, yet I still feel so hollow. Modi and I even managed to kill Fenris Wolf and Jormangandr, but it doesn't feel as if we have won anything. You're gone from my life, and Loki still lives.

"Oh, Freya, what am I going to do without you?" Magni cried. "You know, I could hardly believe it when you did not reject my advances all those years ago. You were the most beautiful creature I ever laid eyes on, yet for some reason, you saw fit to be my lover, my confidant, my soulmate. I was never worthy of you, but I was not about to complain. Many others were envious, and those like Surter were downright hateful that you chose me.

"I know if you were here you would tell me to stop feeling sorry for myself and do what needs to be done. Oh, Freya, even to the last you were so courageous, so valiant. You knew you were going to die, yet that did not deter you. You fought without fear. When you were struck down, I was blinded by hatred. It was not enough to kill Surter. I could only feel satisfaction after decapitating him, and that only served as a momentary respite to the utter despair that has come over me since.

"I will do what is required of me. I know the stakes are high. I know I will face great danger, but none of that will deter me for you will be with me in spirit. And when times are their darkest, I will be brave because I will remember how you lived."

Magni stood. "I will go now, but I will never forget you. I don't know what the days ahead will bring, but I know that I can handle whatever adversity I find because you will be with me always."

Chapter XV

John Madison stood atop a high hill in the city formerly known as San Francisco and looked down at the settlement with loathing. "Welcome and thank you for your attendance today." Despite the distance that separated them, they would have no difficulty hearing him. He projected his voice as if it came from the heavens. That was the benefit of being a deity.

The leaders of the United Freedom Front had gathered below him in the square in the agreed upon meeting place. These humans had dared to defy him. The giants had squashed most of the uprisings around the globe. This strategy worked well in most places, but this settlement proved to be resilient.

When the giants attacked the United Freedom Front, the group had gone underground. Klaus suggested leading an assault team into their stronghold and annihilating their members. Although that strategy had merit, John had a more elegant solution. It was time for him to establish his rule as absolute, not just for this loathsome group of thugs, but for everyone. Some doubted his authority, questioning why he should lead this post-apocalyptic world. His critics did not realize he was not a mere mortal, but a superior being. That was why he was broadcasting this show of force around the world. When the masses saw what he was capable of doing, they would bow to him in subservience.

He brought his palms together. "Much of the strife in this world is borne of ignorance. I can understand your fear and reluctance to accept change. The scars of the disease that killed so many run deep. I am here to tell you that you need not fear this change. I offer you a chance for a better way, an improvement over the life you knew. Together, we can accomplish great things, but you cannot let your fears overwhelm you."

The United Freedom Front had started a propaganda campaign against him, even going so far as saying that he was responsible for the virus that wiped out most of the human population. Of course, he was responsible for the virus, but they had no way of knowing that. Denouncing his laws, they urged others to rise against him.

After having gathered intelligence on their efforts and personnel, he was hardly impressed. They had no military background and lacked armament to fight. Still, they continued to recruit members and incite others. This was a greater threat than a paramilitary group, which could be easily squashed. This group was insidious because their message could spread like a contagion.

Judging by their startled faces, they probably thought it was some trick that they could hear him so well even though he was far away. Perhaps they thought he had installed hidden speakers or used modern technology.

"I have established many new laws and regulations. I assure you that these were not done without thought. They are for the betterment of our world. If we are to live together in peace and harmony, then strict laws must be established. They may seem harsh, but I assure you that they are necessary. I ask you to trust in me. I have your best interests at heart."

These words were directed to the larger audience watching on television and the internet. The United Freedom Front was irrelevant and would soon no longer exist. But those watching had to recognize and unequivocally accept his power.

John Madison looked up to the sky, his face somber. "It is with great regret that I make an example of your group. You leave me no choice, pushing me as far as I am willing to be pushed. You have condemned yourselves with your actions and thus have sealed your fate."

Even from this distance, he could see panic spreading among the rebels.

John raised his hands high in the air and spoke in Old Norse to summon the water in the San Francisco Bay to do his bidding. He was the master of this land, and even the elements recognized that.

A massive rush came from the bay. Any boaters would be in extreme peril as the water roared to life. He gave the water time to take shape as he continued his incantation.

The sound coming from behind John was that of a waterfall. John made an intricate series of hand gestures. He looked back as the water rose hundreds of feet in the air.

The terrified faces of the people below was priceless to behold as the water formed into a massive tidal wave, unlike anything these people had ever conceived of, let alone witnessed. They ran for cover, but it was too late, oh so late, to do anything.

John moved his hands forward. The water gave a deafening roar as it came crashing down on the city streets. He watched in awe as millions of gallons of water smashed these rebellious inhabitants like a sledgehammer. Sure, there would be collateral damage. He could live with it as long as this display of his power left no doubt to the viewers that their obedience was essential if they were to survive. Rising against him would bring upon them a similar fate—one of utter destruction.

The water flooded the street, sweeping away the inhabitants like flotsam and jetsam. They looked like dolls instead of people. Their screams competed with the roar of the rushing water. As much as John had deliberated about this decision, now that he was going through with this severe disciplinary action, he had to admit that he enjoyed it. Having this kind of power was glorious. That was something Odin could never grasp.

John turned and faced the camera. "Today, I did what needed to be to be done. You may find these actions to be harsh, but in these trying times, I assure you that it was absolutely necessary. If we are to rebuild society, then rules must be strictly enforced. As long as you comply, you need not worry. You will find me to be a most benevolent leader, but uprisings will not be tolerated. If you suspect treachery among your neighbors, then proceed to your nearest Assimilation Center and notify the authorities. Together, we will persevere."

After the camera went off, John looked upon the ruined city with a sense of satisfaction. He was quite certain he had sent his message loud and clear.

Chapter XVI

They departed for the underworld that afternoon, Modi on the back of Sleipnir, Magni on his sturdiest steed on what would surely be a treacherous journey.

Magni was concerned at how Sleipnir would react to Odin's absence. She had been with Odin for over a thousand years. Surprisingly, Sleipnir did not seem to mind when Modi took her reigns.

There was no discussion as to who would take possession of Sleipnir. Perhaps because he now owned Odin's spear, Gungnir, each brother assumed Modi would also have Sleipnir. Regardless, the eight-legged stallion immediately took to Modi.

Sleipnir needed no direction on the journey to Niflheim, nor did she tire. The same could not be said for Magni's stallion, so they stopped several times for rest and feeding.

When they stopped for the evening, Magni hunted while Modi created a fire. Perhaps because of his weariness, it took Magni a while to hunt a deer using his spear. Carrying the dead animal on his back, he felt ready to collapse.

Modi raised his brows. "I was about to look for you. I thought you had lost your way, or perhaps encountered a creature of the underworld who had wandered out here and had gotten the best of you."

Magni sat by the fire. "In my current condition, it would not surprise me. My exhaustion has reached unhealthy levels."

"It has less to do with being tired and more to do with how much you ache inside."

"How do you do it, Modi? Nothing ever affects you. You keep going no matter the circumstances. You stay strong regardless of how much adversity you face."

"Do you think you're the only one who hurts inside? I just don't show it." Modi smirked. "To answer your question, you're my inspiration. If I am to do things as well as you, then I must try my hardest, fight my best, think clearly, and work hard to overcome adversity. I strive to be better than you, and it's a battle I usually lose, because you do everything so well. I don't think father would ever have admitted it, but he saw you as his successor. When he was gone from this world, you would carry on in his stead as being the Warrior of the Aesir people."

"That's not true," Magni said.

Modi folded his arms. "Do you know what your problem is?"

Magni shook his head. "But I'm sure you will tell me."

"You have a lower opinion of yourself than anyone else who knows you does. You fail to realize that you're capable of greatness, and in fact, have accomplished many great things. Do you think it's an accident that Odin and Thor chose you for this mission?"

Magni's response echoed with bitter sarcasm. "They chose me because everyone suitable would be dead."

"Wrong. Thor, Odin, and the Norns put this burden on your shoulders because they knew you had the strength, intelligence, and perseverance to see this through."

Magni hung his head low. He knew his brother was trying to lift his spirits, but he had a hard time believing his words. "And what of you? They also chose you."

Modi smiled. "You can't do this alone. Someone has to prop you up when you fall down, to urge you when you falter."

"Now who is selling themselves short? You're as big a part of this as I am. We will succeed or fail together."

Modi tilted his head back and brought out a bottle of wine. "I'll drink to that."

***

The trip to the underworld would have been easier if Magni had a steed like Sleipnir, but no other creature like Sleipnir had ever existed. She never tired despite riding at a blistering pace.

Magni felt sorry for his own horse midway through the second day. He could sympathize with his beast. He often felt inferior to Thor. Since his physical strength had been greater than his father's, it was common for the Aesir to compare them, but he could never live up to the legend. Who could? Thor was the Aesir's greatest warrior. He was the most valiant, the most daring, exceptional in all he did. Despite Modi's assertions, he was none of those things. He could never hope to achieve his father's greatness. He had always thought his father to be invincible, so it had been devastating to see him fall to Jormangandr. Even with the Norns' prophecy that Thor would die at Ragnarok, Magni still did not believe it could happen.

He and Modi continued to speculate about Loki's absence from the Battle of Ragnarok. The answer had to be found in Midgard. It had been over a decade since Magni and his brother traveled there, which was not nearly as long as some of the other Aesir. They were free to travel to the world of mortals, but most chose not to. Midgard society had changed so much that many Aesir felt detached from it.

They rode at a fast pace for the next two days, only stopping to eat and give brief respites for the stallions. Magni worried his poor beast would collapse if they continued at this pace. To make matters worse, the trail was becoming progressively worse.

Much to his relief, by the end of the third night, Niflheim was in sight. He and Modi briefly debated charging straight into the underworld before deciding it would be prudent to stop for the night.

That evening, he and Modi spoke of the Battle of Ragnarok, which turned out to be a poor decision because the image of Freya falling at Surter's hands kept replaying in his mind. That image so tortured him that he gave up on sleep and wandered around their makeshift camp.

The area surrounding Niflheim was devoid of vegetation and growth. It was one rocky crag and canyon after another. There were no animals, plants, or signs of life. There were also no rivers, streams, lakes, or bodies of water to be found. This was as arid and depressing a place as he had ever seen.

He stared into the darkness. Beyond lay Niflheim and hopefully the answers they sought. They would get those answers no matter what it took. The time for civility had long since passed. They had entered a new era, and there was a desperate quality to these times.

Magni climbed a large boulder and stared at nothing in particular. After laying down on the boulder, he surprisingly found sleep. It was only when day broke that he awoke from his slumber.

As he was walking back to their camp, he encountered Modi. Despite the dire circumstances, Modi was whistling.

"Ah, there you are, brother. I thought you had abandoned our quest. Either that or decided to go on without me."

"I sought better company for the evening." Magni motioned with his arms. 'I was surrounded by all of this nothingness."

"I see what you mean. Sometime in the future, we'll have to vacation in this lovely stretch of land."

"Are the mounts ready?" Magni asked.

Modi shook his head. "We're going in alone. Not safe for them. Not even Sleipnir. They'll be waiting for us when we return."

"Then we'll go it alone. No sense doing this on an empty stomach."

"I've already prepared breakfast."

They walked back to camp. Their breakfast consisted of fruit and dried meat. When they finished, Modi told Sleipnir of their plans. Odin frequently spoke to his stallion, and they fully understood each other, but who knew if Sleipnir understood Modi.

The brothers left with their weapons and provisions. The closer they got to the entrance of Niflheim, the more rugged the terrain became. Fortunately, Mjolnir alleviated some of these issues. Instead of climbing sheer rock walls, Modi held onto his brother while Magni used the war hammer to ascend the face of the cliff. The power of flight was spectacular, and Magni was still adjusting to this new ability.

The entrance to Niflheim was not much of a sight to behold. There was no river of fire or moat separating it from Asgard. Nor was there any warning sign at the entrance. If he did not know what to look for, Magni would have missed it altogether. The entrance to the underworld was merely an opening of a cave. Nothing spectacular, nothing noteworthy.

"Shall we enter Hel's domain?" Modi asked.

"I'll lead the way."

Chapter XVII

Magni led the way along the rocky crag to the entrance of Niflheim. At any moment, he expected to be attacked by an underworld minion—and there was no telling which of these indescribable horrors it might be—but there seemed to be none left after the Battle of Ragnarok. The Aesir had dealt the forces of the underworld a severe, perhaps permanent blow. More importantly, Garm was dead. The hellhound gave passage into or out of Niflheim. With Garm present, few could make it into Hel's domain.

Darkness pervaded the cave's entrance. Modi had forged a torch earlier that morning, which Magni now carried. If Freya was alive, she would have used magic to create light, but Magni would have clumsily fumbled around the formation of a spell and the end result would be a ball of fire that would burn them to a crisp instead of providing illumination.

Magni hesitated. Walking into Niflheim could not be this easy. The underworld was a place of legend—a terrifying place of legend. He turned toward Modi and shrugged. Modi nodded, and they proceeded.

Watching his footing on the rocky surface, Magni stepped inside. He moved his torch from side to side, the flickering lights creating shadows. The cave was tall, about twice his substantial height, and wound about like a snake. Nothing adorned the walls or the ground on which they walked.

The air smelled of rotting leaves and had a certain putrid quality that made Magni cringe. A shriek came from the distance. Magni tensed. Using his free hand, he gripped Mjolnir. With the winding cavern and limited visibility, he could not see the source of this noise, so he waited. The noise became louder. He could sense something flying at them, but still could not see it.

As it got closer, Magni could see that it was a winged creature not dissimilar to a bat with coarse brown fur. Magni was poised to strike, but the creature was flying over them, not at them. He would have struck the creature anyway, but Modi tugged at his arm.

After the creature passed, Modi said, "Save your aggression for later. Hel's the target of our ire."

"And Loki."

Modi nodded. "Although I doubt we'll find him here."

They traveled for a half hour without further incident. Magni's nerves remained on edge. The atmosphere inside Niflheim was chilly, not so much in terms of temperature, but the effects it had on his mind. Already fighting off depression from the aftermath of Ragnarok, he became increasingly despondent as they traveled through the underworld.

Interrupting his thoughts, Modi said, "You're rather quiet."

"I'm wondering why we're here. What can we possibly accomplish?"

"I know how you feel."

Magni turned to look at his brother, whose face appeared ashen. That was the last thing he expected to hear.

"It's this place," Magni said. "It feels so dead. It drains all emotion. I remember father speaking about it, but until you are actually here, it's difficult to comprehend."

Modi's voice trembled. "We need to finish this mission as soon as we can. I don't want to spend a minute longer here than we have to."

"We will. I'm surprised Hel hasn't sent her minions to intercept us."

"Perhaps she has none to send," Modi said.

They reached a large, open cavern. Through the middle flowed a river with water the color of gold. The river was at least ten meters wide. Past the river, their path continued.

"We should have brought swimming gear," Modi joked.

Magni shook his head. "We're in Niflheim. I doubt this is an ordinary river. Dangerous creatures probably lurk within."

"Maybe in ordinary times, but I imagine most of these creatures perished at Ragnarok."

"All the same, I think it would be best to use Mjolnir."

Modi gestured with his hand toward the river of gold. "In that case, lead the way."

Modi held onto his brother's shoulders. Magni lifted Mjolnir, and they flew across the river, landing on the ground just past the water.

Modi smiled. "Amazing."

A loud hiss came from behind them. Magni pivoted, holding Mjolnir with both hands, ready to strike. A serpent with gold scales emerged from the river. They probably had not seen it earlier since it blended with the river floor.

The serpent's head was full of spikes. It had deep-set green eyes. Water dripped off its long body. Magni could only see its head and upper torso. Since the part of that was visible to them was several meters out of the water, he surmised this serpent was quite large.

The serpent shot something at them. Magni and his brother ducked, and the stream of fluid flew over their head.

Without hesitation, Magni threw Mjolnir at the serpent. The hammer flew end over end but missed its target as the serpent dove back into the water. Mjolnir flew backward and landed in Magni's hand. The brothers waited for the serpent to return, but it didn't.

Magni moved toward the river, but Modi clutched his arm.

"Let it go," Modi said. "There will be more fighting to come. Save your energy and aggression."

Magni wanted to argue with his brother, but he agreed with the sentiment. They continued on their journey. After encountering the serpent, he kept Mjolnir at the ready. At this point, the lighting was such that they no longer needed their torch, so Magni left it behind.

A strong sulfur odor pervaded the cave. The smell was so strong that it made Magni's eyes water.

After journeying for another hour, they reached a city. It had seven layers, one on top of the other as if chiseled from stone. It appeared to be deserted. From what Magni could gather, each level had houses, machinery, gadgets that appeared to be taken from Midgard, arenas, public squares, and an assortment of things one might find in a typical city.

"Not quite how I pictured it," Modi said.

"I never really thought about what Niflheim looked like," Magni said. "It's not as if I ever intended on coming here."

"You lack imagination, brother."

Paths led from one level to another. The entire structure was massive. The city was several kilometers wide. There was no way of telling from their position its full depth.

"So where do we start?" Modi asked.

"Where would you hide if you were Hel?"

Modi stroked his beard. "Why should Hel hide? Why would she think she had a reason to hide?"

"Because we're looking for her," Magni said.

"And why would she suspect that?"

"For the very reason that we're looking for her. Because Loki is alive. She has to know that the remaining Aesir would not rest until he was dead and will come looking for her to find him."

Modi folded his arms. "There is much area to cover, but I would rather not do so on an empty stomach."

Magni preferred to start searching, but he acquiesced to his brother. They picked a flat spot on the rocky ground and unpacked provisions. If they prolonged this stay, they would have to find food in this desolate place. Thus far, Magni had not seen anything that looked edible.

"So, what will happen to Valhalla now that Odin is no longer with us?" Modi asked.

Magni finished eating his piece of dried meat. "I haven't put much thought into it. I've been a bit preoccupied."

"Valhalla shouldn't go to waste. Perhaps you should take possession of it."

Magni furrowed his brow. "Me?"

"Why not? Odin would approve."

Magni sighed. "Then why don't you move into Valhalla?"

"It would feel strange."

"As it would for me. My own hall suits me fine."

Modi shrugged. "Maybe so, but if you are going to be the new leader of the Aesir, then you should live there."

"Who said that I will be the new leader of the Aesir?"

"I have. The Norns implied as much with this mission. So did Odin and Thor."

Magni tilted back his head. "And what makes you so sure that I should be the one to lead? Why not you?"

"You're more suited for the role. You're strong, intelligent, wise, all qualities needed in a leader. I'm too impulsive. I let my emotions get the best of me. You've seen how I get in the battlefield. I lose control, go into berserk rages."

"It suits you well," Magni said. "It's what makes you an especially dangerous foe."

"Maybe so, but a leader must think clearly at all times, something I am not capable of doing."

"I feel inadequate to lead the Aesir. I am not Odin and never will be." Magni sighed. "Can we visit this topic after we've completed this mission?"

Modi raised his hands. "Of course, but it's something we need to decide."

They finished a bottle of wine before setting off on a systematic search of the first level. Every time they opened a door, went down an alleyway, or stepped into a passage, Magni expected something to attack, but each time was disappointed. He was itching for a fight.

The stench was awful as they crossed the deserted area. The stale air had the smell of raw sewage.

Passing through what looked like an arena full of torture instruments, Modi said, "This must have been their entertainment."

"Hmm. What a cheerful bunch."

Chained to the ground was a creature of unknown origin. Its body was decomposing and, what was left, was rotting flesh and bones.

"Someone must have forgotten about this wretched soul," Modi said.

It took a couple hours to search the first level. Sweat dripped from Magni's brow. His brother's face was red from exertion. Their pace had slowed considerably, and neither of them had much to say.

Modi put his hands on his hips. "I think we've exhausted our search of this level."

Magni shuddered. "We have six more levels to search. And that's only in this section of Niflheim. Just how large is the underworld? We could be searching for days, weeks, months. I don't think I can last that long in Niflheim. In just this short time we have been here, I already feel as if I am crawling out of my skin."

They had no way of telling day from night. It was a morass of twilight.

This search would have been easier if there were obstacles in their path to fight through. Magni feared that not encountering anything for so long would cause them to drop their guard.

"How do we reach the second level?" Modi asked. "When we were approaching this city, I saw paths that led to the upper levels, but now that we are here, I can no longer decipher which paths will lead us upward."

"I have an idea." Magni walked backward toward the eastern edge of the city. After five minutes of walking, he reached a metal door. He stood back looking at the door. "I saw one of these the last time I was in Midgard. I believe the people there called it an elevator."

Modi raised his eyebrow. "And what do these elevators do?"

"They are used for transport, up and down," Magni replied.

"And how does one use this elevator?"

Magni searched for a button. He had seen people press them in his previous encounter with this contraption. He found the button and pressed it. The door opened. He stepped inside, and, after some hesitation, his brother followed. There were more buttons on the wall. They were not numbered, but he pressed the second button from the bottom, figuring that would take him to the second level. The machine groaned and creaked but eventually it moved, taking them higher. After nearly a minute, it stopped, and the door opened.

"The second level?" Modi asked.

Magni shrugged and stepped outside. They began to explore. Not long after entering the second level, the brothers encountered a massive slug, almost two meters long with a wide, round body. Magni contemplated smashing it flat with Mjolnir, but after observing it for a few minutes, felt it was no threat. It didn't appear to have any way of attacking them and smashing it would create a royal mess.

Proceeding past it with caution, Modi gestured to the giant. "I'm guessing that is Hel's pet."

Magni said, "It's a pathetic looking thing. If we killed that creature, we would be putting it out of its misery."

They explored a large hall on the second level. Shabbily decorated, it lacked the stature or refinement of the halls in Valhalla. Instead of trophies or sculptures of great hunts on the wall, they contained dark images of monsters and giants defeating the Aesir. There were even scenes showing Loki defeating Thor in battle. Anger smoldered inside Magni. That coward would not even show at Ragnarok, let alone defeat the greatest warrior among the Aesir.

Modi leaned against a wall. "There's nothing here." The wall shifted against his weight.

Magni's eyes went wide.

Modi tugged at the wall, and it shifted further. Behind the wall were stairs.

Magni felt an adrenaline rush. For the first time since entering Niflheim they had a solid lead.

Magni led the way, wishing he still had his torch. Visibility was poor, and he nearly tumbled down the stairs. There was no handrail, and the steps were narrow.

When they reached the bottom of the stairs, they stood on a dirt floor. The air felt heavy. Something slithered in the corner of the room.

Magni scanned the room but could see little. Modi separated himself from his brother. It was a tactic they commonly employed to prevent an attacker from striking both of them at once.

As Magni stepped forward, something jumped out of the shadows. The thing crawled on the ground. Whatever it was, the creature possessed enormous size that belied its quickness.

Before Magni could react, it jumped on top of him. Its huge jaws suggested it was no serpent. It snapped its jaws at him, its hot breath smoldering. Acidic saliva dripped on Magni's face. From the corner of his eye, Magni could see his brother looming above, but Modi appeared unsure of what to do. Due to the poor lighting, he had an equal chance of striking Magni as their attacker.

The creature had at least six legs. Magni snarled and grabbed two of them. Sharp claws jutted from its paws. When it snapped its jaws again, Magni could not avoid them. He cried out as the creature's teeth sunk into his flesh.

A hot flash of anger caused Magni to wrench the creature away and toss it aside, which gave Modi the space he needed. He thrust his spear at the creature. Judging by the loud yelp, Gungnir found its mark.

As Magni rose, he heard the shuffling of feet. Blood dripped from his shoulder. He took out Mjolnir. His wound made it difficult to heft the hammer, and he struggled with two hands to lift Mjolnir overhead.

The creature swept Modi off his feet. As it was about to pounce on his brother, Magni swung Mjolnir downward, resulting in a large splat. Despite what sounded like a crushing blow, it still moved on the ground. *Resilient beast.* Magni put his foot on top of the creature to get a bearing on his target. He swung Mjolnir and hit it once more.

Modi was back on his feet. He jabbed Gungnir at the creature, piercing the beast's mouth. It stopped moving.

"Dead?" Magni asked.

"I think so," Modi replied.

"What exactly is this thing?"

Modi bent down for a closer look. "My best guess is that it is an oversized alligator with a serious bite. I saw it take a nice chunk out of you."

Magni clutched his shoulder. "I'll live. We have bandages in my pack. Once we get a chance, you can patch me up."

They both turned their heads at the sounds of footsteps running away from them.

Magni's eyes went wide. "Hel?"

Without further discussion Magni and Modi set off in pursuit.

Chapter XVIII

Magni took the lead with Modi right behind him. Unfortunately, the darkness significantly reduced visibility. Magni tripped over a strand of reeds and stumbled to the ground. Without breaking stride, Modi lifted him by his shoulders. They made several turns and wound through a narrow corridor, all the while gaining ground.

From behind, Modi let out a loud curse as he tripped.

Magni glanced back but did not stop his chase. He could not afford to lose the trail, and Modi could take care of himself. The sounds of running came from behind, which meant Modi had recovered from his fall.

Magni turned the corner and faced a long stretch of straight corridor that was better lit than the rest of this labyrinth. With the increased light he could see they were indeed pursuing Hel, daughter of Loki, queen of the underworld.

Hel turned and shot a blast of fire at them from the palm of her hand. Magni hurled himself against the wall and avoided the blaze. Modi carried a shield and used it to defend himself.

Hel continued to run but was losing ground. Turning, she sent icy blasts at them. The air instantly chilled, which came as a relief, since Magni was sweating profusely from the chase. Using Mjolnir, Magni smashed aside the jagged ice coming in his direction.

Magni was tempted to throw Mjolnir at her but he wanted her lucid.

Modi put on a burst of speed and overtook his brother. Continuing to sprint, he dove at Hel. Modi's massive frame collided with her long, thin frame, and they both crashed to the ground. Hel tumbled several times, breaking free of Modi's grip. Magni slowed as he neared her and smashed her face with his fist, worsening her already hideous features. He brought back his fist and slugged her once more. Blood surged down Hel's nose. Magni took another swing at Hel, but Modi put his hand on Magni's shoulder.

"Enough for now."

Hel scampered against the wall and snarled at them. "What do you want with me? You won the battle. Isn't that enough?"

Magni stared at Hel's half black, half white face. Her features were distorted and misshapen. Her crooked nose was entirely too long. Pockmarks covered her face. Her eyes were sunken.

Magni grabbed her by the neck. "Don't play coy with us. You know why we're here."

Hel spat at him. "Leave Niflheim. I still have allies here."

"Like your pet we just killed," Modi said. "No, I think that was your last line of defense. The rest of your friends perished at Ragnarok, just as you should have."

"Except for one of them," Magni said. "Where's your father?"

Despite Magni's hand around her neck, Hel smiled. "How would I know?"

"Because you're his daughter and he trusts you," Magni said. "You're involved in his scheme. Now you're going to tell us where to find him."

"And why would I do that?" Hel asked.

Modi went face to face with her. "Because you don't enjoy pain, and we will torture you for all of eternity if we have to."

Hel spat at Modi. "I would like to see that happen. What do you know about torture? I am the master of torture."

Magni nodded. "Exactly. That means you know that you will eventually tell us what we need to know. Save yourself the agony. Let us know where Loki is, and we will leave you in peace. Our quarrel isn't with you."

"And you expect me to give away my father just like that?"

Magni said, "Your forces were defeated at Ragnarok. You lost the battle. You no longer have an army. My brother and I can slaughter you in combat, and we will do what is necessary to learn Loki's whereabouts. You have nothing to gain by maintaining silence. You won't die easily, so my guess is we could inflict horrible damage upon you before you perish. Do the smart thing, Hel. You may be ugly but you're not stupid."

"Let go of me," Hel said.

Magni released his grip. "So, what will it be? Do you want to test us and see if we have the mettle to bring you unending agony?"

Hel laughed. "You're just boys pretending to be your father. I'll tell you what you need to know, since it no longer matters."

Modi narrowed his eyes. "What do you mean?"

"You weren't paying attention, and now it's too late. What has been done is done, and there is nothing you boys can do about it. You want to know where my father is? I will tell you."

Magni glanced at Modi. His brother's eyes were filled with uncertainty. He figured Hel would put up more of a fight.

"Where's Loki?" Modi asked.

"I will tell you, but not here. I prefer somewhere more comfortable. We will go to my hall."

Magni wondered what devious scheme Hel was concocting, but he knew ultimately her defenses had been decimated. "No tricks, or this will end badly for you."

Hel smirked, a gesture that on her face looked like a sneer. "You boys are all bluster."

Magni knew that Hel calling them boys was her way of reminding them where they stood among the Aesir. But all of that changed with he and his brother surviving Ragnarok while most of the others had perished.

Modi gave her a cold stare. "Tell that to your hound. Oh wait, you can't. I killed Garm."

Magni gestured for Hel to move forward. "Walk. We'll follow."

Keeping a close eye on Hel, Magni followed her on one side, his brother on the other. Now that they found their target, the feeling of utter hopelessness Magni felt earlier was replaced with rage. He felt a strong urge to wrap his hands around Hel's throat and squeeze until she was lifeless. The bitter feelings of losing so many at Ragnarok raged inside him. Hel was personally responsible for killing quite a few Aesir, not to mention she had been a leading force among the opposition, her role even more prominent in Loki's absence. Killing her now would solve nothing, however.

They backtracked through the underground labyrinth, climbing up the stone staircase and going back into the second level of the underworld city, hardly speaking. Hel occasionally tried to bate them with taunts, but neither Magni nor his brother responded. She seemed unconcerned about her capture despite her initial struggle to escape.

Hel laughed as she walked in front of them. "You must really miss your father. Thor was a true hero. I enjoyed watching him die from Jormangandr's venom. At least my father still lives."

Modi kept his voice steady. "Loki is a coward. That's why he's alive. He set the Battle of Ragnarok in motion yet would not fight."

The witch giggled. "You mistake cowardice for genius. It's not his fault he was too smart for Odin. The Allfather. Hah!"

"Odin was a great leader," Magni said. "He had vision, integrity, and loyalty—things Loki is woefully short on. He died with honor, and my brother avenged his death."

Hel rubbed her hands together. "I am glad you ventured into Niflheim. I have been looking forward to gloating. You thought you gained the upper hand at Ragnarok, but you are oh so wrong."

Magni tightened his grip on Mjolnir, fighting a desire to smash Hel in the back of her head.

The severe feeling of depression Magni felt upon entering the underworld was returning. It was more than just being in Niflheim. He was starting to think there was truth in Hel's words. He glanced at Modi, who seemed to be brooding as well.

They ascended to the third level using the same elevator. A massive hall stood in the distance, rivaling those found in Asgard. The closer they got to their destination, the more Magni thought there would be no ambush, that Hel had nothing in her arsenal to offer them resistance. He kept his guard, however, not willing to take chances.

A tall bronze door with a carving of Jormangandr stood at the entrance of the hall. Hel waved her hands, and the door opened.

She made a gesture of welcome. "Please come inside."

Magni and Modi entered the hall. After stepping inside, the bronze door closed behind them.

In a sickly-sweet voice, Hel said, "May I offer food or wine to you weary travelers?"

Modi stared at her with cold eyes. "No thank you. You would probably poison any provisions."

"So paranoid," Hel said.

Magni grabbed her arm. "We're here now. Tell us what we want to know."

"Are you always so rude? We're immortal. We have all of eternity on our side. Well, except those poor souls who perished at Ragnarok. Where were we?"

"Stop playing games." Magni gritted his teeth. "Where's Loki?"

"Oh yes, my father." Hel had a wide smile as she rubbed her hands together. "Well, he has been rather busy of late. You see, he was wise enough to know our limitations and realized that we would not win the Battle of Ragnarok in the conventional manner. Therefore, he excused himself from the battle. He had bigger goals in mind."

Magni's eyes narrowed. What could be bigger than Ragnarok? The battle had been over a millennium in the making.

"While you and the rest of the Aesir were plotting our demise, my father conquered Midgard."

Modi's eyes went wide. "What?"

Hel gave a loud and resounding laugh. "Loki is now the sole ruler of the mortal realm."

Magni was speechless. It felt as if she had stabbed him in the gut.

"How is this possible?" Modi asked.

Hel intertwined her long fingers. "They never had a chance. It was such a well-crafted plan. You see he has been living among them for a number of years. He took over their whole world in one swift motion." Hel tossed her head back in exultation. "You will find Midgard to be vastly different than how you remember it."

Magni and Modi stared at each other. It had been years since they last saw Loki. The Aesir assumed he had been spending his time preparing for Ragnarok and recruiting allies for the battle.

"How did he take over Midgard?" Modi asked in a low tone.

Hel cackled. "He spread sickness amongst them, and they perished by the billions. There was hardly anyone left to fight him. How sad. They were no match for him and the giants."

Magni's eyes went wide. "Giants?" This was getting worse by the minute.

"How could giants gain entrance to Midgard?" Modi asked.

The Aesir had traveled in and out of the mortal realm for years, but giants? That was unheard of. If Loki had accomplished such a thing, that would have been an amazing fete. It would also explain why there weren't as many giants at Ragnarok as anticipated.

Magni clutched Hel's wrist. "How did giants gain access to Midgard?"

Suddenly, she went silent, her previous boastfulness gone.

"You're going to tell us," Magni said. "Start talking."

"No."

Modi held Gungnir to her throat. "Start talking."

"Are you going to kill me?" Hel taunted. "I don't die easily. As you can see, I survived Ragnarok. Not many others can say the same."

"There are worse things than dying." Magni brought out Mjolnir. "How many blows do you think you can sustain from the greatest weapon ever forged. I can start with your feet and work my way upward. I'm guessing I can land a good many blows without killing you."

Chapter XIX

It only took one strategically placed blow from Mjolnir, delivered to Hel's left foot, for her to start talking. Granted, the blow shattered her foot, and she wailed for an hour, but the damage could have been worse.

Magni felt no remorse. Hel had wrought so much misery over the years that she deserved a far worse fate, but they weren't here to deliver the punishment she merited.

She confessed that the giants were able to gain passage into Midgard through a portal in the far recesses of Niflheim. It had taken the concentrated magic of many of Niflheim's inhabitants to create this portal, but mostly through the efforts of Hel and Loki. Of this point, she was quite proud. In her warped mind, it was proof that she and her father were superior to the Aesir, ignoring the outcome of the Battle of Ragnarok.

Modi demanded that Hel take them to this portal, but she protested that she could no longer walk due to the damage done to her foot. Her claim was not without merit, so, being a gentleman, Magni carried her.

The trek was slow moving with Magni and his brother trading off carrying the evil witch. Her incessant chatter did nothing to brighten Magni's mood.

"Too late, too late, too late," Hel said in a sing song voice, as her upper torso dangled over Modi's shoulder. "You're wasting your time. The battle is over. You thought it took place at Ragnarok, but that was merely a diversion. The real battle was fought and lost by mortals."

"I could just as easily break her other foot," Magni said. "What do you think, brother?"

"If it will get her to stop talking, I'm in favor of it."

Hel shrieked. "Do that and you will never reach your destination. I assure you that if I do not lead the way, you will take weeks or months to find it—if you ever do."

Magni grumbled. She had a point, but that did not stop him from wanting to inflict serious pain on her.

"I hope you don't plan on going to Midgard. It will serve no purpose. Return to Asgard. The Aesir need you to rebuild." Hel chuckled.

Modi gritted his teeth. "Let us worry about the fate of the Aesir. You have your own problems to deal with. It appears that the population of Niflheim has grown sparse."

This quieted Hel.

The journey was arduous as they had to climb three additional levels of this underworld city. Apparently, the elevator only went as high as the second level

"How much longer will this be?" Magni asked.

"Not much longer," Hel said. "Another twelve hours of walking should get us there."

"You wouldn't happen to be lying?" Magni said. "I would hate to smash that other foot of yours."

Hel's eyes narrowed. "That won't be necessary. I already told you that I would lead you to the portal. We must walk, and it is quite far from here."

"Then we stop for the night," Modi said. "You do have night in this place?"

"We do. You might find it a bit…frightening." Hel laughed uproariously.

Modi said, "We handled that serpent you had waiting for us. I'm afraid you don't have many arrows left in your quiver. Your friends are all dead."

"As are yours." Hel's retort came off as hollow.

Magni and Modi set up camp, sharing their provisions with Hel. As long as she was their prisoner, they would treat her with dignity, unless she didn't cooperate, and physical pain was necessary.

Not trusting what still may be lurking in Niflheim, Magni and his brother took turns patrolling the grounds. They did not make a fire so as to not attract unwanted attention.

When Modi was on sentry duty, Magni did not allow his captive to bait him into conversation. Instead, he slept, not knowing what the night would bring. Rest might be hard to come by, and he wanted take advantage of any opportunity for sleep.

When Magni relieved his brother of sentry duty, he set up a perimeter around their camp. Having a torch would make life easier. Instead, he let his keen eyes adjust to the darkness.

In the middle of the night, Magni caught movement in the distance. He tensed, his hand on Mjolnir's hilt. He tried to focus on whatever was out there, but it was too far in the distance for him to see.

Magni stood his ground as he tried to determine what he was dealing with. He assumed it would be hostile. This was Niflheim, after all,

The thing appeared to be stalking him in the distance. Whatever it was, it was quite large, bigger than a dog or a wolf, and walked on four legs. When Magni could finally see what he was dealing with, he nearly stopped breathing. He strained to get a closer look. *Impossible.* He whistled sharply to get Modi's attention.

Within seconds, Modi joined him by his side, holding Gungnir. "That's impossible."

Magni slowly nodded as Garm, the hound of Hel, stalked toward them. "I know. I can hardly believe it."

Modi spoke with steel in his voice. "No. This truly is impossible. I killed Garm. He can't resurrect."

Modi turned and ran. Magni spared a moment to look over his shoulder and found Modi running back to their camp. Undoubtedly, he thought this was an illusion created by Hel, a diversion for her escape. If so, it was the most realistic illusion he had ever seen. For the moment, he would keep his eye on Garm, illusion or no.

The hound approached him. Garm looked just the way Magni remembered him on the battlefield. Even on all fours, Garm's height was equal to that of Magni's own substantial height. Drool dripped down his mouth. A pungent aroma of blood and sweat filled the air.

Magni lifted Mjolnir. If Garm was an illusion, then he better find out now. Without another thought, he charged forward.

Magni swung his war hammer, and it went through Garm. He gritted his teeth. Modi's instincts were right. Hopefully, he had been able to catch Hel before she fled.

Putting away Mjolnir, Magni ran toward their camp, not able to see either his brother or the ruler of Niflheim. Up ahead, the thunderous sound of Modi's boots pounded against the paved road. Thinking about the illusion Hel had created of Garm made Magni pause. Just as he was passing their camp, he came to a sudden stop and searched the area. Near a wooden post, he spotted a shadow that should not be there.

He approached warily, confident that Hel had led Modi on a fruitless chase, and she had never left the camp. Keeping the shadow in his peripheral vision, he moved forward. Just as he was passing the shadow, Magni turned and lunged at the spot casting the shadow. As he suspected, Hel had cloaked herself to make herself nearly invisible. Had he not been expecting her treachery, he would have missed her. He tackled a tall and thin frame. Upon contact, the illusion broke, and Hel became visible. She was nearly skeletal in her thinness, with sharp, jagged elbows and knees.

Pinning her down with his knees, Magni said, "I have to credit you for that bit of trickery. It didn't work, but it was a well-crafted spell."

Out of nowhere, Magni felt a blast. Lifting off of what he thought was Hel, he flew through the air, only stopping when his back slammed into a very solid wall of a building.

Magni fell to his knees, trying to maintain consciousness. He looked over. What he thought had been Hel was actually a bed of straw and sticks. She truly had deceived him with a brilliant illusion. His body buzzed with pain, his vision blurred, and his teeth chattered. In the distance, Hel was running with a noticeable limp. Apparently, her foot had healed enough for her to run. He contemplated hurling Mjolnir at her but didn't have the strength to lift the mighty hammer. He struggled to his feet as Hel continued to lengthen the distance between them.

Just as he started his pursuit, up ahead something flashed in front of Hel. The next thing Magni could see was Hel being lifted off her feet in a whiplash motion. She did a flip and went head over heels before tumbling hard onto the cobbled street. Magni blinked as his brother came into view. Modi lifted her off the cobbled street and hoisted her onto his broad shoulders.

He carried her to where Magni stood and dumped her unceremoniously on the ground. "I suppose she wasn't enjoying your company."

Still bruised from smashing into the wall, Magni gingerly knelt in front of Hel. "Can't you put some sort of binding spell on her?"

Modi frowned. "I'm about as well-versed in magic as you are. We're warriors, brother, not wizards."

Magni sighed. If only Freya were alive. She would be more than Hel's equal in the realm of sorcery. He stared into Hel's eyes. "I promise you that if you attempt another escape, I will smash your misshapen head with my hammer."

She gazed at Magni with hatred in her eyes and spat in his face.

After wiping his face, Magni pulled her up by her collar. "I suppose we won't be getting much sleep tonight. We will continue on our journey, and you will take us where we need to go. Understood?"

Hel gazed at him. "I understand. The question is do you understand? Your journey will lead to your own destruction."

Modi ignored her threat. "Do your part, and we will leave you be. Trick us again, and things will not go well for you."

In a calm voice, Magni said, "You are only delaying the inevitable. You can't defeat us, and you no longer have forces to call upon. Let's complete this journey."

Hel got to her feet and started forward. Although it was night, this place never reached full dark, so traveling would not be difficult, not to mention Hel could easily navigate through Niflheim, provided she was a willing participant.

Magni had used threats, reason, and had even attempted flattery. He was tired of dealing with the Queen of the underworld. He was prepared to inflict a fury of pain upon her. He sensed that Hel now realized this. For her sake, he hoped she did.

Hel rose to her feet. "Very well. I will lead you to where you need to go. No more tricks." She let out a loud, cackling laugh.

Magni followed warily, looking over his shoulder.

Chapter XX

They followed Hel through Niflheim into the morning. She was strangely subdued, as if she had given her best attempt at escape and was resigned to give Magni and his brother what they wanted. Magni did not trust her and remained in a constant state of vigilance.

Long after they left the seven layered city, they went through another cavernous trail that seemed to have no beginning or end.

Magni became suspicious when Hel turned chatty.

"Make sure you send word to me after you arrive in Midgard. I'll be worried until I know you arrive safely." Hel giggled.

Modi rolled his eyes. "I can see you're oozing with concern for our well-being, or maybe that's an open sore."

"Laugh now. You won't be so jolly in a little while. Make sure you say hello to my father. You won't be able to miss him."

"We'll be sure to say hello," Modi said. "Except that I don't think he'll be happy to see us."

Magni was getting tired of Hel's little games, her irritating personality, and her underlying malice. Being in Niflheim made his skin crawl. Whereas his brother didn't seem to mind, Magni had no interest in further exchanging banter with Hel.

As they walked around a bend, a brilliant burst of white light assaulted them. Magni averted his eyes. Modi thrust out his free hand, while clamping Hel's wrist. After being surrounded by gloom for so long, it was painful to be in the presence of such an intense and unnatural light.

"What is this place?" Magni asked.

Hel smiled. "It's the place you seek. You wanted to see how giants gained entrance into Midgard. Well, behold my greatest creation."

From what Magni could gather, there were eight massive pillars forming an octagon, spread equidistant about twenty meters apart. At the epicenter of this octagonal formation was light so intense that it was difficult to behold. Each pillar projected beams to the epicenter, which then reflected them outward.

Magni glanced at Hel. "And you were responsible for this?"

"Try to hide your astonishment." Hel sauntered forward. "I can't take complete credit. This is the result of the combined magic of myself, Loki, and a few others." She raised her hands. "This…is the product of monumental efforts, decades in the making. Our efforts came to fruition prior to the Battle of Ragnarok."

"What is it?" Magni asked, still not fully able to look at the structure.

"A portal. An entryway into worlds, not just to Midgard, but for all worlds. For too long, passage was only possible for a limited few using the Bifrost Bridge, which your dead friend Heimdall guarded. No longer. Anyone can pass through this portal, and they most certainly have. Dozens and dozens of frost and fire giants currently reside with the mortals under my father's command."

Magni turned to his brother. "They have to be stopped."

Modi nodded. "I know. We must do it."

Hel shrieked. "Stopped? It's too late. Sorry, boys."

Magni ignored her. "And we must ensure this never occurs again."

Modi nodded. "We must."

"Who goes?" Magni asked.

"What's done is done," Hel said. "Surely even two as simple as you can see the futility of your actions. Return to Asgard."

Magni stared into his brother's eyes. He knew what his brother was thinking and that they were together on this issue.

"I will go," Magni said.

Modi nodded. "I will join you when I can."

They clasped hands and embraced. The last thing he wanted was to be separated from his brother in this time of crisis. They functioned much better as a unit. He thought clearer, fought better, and was generally at peace with Modi nearby.

"When will I see you again?" Magni asked.

"After destroying this portal, I will travel to Midgard in the traditional way using the Bifrost Bridge. That will take time. The bigger issue is that we will likely be entering at entirely different places. Even once we are both there, we will have little way of finding each other. We will have to try to stop Loki independently. With luck we will find each other."

Magni took a deep breath and prepared to enter the portal. There was always a chance that this was a trap, but he believed that Hel spoke the truth.

Chapter XXI

Upon stepping into the portal's epicenter, Magni felt as if a tremendous force was crushing him, his body caving in upon itself. He gritted his teeth, trying to withstand the force. Blinded by darkness, Magni reached for his brother.

Magni flipped end over end, his skin and muscles stretching. Before long, he would be torn to pieces. Just when he thought he could no longer take it, the pressure subsided. The darkness around him brightened. As things became clearer, he could see his initial impulse was correct. He was hurtling toward Midgard at a frightening speed.

He would have preferred a more pastoral setting instead of the city street filled with buildings and motorized vehicles that he was descending toward. He tried to control his trajectory but had no way of doing so. Clutching Mjolnir, he braced for impact. He spread his arms and legs to give himself a wider base as he neared the city street. When he landed, the impact cracked the asphalt beneath him.

Magni checked himself for injury, amazed the landing had not crushed his body. Perhaps that was part of the portal's magic. After all, it had been created to transport giants. He shuddered, thinking the damage they could wreak upon this world.

Magni slowly rose to his full height.

A slender, dark-skinned woman approached him, her jaw hanging open, her eyes as wide as they could be. "Oh my Lord! Where'd you come from, big boy? You just drop in here from outer space or something?"

The woman was speaking English. Magni was familiar with many languages used in Midgard. This narrowed the possible nations in which he could have arrived.

Magni looked up the road. The city appeared to be deserted, this woman the only person present. Cars were abandoned on the street. He had marveled the first time he had caught site of these automobiles on a trip from Asgard. All of their technology amazed him.

Magni regarded the woman, who was looking at him as if he were an alien creature. "I suppose in a fashion I have. Where am I?"

The woman bobbed and weaved her head. "Honey, you don't even know where you are? You really must have fallen from the sky. Well, that John Madison cat can call it whatever he wants, but it's still Philadelphia to me."

Magni gave a slight nod. Philadelphia. If memory served him correctly, that was the location of the first capital of the nation of the United States of America.

"Where is everybody?" Magni asked. "These metropolitan areas are generally more populated."

"Child, where have you been?"

"Not anywhere near here." Magni looked up and down the street. The houses and buildings had smashed windows and showed signs of vandalism. The stores looked abandoned.

The woman frowned. "Are you being serious, or are you pulling my leg, 'cause I ain't in the mood for joking."

"I can assure you that I am not pulling your leg or any other body part, however I am enshrouded in confusion."

"I can see that."

"So, where have all the people gone?" Magni knew the answer but still needed to hear it.

The woman gave him a long, hard stare. "They're all dead. The sickness got 'em. What rock have you been hiding under, child?"

"No rock, my lady. I have been in Asgard." The woman frowned. "Don't know no Asgard, but it shouldn't matter. This sickness hit the whole world. It took out most everybody. I'm talking billions and billions of people worldwide. Nobody was safe. Now they say they got a vaccine, but where was they with their vaccine when this was going down?"

Magni closed his eyes. Emptiness filled his soul. Loki was the ultimate deceiver. The Aesir had been so caught up in legend and prophecy that they forgot Loki never played by the rules. So consumed in their preparation for the Battle of Ragnarok, Loki had played them for fools. Now, most of his brethren were dead. Meanwhile, Loki had control of Midgard and had an army of giants at his command.

"You okay?" the woman asked. "You don't look so good."

Magni shook his head. He felt weak. Perhaps it was the travel from Niflheim. Perhaps it was the enormity of the situation he was facing. His massive frame collapsed.

***

Not sure how long he had been unconscious, when Magni awoke the same woman he had been speaking with earlier was hovering over him with a look of concern.

"Glad to see you're awake again. You're too damn big for me to move. I was going to get my nephew and his friends to help. Can you get up on your own?"

Magni nodded.

"Where did you come from anyway? I've never seen anybody as big as you?"

Slowly and gingerly, Magni rose. "I am from Asgard."

"Right, Asgard. Wherever that is. You never told me your name, by the way."

"I'm Magni." He extended his hand to the woman.

She shook his hand. "Magni? That sounds like it's from Sweden or Norway or something. Is Asgard near any of those places?"

Magni shook his head. "Far, far away I'm afraid. And never has it felt so distant."

"I'm Sheila. We need to get out of here. These streets ain't safe. If the government goons don't get you, then the gangs will. We've been here too long already."

Wherever Sheila would take him was as good as any other place. He needed more intelligence. The more he knew, the better chance he would have of achieving his ultimate goal—destroying Loki.

"How did it happen?" Magni asked. "This sickness that you speak of."

"Are you sure you ain't playing me? How can you not know? I mean people all over the world died by the billions. They dropped like flies." Sheila paused. Her voice dropped. "I lost everyone—my husband, my mom, my two children. Only one I got left is my nephew, Dante."

"How does the sickness work?"

"If ya ain't seen it, then trust me, you don't want to know."

"I do want to know," Magni said.

Sheila paused. Her face appeared aged beyond her years, and her eyes were distant. She must have suffered greatly. He wanted to comfort her, but first he had to hear her story.

She shook her head. "It's the most horrific thing I've ever seen. Forget whatever you might have seen in one of those scary movies, because this is way worse. The people who get the sickness, it's like their insides turn to mush. They start bleeding…everywhere. It comes out of their mouth, their eyes, their nose. Anywhere blood can come out, it does. It's…"

Magni raised his hand. "I understand."

Sheila looked down. "Well, you wanted to know how the sickness works."

"Thank you for informing me. I appreciate your candor in what must be a distressful time."

"Well, yeah, it definitely has been that. Do you have a place to stay?"

"No, I do not."

"You can stay with us until you get yourself settled. Of course, you'll have to pitch in. Everybody works."

"I would appreciate that, my lady," Magni said.

Sheila chuckled. "You sure talk funny. Is that how all people from Asgard talk?"

"I suppose we do."

"Well, in West Philly we talk a little different, but I think we'll be able to understand each other just fine."

"I understand you perfectly well," Magni said.

After walking a couple of blocks, Sheila suddenly stopped. Up ahead were half a dozen young men wearing tattered clothes and carrying weapons.

"Oh, shit," Sheila muttered. "We got trouble."

"What is this trouble you speak of?" Magni asked.

"These thugs are in a rival gang to my nephew's. Well Dante doesn't run with a gang. It's more like a group of people livin' off the grid looking after each other."

"These ruffians do not concern me," Magni said.

"Well, they should. They're bad news. Look, if we cut across the playground, we might be able to shake these guys before they catch up with us."

Magni shook his head. "We'll do no such thing. There's no reason you should live in intimidation. While you're in my presence, you have no reason to be afraid by ruffians such as these."

"Are you crazy? You don't want to mess with these guys. Their leader, K-Dog, flayed a man alive. They abduct children and turn them into sex slaves."

"Perhaps they have yet to learn a proper lesson. I feel obliged to teach them one."

"Look, Magni, I can see you ain't intimidated by anyone, but you need to trust me on this."

"And you need to trust me. I assure you, I will not allow harm to come to you."

Sheila took a deep breath. "Okay, big boy. I hope you know what you're doing. Otherwise, we're in big trouble. The one in the middle of the pack with all of the rings in his eyebrows is K-Dog. He's their leader. Look, we can still make a run for it."

"My lady, you have my solemn vow. I will protect you."

The one Sheila called K-Dog had a half beard and wore a mean scowl. Magni supposed this was supposed to scare other mortals, but it had no such effect on him.

K-Dog and his men slowed as they approached. He sneered. "Look if ain't Dante's aunt and some giant freak. Who the hell are you, freak?"

Magni pointed at his own chest.

"Yeah, I'm talkin' to you, you giant mutant freak." K-Dog spat on the floor. "You guys see any other giant freaks here?"

This rather witless comment drew chuckles from K-Dog's dim looking friends.

One of K-Dog's friends sporting sunglasses and a mohawk walked to Magni's side. "Hey, what you got there?"

Magni clutched his war hammer. "You must be referring to Mjolnir."

The man with the mohawk motioned to Mjolnir. "That's a weapon?"

Magni nodded. "You're not as dim as you look, although calling this a weapon is a considerable understatement."

"Who you calling stupid?" Mohawk asked.

"You, of course," Magni replied.

"Enough." K-Dog pulled out a pistol and pointed it at Magni's head. "Give me that weapon."

"You want Mjolnir?" Magni frowned. "I don't think that's such a wise idea."

"I said give me the weapon right now or I'll blow your brains out."

"Well, since you put it in those terms, I suppose I have no choice but to comply."

"That's right," K-Dog said. "You don't have a choice."

Magni removed Mjolnir from its side holster. Holding it by the hilt, he handed it to K-Dog.

Magni tried not to laugh as Mjolnir slipped out of K-Dog's hands and crashed onto the road, cracking the asphalt.

"What the hell you pullin'?" K-Dog asked.

Magni shrugged. "You did ask for my weapon."

K-Dog motioned to a large man standing behind him. "Pick that up, Dre."

Dre stepped forward, squatted, and tried to heave Mjolnir. Dre pulled and tugged, his face turning red, yet he could not budge the war hammer. Dre cursed under his breath and gave another mighty heave but came no closer to moving Mjolnir. He looked up, sweat dripping from his brow. "What is this thing?"

K-Dog turned to Magni, still pointing the pistol at him. "I'm tired of this shit."

Magni summoned Mjolnir to his hand and, without hesitating, swung the hammer at K-Dog's hand, shattering it, sending the pistol flying. Magni's next move was to take out Dre. Knowing that a blow to the head with Mjolnir would kill him, Magni swung at his knees, chopping the big man down like a tree.

From the top of the street, an automobile came roaring toward them. Magni threw Mjolnir at the vehicle, indenting it. A burst of smoke came from its engine.

Magni held out his hand, and Mjolnir flew back to it. He did not want to kill any mortals, but it was against his nature to back down from a fight. At the core, he was a warrior. He raised Mjolnir and released a burst of lightning.

K-Dog shouted, "Let's get out of here. Move. Now!"

Thor would have crushed K-Dog and all of his followers, but Magni did not wish to shed unnecessary blood. He would be more subtle in his opening foray in his war against Loki.

Three of their group dragged Dre and K-Dog off the street. With the automobile no longer operable, the passengers leapt out of the car and made an escape.

Sheila gaped at Magni. "What was that all about?"

He put away Mjolnir. "I am Magni of Asgard. I am here to save you and your brethren. Lead me to your people."

Chapter XXII

Magni followed Sheila, convinced that K-Dog and his followers would not be eager for another confrontation so soon.

As they walked, Sheila would steal an occasional glance at him. Her look contained awe mixed with fear. "What was the deal with that lightning? That come from your hammer?"

"Indeed, it did," Magni replied.

"Well, I'll be damned. And how come Dre couldn't budge it?"

"He not only lacks the required strength but is not worthy to wield it." Magni remembered fondly the amazement the other Aesir showed the first time he had wielded Mjolnir, having thought Thor was the only one capable of possessing the mighty hammer. That memory filled him with pride and some regret that his father would never pick up his hammer again.

"Then you must be one strong fella. Dre's as strong as an ox and he couldn't do anything with that hammer. What did you call it?"

"Mjolnir. It was my father's hammer. When he died, I took possession of it."

"You might not know about the sickness, but I guess you're no stranger to death," Sheila said. "There's nobody innocent no more."

"I suppose not."

"We're close now. We stay at a converted boxing gym. So far none of the government people have come to harass us."

"What issue do you have with your government?" Magni was starting to piece together what had occurred but wanted unbiased information.

"My nephew, Dante, can talk for hours about John Madison and this new government. Don't get me wrong, I don't trust them either, but Dante is constantly spinning one conspiracy theory after another."

"I look forward to meeting your nephew," Magni said.

"And you mean what you said earlier? You're here to help us."

"I am, my lady. I will do what I can to rid you of this misery."

Sheila snorted. "Well, that's a good thing. We can use all the help we can get."

They walked a few more blocks until they reached what appeared to be a large, abandoned building.

"We purposely try to make it look like this on the outside. This way, nobody notices us. There's actually a lot of people living here. We tend to pick up drifters and people surviving on their own."

"I thank you for your hospitality," Magni said.

"Well, don't thank me yet. If the others don't want you around, then you won't be able to stay, but after what went down today, I'm sure they'll take you in with open arms. We can use someone like you on our side."

Sheila used a key to open a door at the rear of the building. Inside, the building was quiet. So far, Magni had not seen anything to support Sheila's claims that many people lived here.

It wasn't until they descended stairs that Magni finally heard voices.

They encountered a man with thick, wavy black hair and a mustache.

Sheila waved. "Hi, François."

François's eyes went wide. He tensed and reached into his jacket, presumably for a weapon.

At the same time, Magni reached for Mjolnir.

Sheila raised her hands. "No, no. It's okay. His name is Magni. He's a friend."

A dark-skinned man wearing glasses and a goatee emerged from a room. He also reached for a weapon. "What's going on?" He took a step back. "Holy mother of God. Who the hell is this?"

"That's what I was wondering," François said.

"You boys just relax. Magni saved my bacon. K-Dog and his crew were about to do me in for sure until he sent them running with their tails tucked between their legs." Sheila turned toward the dark skinned man. "Dante, you need to trust me here."

Dante folded his arms and frowned. "Where did he come from?"

"Would you believe it if I told you he landed from the sky?"

"Landed from the sky? Aunt Sheila, have you been drinking again?"

"I haven't touched a drop in weeks. And he did land from the sky."

François arched an eyebrow. "He certainly is the biggest fellow I've ever seen."

Magni watched the discussion in amusement. He always had this type of effect on mortals. Given time and the aid of magic, he could have altered his appearance prior to entering Midgard. They were seeing him in his true form, and he towered over any of their kind by at least two heads.

"So, who are you?" Dante asked. "Other than the jolly green giant who popped out of the sky?"

"I am Magni of Asgard."

Dante rolled his eyes. "Really? Asgard? You gotta be kidding me."

"I do not kid you. My name is Magni, and Asgard is my home."

"Oh. Okay. I guess the next thing you want me to believe is that you hang out with Thor and Odin and those other Norse gods."

"Thor is my father. Odin is my grandfather."

"Come on," Dante said. "Who you trying to fool? And I guess you got Mjolnir in your back pocket."

Magni pulled out his war hammer.

Dante's jaw dropped. "You have got to be kidding me. Are you for real?"

"What are you two going on about?" Sheila asked. "Will someone clue me in on all of this?"

Dante narrowed his eyes as he appraised Magni. "Asgard is the home of the gods of the Nordic people. Odin was their leader. He was mainly worshipped by the aristocracy in and around Norway and Scandinavia around a thousand years ago. Thor was the god of thunder, and the main god of the farmers and warriors."

Sheila frowned. "Thor? Ain't he like a superhero?"

"Before he was popularized by Marvel Comics, Thor was worshipped as a god. He was reputed to be a fierce warrior. His weapon was Mjolnir, a war hammer that was supposed to be the most devastating weapon ever created."

"Hold up," Sheila said. "Are you trying to say that you're some kind of god?"

"I am an immortal," Magni said. "And this is Mjolnir, the hammer that once belonged to my father."

Sheila laughed. "You shoulda seen him use that thing against K-Dog and his crew. For starters, none of them could lift it up. Then he nearly chopped off K-Dog's hand with it and destroyed a charging car. Then it shot out a burst of lightning. I almost wet myself when I saw that."

Dante stroked his goatee. "Those things really happened, Aunt Sheila?"

"They sure did."

"So, you're serious about this?" Dante asked. "You truly are from Asgard? And you really are the son of Thor?"

"I would not deceive you, my friend."

"I'll be damned. Can I see that?" Dante motioned to Mjolnir.

"You will not be able to wield it," Magni replied. "But you may look upon my war hammer."

The look in Dante's eyes changed from skepticism to awe. Just by their brief conversation, how he spoke and carried himself, Magni could tell that Dante was intelligent and learned. He sensed a strong ally in this young man.

Dante lightly ran his hand over the hammer. "I'll be damned. But I thought…according to mythology, Thor is the only one capable of possessing Mjolnir."

Magni sighed. "I always have been capable of possessing it, even when he was alive. But alas, my father passed at Ragnarok."

Dante's brows rose. "The Battle of Ragnarok?"

Magni nodded.

Sheila said, "I have no idea what you two are talking about. You see, my nephew, Dante, is the genius of the family. Before this sickness broke out, he was going to Princeton on a full scholarship. Half the time, I don't know even what he's talking about."

Magni smiled. "Your nephew is an astute young man. I can see that you are starting to piece this together. Let me ask you? Have there been an influx of giants into your world?"

François responded, "Oh, yes. We have giants. I saw one in New York about a month ago. It was the biggest damn thing I've ever seen. It even makes you look small in comparison, and you're an enormous fellow."

"So, my friend, Dante, you know of Asgard and Ragnarok. I can see that you are well read on the subject. Then you must also know of frost and fire giants."

Dante nodded. "In Norse mythology, the frost and fire giants are enemies of the Aesir and were believed to oppose them at the final battle."

"Is the picture becoming clearer for you?"

Dante nodded. "I guess it's not too much of a stretch that if we can have giants, then why can't we have gods of mythology? Except it isn't mythology, is it?"

"No, it is not," Magni said. "My people have been around for a very long time."

"So, you're Thor's son?" Dante asked. "I apologize, I'm well versed in Norse mythology but I'm not familiar with you."

Magni shrugged. "No need to apologize. My brother, Modi, and I were worshipped by few mortals. I never felt the need for such adoration."

"So, what happened?" Dante asked.

"The Battle of Ragnarok indeed took place. My father, my grandfather, almost all of those I loved so dearly died. Yes, the Aesir won, but the price was steep. My brother and I were among the few survivors. There is one other key figure who survived. Loki. He elected not to fight, and he is the source of the misery that has befallen your world. He is the reason I am here."

Dante narrowed his eyes. "Hmm. Loki, the trickster god."

"This seems far-fetched," François said. "How can this guy possibly be on the level?"

"As far-fetched as giants?" Magni asked. "As far-fetched as a sickness which has destroyed your world?"

"I don't know about all that," Sheila said. "But I can tell you one thing, I saw that hammer shoot out lightning. I also know that Dre and K-Dog couldn't budge it, and it flew into Magni's hand from the ground. You tell me you're some sort of god, well, I believe you. I sure ain't never seen anyone like you before."

"Aunt Sheila, I think you might be right. It certainly fits in with the appearance of these giants. Prior to the doomsday virus, we had never seen anything like them. Or you."

François shook his head. "You're all loco."

"Maybe later you can give a demonstration to the non-believers." Dante motioned to François. "So, what happened? The Battle of Ragnarok was supposed to be the final battle, which would signify the end of the world, followed by a rebirth and renewal."

"All went as it was destined to go. All except Loki. He was not there. I have not seen him since."

"And that's why you're here? To find Loki?"

Magni nodded. "Loki is responsible for the sickness as well as the giants. I am here to stop him, but I need your help."

Dante let out a snort. "Help? Listen, even if I were to accept the fact that you're an Asgardian god—which, by the way, the concept is mind-bending—how are we supposed to help you? We're barely surviving. We're living outside of the government's clutches, but sooner or later, they'll find out about us. Even if they don't do, K-Dog and his goons or some other street gang will. I'm afraid if you came here for support, then you came to the wrong place."

Magni put his hand on Dante's shoulder. "No, my friend. I don't think it was an accident that I landed where I did and encountered your aunt. These things do not happen by chance. I have lived long enough to recognize the hand of fate. I was destined to meet you. I will do all I can to stop Loki, and you will help me. Now you must tell me everything that has happened to lead to the current state of your world. I have not travelled to Midgard in many years and I am badly out of touch."

Chapter XXIII

Dante led Magni through the surprisingly large facility. Connected by underground passageways, it extended more than a city block. By his estimation, nearly one hundred people lived here, off the grid, as Dante had described. Magni was still trying to get used to the modern vernacular. Although fluent in English, many of the terms had changed since he had learned it.

The people living here were like huddled refugees from a raging war. They had a defeated look about them, their eyes displaying constant fear. It reminded him of when he had been in Europe during the second World War.

"What is your source of food?" Magni asked.

"Forage what we can," Dante answered. "John Madison's government controls the food supply. That's one of the ways they keep the populace under their boot heel. If you want food, you have to go through them. Fortunately, we've found a way around that. There's a thriving black market, not to mention we've gotten pretty good at stealing from the government. Normally I don't condone thievery, but you do what you have to if you want to survive in this new world."

"Why are you so fearful of your government?" Magni asked.

"Are you kidding me? They're a bunch of fascists. They make Joseph Stalin look like a choir boy. They want to control every aspect of your life: what kind of work you do, where you live, what you wear. They've banned all organized religions.

They want to control everything you can or cannot do. Their book of laws is about three hundred pages long."

"I can see how that would be oppressive," Magni said.

"Oppressive isn't the half of it. I can't live like that. That's why I started this group. We're all people who refuse to live under the current system."

Magni smiled. "Then you are my kind of people."

"So, you're really an Asgardian god? Does that mean you can't die?"

Magni cast his eyes downward. If only that were so. Freya would still be with him. "No. My kind can be killed. Unfortunately, I witnessed far too much of that recently."

Dante put his hand on Magni's arm. "Right, the Battle of Ragnarok. My sincere condolences for your loss."

Magni shrugged. "We have all experienced loss. Mine is no worse than yours."

"I guess. So, can you demonstrate how you use that hammer?"

The others that had gathered around murmured their ascent.

"Not here," Magni said. "Mjolnir is a destructive force of nature, capable of utter devastation. Somewhere outside in the open would be more appropriate."

Sheila frowned. "I don't know if that's such a good idea, either. I saw for myself what that hammer can do. Unless you got someone you want to put a serious hurtin' on, I suggest you put that away."

Magni noticed they used electrical lights and other tools that required the use of electricity. He was well acquainted with the physics of electrons and the transmission of current, even though in Asgard there was no need for such things due to the presence of magic. Still, he enjoyed learning about the sciences of the people of Midgard. Their advances over the years were nothing short of staggering. It was little wonder they stopped worshipping the Asgardians as gods.

Magni pointed to the lights. "With much of your society in chaos, how do you obtain electricity?"

"I wouldn't think an Asgardian would know much about electricity," Dante said.

"I know much about your world. Remember this; it is the solemn duty of all Asgardians to be the guardians of your realm. It is the reason I am here."

"Well, we could have used you before all hell broke loose." Dante waved his hand. "Yeah, I know, you were busy with the Battle of Ragnarok. Anyway, to answer your question, we found a way to tap into the government's electrical grid. We have a lot of smart people living here and we're pretty resourceful."

"I can see that."

"Well, that's the tour. Maybe some other time I can take you to some safe spots in the city. We have allies, people like us living underground."

"I would enjoy that," Magni said. "I have a feeling that before long, I will need to assemble an army."

"Woh, back up," Dante said. "Who said anything about an army? After all that's happened, I don't think people are going to be too keen about fighting other people."

"Who said anything about fighting people? I have much larger targets in mind."

As they were walking, they passed by a television set. Magni stopped in his tracks at the sight of an image on the screen. He pointed at it, hardly able to speak.

"What is it?" Dante asked.

"It's him," Magni said.

"Who? John Madison? Yeah, he's the fascist bastard who appointed himself the new king of the world. He's president, prime minister, pope, whatever he wants to be. We all have to bow to him."

"That's Loki," Magni said.

Dante cocked one eyebrow. "What do you mean?"

Magni pointed at the screen. "Loki. That's him."

The entire picture was now coming into focus. Loki masterminded this plot, ridded the planet of most of its population, killed off the world leaders, brought in frost and fire giants as his muscle, and put himself in charge of everything.

"If you're Thor's son, then I don't suppose it's a big stretch that Loki can be John Madison. Why didn't you gods stay in Asgard instead of meddling with us people? We all would have been better off."

Magni took a deep breath. "I can't argue the point. It has never been our way to let your people to their own devices. We have always been here throughout your history, even though you have not been made aware of our presence, with the exception of nearly a thousand years ago in your land of Scandinavia. From time to time, we have intervened for the benefit of humanity. This time we failed to protect you in our roles as Midgard's guardians."

"You did some job of protecting us. If what you're saying is true, you allowed Loki to decimate us. I can't believe I'm talking about mythical beings like they're real."

"To call it myth is to deny what you see in front of you. Your eyes don't lie. Normally, we Asgardians would travel to Midgard in disguise and try to blend in, but the time for pretenses is over. There is much work to be done to restore what once was, and right the horrible wrongs that have been perpetrated."

Magni continued to watch as Loki spoke about how they must come together as people, how he was a benevolent leader, and that his rules must be followed if they were to rebuild society. The trickster was doing what he did best. Judging by the group Magni had settled in with, not everyone believed his lies.

François came running toward them.

"What's going on?" Dante asked.

François struggled to catch his breath. "I have horrible news. It's Erin. She's been murdered."

Dante's eyes went wide. "No! How?"

"K-Dog and his crew," François responded, fighting back tears. "They killed her and sent her back with a message. They want vengeance in the form of an old school street rumble. Said they would meet us at the old Tyler playground at dusk to settle things once and for all between us."

Dante's hands began to tremble. His aunt immediately went to comfort him. Magni did not know what relationship this woman, Erin, had with Dante, but it was clear that her death shook him deeply.

Spit flew out of François's mouth as he spoke. "We have to pay them back. If they want to fight, then we'll give them one."

"No," Magni said.

François, who to this point had ignored Magni, turned toward him. "Excuse me?"

Magni stared at François, whose wavy hair looked disheveled. "No. You will not fight them."

"Hey, you just got here, pal" François said. "This isn't for you to decide."

"I realize my time here has been short, but you must listen to me. There has been enough death amongst your people. There is no reason to shed unnecessary blood. Fighting each other will solve nothing when you have a much bigger enemy."

François folded his arms. "Look, man, times have changed. I was against the wars in Iraq and Afghanistan, but there's no room anymore for pacifism."

"I am hardly a pacifist. A few weeks I engaged in a battle bloodier than most would see in ten lifetimes and I slew more than my share."

"What do you know?" François asked.

"I know your true enemy —Loki, under the guise of John Madison."

"What are you talking about?" François asked.

Dante vigorously rubbed his face with his hand, as if trying to remove the hurt. "If you don't want us to fight them, then what do you propose?"

"We will meet them at the time and place they requested, but we will not bring an army prepared for battle. You will go with me, Dante, unarmed."

Dante folded his arms. "Are you crazy? You got a death wish or something?"

Magni shook his head. "I have no wish to die. You will go unarmed. I will bring Mjolnir. By the time this is over, they will no longer be a threat."

Chapter XXIV

As Magni sat in meditation, Sheila approached him. "You mind if I sit next to you?"

He extended his hand to the spot next to him.

Sheila frowned. "You sure you know what you're doing? I know you handled yourself last time, but now they're going to be coming armed and looking for a pound of flesh. They're meaning to kill you and Dante."

Magni stared into Sheila's eyes. She had ebony skin and deep, brown eyes. Her face was etched with concern. Her hair was curled and well-maintained. He could tell she was a proud woman, who, despite the dire circumstances, was continually trying to make things better. "I realize that. Their intentions will not deter me."

Sheila grabbed his hand. "Dante is all the family I have left. I can't have him getting killed out there."

"I promise that I will deliver him safely to you."

"Why can't you just handle this business yourself?" Sheila asked. "You seemed to do fine last time."

"If Dante is to be an effective leader, he cannot hide while I do his fighting for him. He does not object to being there."

"That's 'cause he's bull-headed like the rest of you men."

For a while, neither said anything. Magni asked, "Who is Erin?"

Sheila took a deep breath. "Erin's a wonderful young woman. She and Dante were close. I suspected they may have been, you know, romantically involved if you follow what I'm saying, but if they were, he never fessed to it."

Magni remembered the rage he felt when Surtur had killed Freya. "Then his loss is deep and personal. I am very sorry to hear that she is no longer alive, and I am sorry that Dante has to suffer more than he already has. I will not deny him the revenge he seeks."

Sheila looked away from him. "Do you have a plan? I hope you know what you're doing."

"I have a plan. As far as the wisdom of it, I can only hope it works. I would feel better if my brother were here. He always helps me see things clearly."

"Where's your brother?" Sheila asked.

"In Niflheim."

"Is that anywhere near Asgard?"

"It is far from Asgard, just as we are far from Asgard."

Sheila regarded him closely. "Magni, don't make me regret coming across you on the street and taking you in. You know, when I saw you, I knew there was something special about you, which had nothing to do with the fact that you're eight feet tall and as thick as an oak tree."

"I am glad you made that decision."

Sheila stood. "Take care of Dante." She walked out of the room.

***

Two hours later, Magni entered Dante's room. Judging by his red eyes, the man had done his share of crying. Magni, on the other hand, was in full battle mode.

"Are you ready to depart?" Magni asked.

Dante shrugged. "Why did they have to kill Erin? She never did anything to them."

"They were attempting to hurt you. It has always been the way of the cruel and vicious not to strike a direct blow but an indirect one that will damage the psyche. I am sorry they chose to hurt you in this manner."

Dante nodded. "Thanks, man."

"Will you be able to do what we must be done or would you rather I go alone?"

Dante shook his head. "No way. I'm coming. This is personal."

"Very well. I must ask you another question. I do not wish to shed unnecessary blood. Would it suffice to have K-Dog's head for you to satisfy your thirst for revenge?"

"What are you getting at? What do you have in mind?"

"Even if you did not seek revenge, their leader must be eliminated. I ask again, will killing K-Dog satisfy your thirst for revenge?"

Dante nodded. "Yeah. He's the one I want."

"Good. Then let's meet our foes."

Dante's eyes went wide. "Wait. Shouldn't we have a plan? We're just going to go over there and wing it?"

"Once they draw their weapons, grab hold of me. I will handle the rest."

"You're going to get me killed."

Magni shook his head. "I already swore to your Aunt Sheila that I will deliver you safely home. It's a vow that I fully intend on keeping."

"Well, that's reassuring. You don't want to piss off Aunt Sheila."

"Indeed. Now guide me to our destination."

***

They walked a couple of kilometers through deserted streets. It was hard to tell what his mortal companion was thinking or feeling since he hardly spoke.

Magni, on the other hand, was calm and confident. He was bred to fight. Like many of his Aesir brethren, he thrived on combat.

When they were a few blocks from their destination, loud voices along with the revving of automobile engines emerged.

They reached what used to be a playground. Magni imagined that once upon a time the children of this city enjoyed themselves with the slides and swings and ball-courts. Now, at least fifty men and women armed with wooden bats, knives, chains, and pistols confronted them. They might not be giants, but they were still formidable. Dante stood tall next to him.

As they approached the wall of humanity, Magni went straight to K-Dog.

K-Dog sneered. "What is this, some kind of joke? This all you got? The egghead and this giant, mutant freak."

Dante did not back down in the face of adversity. "This is all we need. I heard your run-in with my friend didn't go so well last time."

"Yeah, well we weren't ready then." K-Dog removed his gun, which was much larger than a regular pistol. Magni guessed it to be one of those machine guns that could fire many bullets in rapid succession.

"I'm glad you brought your heavy artillery," Magni said. "It will do you no good, but I am sure that it will make you feel better."

K-Dog gave a nervous laugh. "What, you think that hammer's better than this? I don't think so. Neither one of you makes it out of here alive."

Magni raised his brows. "Who are you trying to convince, us or yourself? I will say this. You may lack intelligence or any sense of morality and decency, but you do not lack courage. I was convinced after our last encounter that you would not seek retribution any time in the near future, but you have proven me wrong. Ultimately, it will lead to your demise, but I am quite certain it will be nobody's loss."

K-Dog's upper lip flared. "You sure talk a lot of smack, you giant, mutant freak. Now you're gonna die."

Magni turned to Dante. "Now."

Dante wrapped his arms around Magni's waist. Magni could not tell for sure if K-Dog started firing or if someone else did, but bullets flew from every direction. He lifted Mjolnir, and he and Dante flew into the air well above any of the nearby buildings. The bullets targeted for Magni all missed their mark. Magni had never been shot before but did not imagine it would feel pleasant, although he highly doubted it would be fatal for him. Also, he promised to keep Dante alive.

Magni swung Mjolnir overhead and hurled it at K-Dog. His aim was true, and the war hammer decapitated the leader of this rogue group.

A stunned silence enveloped what had been a deafening roar of gunfire. The others that had come here to fight now looked at their fallen leader, who lay twitching on the ground. The head that had once been sitting between his shoulders rolled on the ground.

Mjolnir flew back into Magni's outstretched hand. He slowly lowered himself and Dante back to the surface and the awestruck eyes of the people below. They no longer had their weapons raised.

"I had to kill your leader because he was a contagion among your group. I offer you a different way, a better way. Dante and his people are not your enemies. They are not the ones who destroyed your world. Your enemy is the one who calls himself John Madison, he who is known to me as Loki."

Magni put away Mjolnir. He was certain his foes would not attack him now.

"If you choose to join me, I will offer you a better path. You live in a state of constant fear. Having already been victimized, you now prey upon those who you perceive as weak. If you help me bring down John Madison, you can return to the life you once knew."

Magni made eye-contact with individuals in the crowd and found reluctant acceptance.

Dante spoke up, "If you're willing to work with us, then I would be willing to let bygones be bygones. Things have been tough for everyone. We're all just trying to survive in this crazy world."

"Will you join us?" Magni asked.

Although some walked away, most laid down their weapons and joined them. It was a small victory, but he hoped it was the first step in uniting the survivors of Midgard against Loki.

Chapter XXV

John Madison's anger rose as he watched Yuri Uzelkov, the former Russian president, place markers on the map that covered a wall of the conference room. The markers represented locations that had recently experienced a protest, an uprising, or some other form of dissent against him or his government. It was unnerving to see all the red markers on the map.

"South Africa continues to be a problem." Yuri used his laser pointer to highlight the area near Johannesburg. Normally Madison used English to speak with his aids and lieutenants, but Yuri's English was barely understandable, so they conversed in Russian, one of the many languages in which John was fluent. "In the past month, we raided and destroyed a meeting center used to start a new local governing council. Then, despite the ordinances against it, the people continued to have services at one of the churches. My understanding is that this was non-denominational and open to all."

John tapped his fingernails against the mahogany table. In his compound, located in the former capital of the United States, everything about the place suggested luxury and opulence. From the Persian rugs to the Dali paintings and sculptures sourced from various museums throughout the world, John Madison demanded the best, not only here but in other similar buildings in Moscow, Abu Dhabi, and the city formerly known as London, which he officially renamed Madison in his own honor. He was considering renaming New York City as Loki City.

"What action are you taking?" John asked.

"Leveling the church," Yuri replied. "I plan to bring it down with a massive bomb."

John tilted his head, his long blond hair flowing down his back, as he thought about the ramifications of the actions. "Proceed but minimize the collateral damage. I don't want to create martyrs for these people, just enough to send a message."

Yuri scanned a notepad before speaking again. "There have been pockets of protests erupting in major European cities: Paris, London—I mean Madison—Brussels, and Munich."

"What is wrong with these people? Why is it so hard for them to accept me as their leader? Is it too much to ask to have some devotion after all I've done for them? The general lawlessness that had corrupted society after the release of the virus has ceased to exist. We have provided food, clothing, and shelter to those in need. We have created order from chaos. They would be living in squalor without me. What more do I need to do for them?"

Yuri raised his hands. "Nobody should question your benevolence. People are fickle. Never satisfied. It sickens me."

John folded his arms. This was a constant source of irritation for him since becoming the undisputed ruler of the planet. He wanted to be adored and revered, but that type of adulation had been fleeting and hard to find. Oh, he had devoted followers, but it wasn't enough.

"All is not bad," Yuri said. "Construction on several of your ideological and cultural centers has begun. They will be devoted to teaching your principals. Numerous volunteers among the populace have stepped forward to work on the construction and operation of these centers. We have also made significant strides in creating a network of informants throughout the globe to expose of dissidents. We have detained and arrested dozens thus far and have squashed movements before they have had a chance to sprout."

This was where Yuri Uzelkov's former role in the KGB came in handy. Prior to becoming the president of Russia, he had been a major force in the intelligence arm of the Soviet Union. His abilities in the area of espionage and developing information networks were invaluable. He was glad to have Yuri as part of his inner circle, having given him the role of Director of Intelligence.

John sighed. He supposed these were positive things, but the negativity was bringing him down. When he had descended into Midgard, removing himself from the dealings of Asgard, he had high expectations. He had achieved most of his goals, cultivating a core group of followers, supervising the production of the virus, and successfully seizing power from all the world leaders. Nevertheless, he craved the love of the people, just as Thor and Odin had more than a millennia ago when they had made themselves known among the Scandinavian people.

He vowed to solve this problem and make the people adore him.

Yuri continued with his report, most of which was of little concern to John. He did not have time for minor details. That was why he had people working for him. He was a big picture thinker, his focus achieving his vision of the world. As the former Russian president spoke, John was sure there was something he was holding back.

"Is there anything else?"

Yuri hesitated. "There is something that concerns me. It may be nothing. It may be something."

"What is it?"

"I was expecting more frost giants to arrive this week from Jotunheim, but they have not appeared."

John frowned. Since logistical issues such as providing shelter for the giants could be problematic, he was staggering their arrival. Thus far, they had all arrived according to schedule. He would have to contact Hrugnir to investigate this matter.

"Very well," John said. "I will look into it. Continue with your work."

As Yuri left the spacious office, John pondered the cause of this disruption. He was beginning to develop a feeling of dread that all was not well in his empire.

Chapter XXVI

After killing K-Dog, Magni spent the next couple of weeks meeting with other underground factions in Pennsylvania and New Jersey. Dante and François had numerous contacts with whom they traded or worked together on certain endeavors. When he informed them that John Madison had brought about the sickness that killed their brethren, and that with their help he would bring Madison down, he encountered fear and reluctance. Even though these people did not like Madison and his authoritarian rule, they were not ready to join a resistance movement.

His frustration mounted with each meeting. It was hard for him to relate to this unwillingness to fight back. The people were clearly unhappy with their current situation but were not willing to take to arms to change it. That attitude went against his warrior's code.

After one such visit, Magni returned to the converted boxing gym that was now his headquarters and shared a meal of rice, beans, and stewed rabbit with Dante, Sheila, and others.

Dante sipped local wine that made Magni cringe every time he tasted it. It was nothing like the great tasting wine from the vineyards of Asgard. "I hate to say I told you so, but I did tell you these people weren't going to join with you to fight against John Madison, let alone the giants. Have you seen those things?"

Magni raised his brows.

"Dumb question. Of course you have." Dante waved his hand. "Regardless, if you weren't around during the early days of the virus, then you don't know what it's like. People died horrifically. Your family members being wasted, bleeding out in front of you. The people who survived, it's like you just got out of a horrible car accident and you're still shell-shocked, glad that somehow you made it out alive. I lost my mother, my father, my grandma, my two sisters, my nephew and niece, pretty much all of my relatives except Aunt Sheila."

Magni regarded his new ally. "I do not deny the terror you experienced and I don't want to minimize your lost since I know very keenly what it is like to lose those you care dearly for, but now is the time to reclaim what is rightfully yours. Loki is not of this world and does not belong here. The daily suppression you experience is unacceptable. I have witnessed the conditions of those in the work camps. Dogs should be treated with more dignity. You may have survived, but you are not living. You need to fight for what belongs to you."

"I'm with you," Dante said. "You have my support, and after taking out K-Dog, you have my gratitude. Whatever you do, I've got your back. The same goes with the people living here. Even François has come around."

The Frenchman chuckled. "Who am I to oppose the mighty Norse god and his powerful war hammer?"

"You are with me, as you say, because you have seen what I am capable of doing, even my good friend, François, who was hesitant at first." Magni ran his hand through his beard. "The others have not. They need a demonstration and a gesture of good will. And they need food. We need a show of force taking from the government's food supply. We will then distribute the food among those who need it."

François raised his hand. "Well, we need food too."

"We will take our share, but we will give the rest away. If we show that we can stand up to Madison's government and provide something that is much needed and valued, this will gain us the support we need."

Dante removed his glasses and nodded. "I like it. We can fight Madison with his own game of propaganda."

"Please explain," Magni said.

"Well, Madison is big on instilling fear in the people by showing on their television station just what he can do. There's footage of giants crushing a village of guerillas in Ghana that opposed him. Then he did this impressive display of force where he flooded a portion of San Francisco when he was supposed to be meeting with members of a group who opposed his rule. I don't know how he did it. He just brought these tidal waves down upon them."

Magni nodded. "Loki is a skilled sorcerer. That is well within his capabilities."

"Well, it certainly surprised the hell out of us. I had never seen anything like it. Anyway, we may not have our own television station like Madison does, but we have the internet. We've been active on forums and websites that speak out against Madison. We can record footage of us breaking into the food storage center, create a video, and have it go viral. That way, everyone can see what we have done."

Magni ate a large chunk of rabbit as he pondered this. The internet and the messages and videos they contained was still a new concept to him. Dante had been demonstrating some of this to him. He referred to himself as a hacker, which apparently was a good thing. Magni put down his fork. "I don't think this would be a wise course. I do not profess to have the same knowledge that you do regarding the internet, however I do not wish to reveal myself to Loki. The longer he remains unaware of my presence, the more favorable it will be for us."

"That won't be a problem. I can edit the video so that you or Mjolnir won't be seen. We can make it look like you're not there at all. That might even work better if you wreak all kinds of havoc, but nobody can see what's causing it."

Magni nodded. He looked around at the large, sterile room lined with metal folding tables that served as the communal dining area. Putting together meals for the people living here was a challenge. Ever since Magni had killed K-Dog, there had been more people asking to live with them. What they served was a far-cry from the elaborate feasts he was used to eating in Valhalla, but his people were doing the best they could.

"Is there any objection to this course of action?" Magni asked.

"Certainly not from me," Sheila replied. "I'll tell you this much. If you hit them, then hit 'em hard. Really send a message."

"Then we will do this," Magni said. "Dante and François, I will rely heavily upon you since you know far more of the logistical details than I. However, when it comes to the heavy lifting, as you call it—that is where I will come into play. I would like to minimize the risk to your people."

"No problem there," Dante said. "I have some ideas on how this needs to go down."

***

Magni set off with his group of twelve under the cloak of night. They all wore dark clothing and had their faces painted. This type of operation was entirely new for him. He was used to facing his enemy in the battlefield, using force to smash them. He fought his battles with honor.

He had agreed to defer the logistical planning of this operation to Dante and François. They were more familiar with not only the area but also the modern devices needed to send their message. One of their members carried a device smaller than Magni's hand that would record the footage.

They took several vehicles to the destination. Magni had only been in a motor car a handful of times on prior trips to Midgard. He enjoyed travelling in them, the ride more comfortable than a horse-drawn wagon or the back of a stallion.

There were no other vehicles out this evening. The decrease in population had created a sense of desolation, something he had felt while walking through the streets of Philadelphia. The city had a vast emptiness to it with the abandoned buildings and streets, signs of the people who had once resided here before Loki and his virus had killed them off.

There was little conversation on the ride. Besides Magni's vehicle, they employed two large trucks to haul their bounty. The men and women aboard were armed with handguns.

The government kept the food supply in a three-story building with a fenced-in perimeter where guards carried machine pistols. Two were in a booth by the road leading into the building. In addition, guards wearing black and grey uniforms patrolled the area in convertible Jeeps.

The car stopped a few blocks from the food storage building. Dante put his hand on Magni's shoulder. "You ready for this?"

"You need not worry, my friend," Magni said. "I will do my part. Be ready for yours."

Dante nodded. The rear doors of the van opened, and his group exited. Magni was the last to leave. He waited as the others took their positions. The videographer stood next to Magni. She provided last minute instructions as to where he should be placed for proper recording.

Magni lifted Mjolnir and shot a large lightning bolt. It cracked the sky, illuminating the dark night. Advancing toward the building, he shot bolts of lightning near the booth that held the two guards.

The confusion among the guards was apparent when they ran out of their booth shouting. They drew their automatic weapons but did not fire. Magni continued to fire lighting near them. A direct shot obliterated the booth they had been sitting in moments earlier. One of the guards spotted him and was about to shoot but fell to the ground in a twitching heap after Dante struck him with a weapon called a Taser, which shot electricity in much lower voltages than Mjolnir. The other guard similarly fell down after someone zapped him from behind with a Taser. François handcuffed the men while Dante removed their weapons.

A Jeep raced toward them. Magni flung Mjolnir at the oncoming vehicle, smashing its front end. The Jeep jerked into the air and flipped over, crashing onto the paved road.

François put his hand on Magni's shoulder. "I can't believe what I just saw."

"Believe it, my friend," Magni said. "Do not underestimate Mjolnir's power."

"I don't think I'll be doing that anytime soon."

Dante and two others from their party raced out to the overturned Jeep and dragged away the guards who had been inside of the vehicle. The two men looked bruised and bleeding. Magni had done his best to destroy the vehicle, but not kill the passengers.

"Don't worry," François said, as if reading his mind. "They're still alive. Let's move inside."

They carried flashlights, although the facility had electrical lighting. They walked unimpeded to the locked front door. Of his various options to enter the facility, Magni chose to bust through the door with a massive kick.

François spoke into his black radio and told the others to bring the trucks to the front of the building.

Magni thoroughly enjoyed all of the electronic devices and gadgets the people of Midgard employed. He frequently asked Dante about the function of these devices and had even used a computer to read Loki's propaganda.

Inside the facility, they found room after room with produce and canned food, in addition to refrigerators and freezers filled with meat and fish.

Dante whistled. "Damn. We can feed ourselves for months." He raised his hands before Magni could speak. "I know. We're going to share it with other groups."

"Do you have enough room in your refrigerated machines to store all of this?" Magni asked.

"We'll figure out a way to store everything," Dante replied. "Let's take as much as we can and be quick about it in case there are more guards in the area, or some coming to relieve these guys."

Magni assisted in bringing the food into the trucks. He expedited the process by carrying several large boxes at a time.

When they finished, Dante donned a mask and stood in front of the videographer. At the videographer's command, Dante started his pre-rehearsed speech. "The time has come to stand up against John Madison and his evil regime. He is not the savior he preaches to be. He's a madman who created the virus. He claims he's here to help us. Well, he's here only to suppress us.

"We're not going to take his fascist oppression anymore. We ask that you stand with us. We are called *Freedom For All* and with your help, we are going to bring down John Madison. Join us to stand against his tyranny. He can't hold all of us down. Tonight is the first step in overthrowing the dictator. You just witnessed how we took the food he has been withholding from us. Well, we're going to distribute this food to those who need it. And now, we're going to bring down his building, just like we're going to bring down John Madison." Dante held up a clenched fist to the camera.

"And cut," the videographer said.

Dante removed his mask and turned to Magni. "All right. Time to do your thing. You sure about this?"

"I would have thought by now that you would no longer doubt me," Magni said. "Just be certain that you are clear of the area."

Magni wanted a show of strength, both for the people watching this video and for Loki. However, he did not wish to destroy the building storing the food, since they had not been able to take all of it, not to mention it contained valuable refrigeration equipment. Instead, they targeted the building next to it, which was similar in size and appearance. Those who observed the footage would not notice the difference.

When his group cleared the area, Magni went to the rear of the building and removed his hammer. With a mighty smash, he shook the building. Bricks fell, but it still stood. Another strike wobbled it further. Magni smiled. *Stubborn building. Well-constructed, too.* This would require just a bit more force than he had given it before. He reared back and smashed the base of the building. The result was a concussive blast and an explosion of brick and mortar. Debris flew in every direction, and the once sturdy building collapsed to the ground in a heap of rubble.

In the background came shouts of triumph from his compatriots. Their attitude and demeanor had undergone a revolutionary shift since he first joined them. All they needed was confidence that they could make significant changes. If he could instill this confidence in them, then he could instill it in the rest of the people as well.

Chapter XXVII

Magni kept his eyes trained on the large man sitting behind the desk. He wore gold rings on each finger, diamond studs on each ear, a fedora, and had gold-plated teeth. Magni was hardly impressed with Hector Pedroza, but kept his opinion to himself, knowing how hard Dante worked to make this meeting happen.

Dante was pleading their case to Hector, whose henchmen stood on either side of the room holding machine guns. If they made a threatening move, he would not hesitate to bring Mjolnir into the conversation.

Dante wore a shirt and tie for this meeting. Magni could not understand his choice of formal dress, considering that Hector wore baggy pants and a sports jersey.

"I fully respect the operation you're running here and the strides you've made," Dante said. "I wouldn't be here otherwise, but I think it would benefit you to join *Freedom For All*. We have made alliances with groups in Pennsylvania, Maryland, New Jersey, D.C., and Ohio. We need to stick together. John Madison and his government can't fight us all."

Hector folded his arms and leaned back in his chair. "Who said I want to fight the government? They've done all right by me so far."

"You're under their thumb," Dante said. "You can't do anything without their consent. They tolerate you because of your influence in the community."

Hector spread his arms and gestured. "Look around. I'm the King of New York."

Magni could no longer hold his tongue. "You are the king of nothing. You allow this dictator to control your life and the lives of your people. You are merely his servant boy. If you weren't such a coward, you would standup up to Madison."

Dante winced.

"You got a lot 'a balls comin' here and talking to me like that." Hector's voice was level and even.

"Look, my friend means no disrespect," Dante said.

"Actually, I do," Magni said. "You need to remove your head out of your posterior. As long as John Madison rules your world, you have nothing. You are a slave to his whims. Let me ask you, can you travel as you please? Can you live where you want? Can you worship as you please? Can you choose your own occupation? The answer to all of these questions is no. If you are willing to accept these conditions, then you deserve to be John Madison's slave."

The men standing at either side of the room clutched their weapons. Hector raised his hand, and their stances relaxed.

He folded his large arms. The man was not fat, but neither was he muscled. "You guys are responsible for all those bombings and terrorist attacks against the government?"

Dante nodded. They had been quite busy during the last two months since leveling the food storage building in Philadelphia. Since that time, they had staged numerous acts of defiance against Madison's government.

"I could turn you guys in," Hector said. "There's a massive bounty on your heads."

Magni shrugged. "You could, but you wouldn't live very long."

Hector smiled. "That's some impressive stuff, taking down buildings, distributing food, releasing prisoners. You people are fearless. I like your style. Let's get serious. What can you offer me?"

"You said you were the King of New York," Magni said. "After we bring John Madison down, society will have to be rebuilt. We will need people to lead this effort and create a real government. If you help us, you will be a big part of that. We can offer you real authority, real political power."

Hector sat silently, his massive brainpower at work. Magni could almost feel the gears grinding. Unfortunately, Hector did not strike him as a great thinker. "All right. You sold me. As part of the deal, I want a constant supply of food and medicine for my people. Let me give you a tour of the facility."

Dante glanced at Magni, who gave a slight nod in reply. Magni did not think Hector would betray them. The man was greedy, but he was also an opportunist, and this was a better opportunity than what he currently had.

***

Much of Hector's network was underground, quite literally. They made extensive use of the area housing New York's old subway system. The subways were no longer running, but they used the existing tunnels. Rats scurried back and forth. The tunnels were dirty and had a bad odor. As Magni told him earlier, Hector Pedroza truly was the king of nothing.

Their living quarters were crammed with people clustered together despite the large area with which they had to work.

The citizens were dirty and poorly dressed. They lived much like the rats that ran across the floor.

Fortunately, Hector had a nice cache of weapons. Besides guns and ammunition, they had explosives, knives, and other hand-to-hand weaponry in abundance. Despite this, Pedroza had no combat background unless he counted being the leader of a street gang. In recent recruiting missions, Magni and Dante sought people with military backgrounds. If they were going to put together an army, they needed trained men and women to lead it. They recently started boot camps to train the new recruits. When they encountered individuals with extensive combat experience, Magni put them in charge of training, maintaining regular communication with them.

They exited the subway and walked to an old school, which housed more of Hector's people and stored supplies. The sense of desolation felt overwhelming in the empty streets of New York. *So much loss of life. What a tragic waste.* All because of Loki's unquenchable thirst for power. The trickster had done many treacherous things in the past, but nothing compared to this. What he had done to the people of Midgard was unthinkable, inexcusable. The only acceptable punishment was death, one that Magni vowed to deliver.

Before they entered the school, a dark-skinned woman holding a radio approached Hector. "We got problems. It looks like a whole squadron of government people are coming this way. They're armed and motorized."

Hector frowned. "Damn."

"And they have giants with them," the woman said.

A panicked look entered Hector's face. "We need to go to ground."

François, who had been talking on a radio, said, "Our people have confirmed the same thing. There are giants and soldiers coming this way."

"We need to go," Hector said.

Magni grabbed his shoulder with a firm grip. "Now is not the time to run. Now is the time to fight. I have seen your armament. You claim to have trained fighters. We must put them to the test. Madison's forces have come here for a reason. Going underground will solve nothing. They will merely flush you out and destroy you."

"Are you crazy?" Hector asked. "They have giants out there."

Magni gazed into his eyes. "Leave the giants to me. I will battle them."

"Trust him," Dante said. "This guy has killed more giants than you can imagine. He's right. Going to ground won't solve a thing. They'll follow us and eradicate us. At least this way we have a fighting chance."

Sweat dripped from Hector's brow. "I hope you guys know what you're doing, otherwise it's the end for all of us." He turned to the dark-skinned woman who reported the news. "All right. Gather everybody you can. Bring out the heavy ammo."

"You ready for a fight?" Dante asked.

Magni stared into the distance. "I have been bred for this. Thor and Odin have taught me well over the centuries. I welcome the opportunity to shed more giant blood."

Hector snarled. He had the look of a feral animal. He went up to Magni and glared at him. "You better know what you're doing. If not, we're all dead."

Magni ignored him. He did not need a pep talk from this man. He sat at the top of paved steps leading to the school building, leaned his head against the brick wall, and closed his eyes, remembering the Battle of Ragnarok and how he broke through line after line of frost and fire giants, how he slayed Surter, and finally felled Jormangandr. It felt like a lifetime ago.

While the others bustled about in preparation, he channeled the mindset he would need today. He had not come to New York thinking he would battle Loki's forces for the first time, but it did not matter. He would eventually have to defeat them in the field of combat, and this rainy, chilly April afternoon was as good as any.

Chapter XXVIII

He was not sure how long he sat on those steps in contemplative meditation before Dante shook his arm.

"Time to fight, Magni. They're a few blocks away."

Magni opened his eyes and rose, still feeling bitterness and hatred toward the enemy he faced at Ragnarok. If only Loki were here. Instead, he would have to focus his rage against the giants, a poor substitute.

He stretched his arms, back, and shoulders before removing Mjolnir. He would put his father's hammer to good use today.

By now, dozens of armed humans with firearms had gathered on the street. Mostly they were Hector's people, along with the eight individuals who accompanied him on this trip. He would do his best not to fight humans. Even if they were following Loki, they were not his enemy.

He stood and faced his compatriots. "Today we must strike a blow to the heart of our enemy and begin to take back what is rightfully yours."

Magni froze. He couldn't believe his eyes. It was her. But how was that possible? She was dead. His eyes had to be deceiving him. With the sounds of the impending army advancing, he could not stop now to speak with her.

He glanced at the army on the city streets. The reverberations coming from the giants shook the buildings, streetlights, and vehicles. As they came into view, Magni focused on them. He recognized Mangor, an ally of Thrym, the former leader of the frost giants, at the front of the pack. There were six giants in total, and he meant to kill them all.

He marched forward to meet the charge, hoping to radiate confidence. It seemed to work as the others followed him with purpose. As he got close, he shot lightning bolts at the enemy.

When the opposing army opened fire, he lifted Mjolnir and let it take him into the air. As they made a futile attempt to shoot him in the sky, he answered back with more lightning. One bolt exploded an oncoming truck. Another blasted the hood off a Jeep. He continued raining down lighting on his foes. Some attempted to scatter, but the giants would not allow them to flee. Meanwhile, Magni's forces opened fire.

Using Mjolnir to propel himself, Magni shot down directly at Mangor. He was a firm believer in taking the head off the enemy. He hit Mangor like a missile, toppling the frost giant.

The giant's skin was as white as porcelain. He was about five meters tall and as thick as an oak tree. His hair had jagged spikes. He wore plated mail armor and had a battle-axe in hand, the weapon of choice for most frost giants. He also had a sheathed sword and, more likely than not, a few knives for close combat.

Despite the size disadvantage, Magni was able to outmuscle him on the ground, shoving his forearm into the giant's face, digging an elbow into his throat. As they fought for position, Mangor used his knees to thrust Magni off him. Magni took a swing at Mangor's head with his war hammer, narrowly missing.

Mangor reached for his fallen axe and took a swipe at Magni. Anticipating the attack, Magni dodged right, then took another swing at the giant to no avail. In close, he holstered Mjolnir and unsheathed his sword.

He barreled his way forward, the blade of his sword quicker than Mangor's axe. In the process of driving the giant backward, Mangor knocked over an unsuspecting human, one of Madison's soldiers. Somehow, Mangor maintained his balance.

Just as Magni was about to go in for the kill, a massive fist cracked the back of his skull. He fell to the ground, dazed. Getting to one knee, he tried to regain his senses. The frost giant that hit him from behind wrapped her furry hands around his throat, leaving him breathless. He got to his feet, turned, brought a knee into her abdomen, then lowered his shoulder and rammed into her, knocking down the frost giant. He kicked the giant's head.

He brought out Mjolnir once more, the sword now lying on the ground. With one mighty swing, he smashed the top of the frost giant's head, ending her miserable existence.

Magni collected his sword and looked for Mangor, but the giant was gone. Glancing at the chaotic street, much of the fighting had turned into the hand-to-hand variety. It was hard to tell which side was winning the day. The only thing he knew with certainty was that if his allies were to gain victory, he would have to eliminate the frost giants.

Ten meters in front of him, a frost giant was mauling one of Hector's people on the ground. Magni swung Mjolnir once in the air and flung it at the giant. The impact was devastating as the hammer's momentum sent him flying backward until he crashed into an enemy vehicle. The vehicle reared up and flipped over, its passengers crushed by the giant's hulking frame.

Magni held up his hand to catch Mjolnir on its return. As he was about to advance on his next target, one of Madison's soldiers opened fire on him using a machine pistol. He elevated out of the path of bullets with Mjolnir's assistance. The man continued to shoot. The bullets missed their mark, but Magni could not count on his inaccuracy for long. He did not want to kill this man. He was here to save the people of Midgard, not to kill them, but he did not see a way out. He was relieved of having to make this decision when François shot the man twice in the chest.

With a better view from up above, Magni surveyed the battlefield, pleased to find that his forces were carrying the tide of the battle. Advancing, they now outnumbered the opposition. The only problem was that the frost giants were still wreaking havoc. He set down on the ground, only to receive a spear in his thigh.

Magni cried out in pain, staring at the metal shaft. With the frost giant who had hurled it at him advancing, he tore out the spear, cursing loudly. He winced and tried to take a step, but the pain became more intense as he walked.

Before Magni could brace himself for impact, the frost giant tackled him. The giant smashed Magni's head against the hard concrete. Out of desperation, Magni threw a blind elbow, which caught the giant on the bridge of the nose. Magni crawled on his knees, trying to regain his senses. The world around him was fuzzy. Shouts, screams, and cries filled his ears.

When the giant reached for him, Magni backhanded him to the face, staggering his foe. Magni got to his feet, twisted, and swung Mjolnir, cracking the giant's skull. The echo from the blow reverberated over the gunfire and sounds of fighting.

The giant crumpled to the ground in a heap. Magni went to finish the job, but the giant was clearly dead, its face indented from the blow.

Magni shook his head once more, trying to clear his mind. His leg ached. Blood dripped down his thigh. He looked for Mangor but could not find him.

Nearby, a Madison soldier held a long knife to Anthony, one of the men who had accompanied Magni from Philadelphia. Magni rushed over, lifted the soldier by the back of his neck, and flung him against the side of a car. He helped Anthony to his feet. The young man's blond hair was red from a gash on the top of his head, but he looked like he would survive.

An oncoming vehicle coming from the top of the street drove straight at Magni. He had the distinct impression the driver was planning to flatten him. Magni put away Mjolnir and stared at the driver, who suddenly had a look of naked fear. He planted his feet on the ground, took a wide stance, and lowered his shoulder. When the vehicle neared him, he took the brunt of the impact on his shoulder, grabbed the front bumper, and snarled as he put all of his strength into stopping the vehicle from moving.

He lifted the vehicle into the air. Walking forward, he continued to raise the vehicle. Its front wheels spun as the driver tried to accelerate. His shoulder throbbing from the collision and his leg aching from the wound, Magni flipped over the vehicle. A loud screech sounded as metal grinded against asphalt.

Magni turned at the sound of loud footsteps behind him and caught the sight of whirling metal. His keen reflexes saved him from the frost giant's axe. He pulled his head back just enough for the axe to miss its mark.

The frost giant remained on the offensive, taking another swipe at him with its axe. This time, Magni spun to his left to avoid the blow. The blade clanged against the road.

As the giant tried to wrench his blade from the street, Magni clenched his fist and cracked the giant's jaw, snapping back his head. He then grabbed the giant by the neck, lowered his head, and landed a knee to the giant's face, smashing his nose. He followed this with another knee to the face that sent the frost giant tumbling to the wet street.

Grabbing the axe that fell from the giant's grip, Magni lifted it overhead. The weapon was huge, even for someone his size. He swung it, and with one swipe, cleaved off the giant's head. With some pleasure, he watched it roll on the ground.

Magni tossed the axe aside. With a limp, he moved forward, searching for another giant to slay. A blinding pain surged through his body. He fell to the ground, not sure what had just happened. All he knew for sure was that something had struck him with devastating speed and force. He looked around and found a large crimson stain on his tunic. He clutched his arm and cried out in pain. It took him a few moments to realize that someone had shot him. He could not see a bullet, but the wound was clear enough.

Magni smashed his fist on the ground. He had been hoping to get through this fight without being shot. If he knew which human had done this to him, he would crush them with his bare hands.

Magni got to his feet and encountered a frost giant he had fought before in Asgard named Bentonil, who thrust a spear the length of a car at him. He avoided the spear and backed away from his larger foe. When fighting giants, because of their substantial size advantage, he preferred to either fight them from a far enough distance so they could not reach him, or in close to nullify their height and reach advantage.

Magni backed away against a light pole. Bentonil lunged at him. Magni jumped to the side, and the giant crashed into the light pole. The structure groaned and creaked, and eventually tore out of the ground, landing onto an unsuspecting Madison soldier. Magni seized the advantage, took two steps forward, and swung Mjolnir. The blow found its mark, giving a solid crunch when it connected with Bentonil's ribs.

The giant cried out and blindly thrust his spear. The spear caught Magni in the chest. For a moment, Magni could hardly breathe. His mail armor absorbed part of the blow, but it still pierced him. He staggered backward as Bentonil ripped the spear out of him.

The giant pressed the attack, continuing to jab the spear at him. Magni's normal agility had lessened from the blows he had taken. Despite that, he managed to avoid Bentonil's attack. Magni took an upward swing with his hammer but could not connect. He continued to back away until he bumped into an abandoned vehicle. After climbing on top of the vehicle, he was nearly the same height as Bentonil.

He jumped at Bentonil and planted his good shoulder into the giant's chest, knocking him to the ground. He used his weight to pin the stunned giant. With his right hand, he punched Bentonil in the face repeatedly, bloodying him. Magni got up and stomped his heel into Bentonil's abdomen, then reared back with Mjolnir and smashed the giant just above the chest. One more solid whack, this time to Bentonil's face, slayed the giant, his face crushed.

Magni looked around but could not find Mangor. He grunted. It was unlike a giant to skirt away from a fight. They relished the opportunity to battle Asgardians. He had tangled with Mangor in the past and had found him to be a formidable foe.

As he surveyed the battlefield, it became clear that Madison's troops were on the retreat as Magni's human allies drove them back. His gaze on the battlefield lingered too long, and he did not notice the remaining frost giant as she smashed him from behind with a weapon.

Magni crashed face-first into the asphalt. Still woozy from the blow, he tried to get to his feet, but all he could manage was to flip onto his back. Through clouded eyes, he could see the giant's ugly face, scarred from battle-wounds. Blue blood covered her knobby nose and protruding forehead. Her black eyes were sunk deep into their sockets.

She held a metal-plated spiked mace, forged by frost giants from ancient times and considered unbreakable. It only added to the ferocity of the giant's blows.

She attempted to smash him once more with her mace. Magni put up Mjolnir to defend against the blow but was only partially successful. She blasted him time after time with the mace. He was taking heavy damage from the attack. If he was going to make it out alive, he would have to think of something quickly.

She staggered back a step as a bullet ripped into her gut. Magni glanced back and found Dante behind him on one knee pointing his pistol at the frost giant. Blood was flowing down his nose, and his shirt was torn, but he did not fear the giant in front of him. He shot her in the chest this time.

The frost giant gave an angry roar that emerged from deep within her ample belly. For a moment, she took her attention off Magni and advanced toward Dante. That was the opening he needed. He raised his hammer and shot a bolt of lightning. She swayed and nearly fell.

Dante took another shot at the giant and missed, despite the large target. She charged at Dante. Magni grimaced and got to his feet. If the frost giant reached his human friend, she would crush him.

Magni lunged at her. Their collision was violent. Magni fell to a knee. Although wobbled, the giant still stood. She wrapped her large hands around Magni's neck and began to squeeze. Mjolnir hung uselessly in one hand.

Dante shot her in the shoulder, which caused the giant to release her grip. Magni grunted and punched her abdomen. With the separation created from the blow, he swung Mjolnir with a massive uppercut of an arc that connected with her chin, sending the giant off her feet. He could not tell if she was alive or dead but he was not about to take any chances. He raised Mjolnir, about to finish his foe, when bullets punctured Magni's shoulder, chest, and abdomen.

The pain was beyond excruciating. He could hardly breathe. The world around him became dark and frightening. He tried to move forward, vaguely realizing that Mjolnir was no longer in his grasp. When his legs gave out entirely, he collapsed. Loud noises and movement came before him as he tried to keep his eyes open. He had the sensation of being carried, but by whom and to where was a mystery.

When he looked up, he saw the familiar faces of Dante and François. He also found unfamiliar faces, which seemed friendly enough. He tried to keep his eyes open but was forever on the edge of having his consciousness ebb from him. The one image that remained engrained in his head, the one that made him wonder if this was all a dream or if he had passed to great beyond, was her image. He thought he had lost her forever, but now she was back. He found Freya and never wanted to leave her again.

Chapter XXIX

For a while, Magni was back in Asgard. He flashed from battles against giants, feasts in Valhalla, competitions of strength and skill, great hunts with his Aesir brethren, and time spent with Freya, never staying in one place for long before being yanked back into Midgard where he was in the presence of his new allies, who expressed concern for his well-being. He could not tell what was real and what was conjured by his imagination. Was he alive or had he passed to the great beyond? How could Freya be in both Asgard and Midgard?

He longed to return to the way things were before Ragnarok. Although not always peaceful, he had enjoyed his life, felt in control of things. Ever since the Battle of Ragnarok, things had been in turmoil living in a foreign world, his loved ones lost to him, taking part in a mission that seemed daunting if not impossible.

He opened his eyes and, this time, kept them open.

Dante's voice rang in his ears. "I think he's coming back to us."

"Get Dr. Harris," François said.

A small hand gripped Magni's large one. Dante peered down at him. "Thank God. Magni, I thought we lost you. You took more damage than any person can possibly sustain, but then again I guess you're not human."

Magni grimaced as he tried to elevate himself. He looked around at the sterile, white room and groaned. "How did the battle end?"

Dante's face brightened. "We defeated them. We turned them away. Keeping it real, we all owe it to you. You were amazing out there. You chopped those giants down. One escaped, but you killed the rest of them."

"Mangor," Magni muttered. "I tried." He cast his eyes down.

"Hey, don't be down on yourself. You did everything you possibly could. You were the difference maker, and everybody here knows it. You certainly convinced Hector Pedroza. That guy was talking about you like...well you're a god."

"I'm glad we prevailed. Mjolnir."

"Still on the street. Nobody could budge it. I have people guarding it. Once you get better, you can collect it. Man, I can't believe you're still alive after the damage you took."

"I am hard to kill."

"You can say that again."

Just then, Freya entered the room wearing a white coat the physicians of Midgard typically wore.

Magni lay there, open-mouthed, staring at her. "Freya."

A severe frown enveloped her face. "What are you doing sitting up? You need to lie down. Help me get him down."

Magni felt too weak to protest.

Using a stethoscope, she examined his chest. "Your pulse is normalizing and you're breathing better, which is something of a miracle considering the condition you were in just a few hours ago, but then again they tell me you're not human."

"Freya."

She turned to Dante. "What is he talking about?"

Dante stared at Magni. "Well, you see, Freya was his lover for centuries. They were involved in this cataclysmic battle in which she died. Magni survived the battle and has come here to help us, to liberate us from our current oppression."

She stared at him wide-eyed. "Are you serious?"

"I know it sounds far-fetched," Dante said. "But is it any crazier than the things you've seen lately? We did fight giants today, after all."

She frowned. "So, he thinks I'm his dead lover? Oh, boy."

Magni propped himself up again. "You are Freya."

"You need to lie down. I don't even know how you're still alive." She ran a device across his forehead. "His temperature is one hundred and forty degrees, which is down a bit. Is this normal?"

Dante shrugged. "Beats me."

"I am fine." Magni struggled to a sitting position.

"You're not fine. Now lie down, for the love of God. You should have been dead five times over with what happened out there." She folded her arms and stared at him. "I'm sorry that this Freya died, but I'm not her. My name is Susanna Harris. I'm a physician; at least I used to be before hell broke loose with the virus. Now I'm doing what I can to help the people here."

Despite her denial, he knew Freya as well as he could possibly know another person. Everything about her: the way she spoke, her physical appearance, her mannerisms all were the Freya he had known for centuries. He didn't understand why she insisted she was a physician from Midgard. "Listen, Freya…or Susanna if you call yourself that, you need not worry about my health. I heal quickly. I am nothing like the people of Midgard. That I survived the battle is what mattered."

Gritting his teeth, Magni managed to stand with great effort. Those gathered in the room stared at him in awe. Once standing, he felt better. He needed a good meal and a bottle of wine, and he would be ready for another fight.

"Can you remove the gown," Susanna said. "I need to take a look at your wounds."

Magni did as she requested.

She gasped as she felt his chest and abdomen. "Your wounds. They're almost healed."

Magni smiled. "As I said, I am no mortal. Now, if I am to recover and be of some use to you, I need nourishment."

"Sure thing," Dante said. "I'll get you some food and beverage."

Susanna pursed her lips. "I don't understand how this is possible."

Magni put a hand to her cheek. "Dine with me, and I will explain."

She stared at him. "I think I will."

***

Susanna took bite of the beef stew and drank her wine. They were dining in a back room near her medical office where she kept supplies. "So, I'm still trying to wrap my head around this whole Asgard thing. Your friends readily accept it, but it seems crazy to me."

"I wouldn't say that they readily accepted it, but after seeing what they have seen, it was impossible to not. I take it you witnessed today's battle?"

Susanna nodded.

"And what do you think?"

Susanna looked into his eyes. "I saw you fly and shoot lightning from your hammer. I also saw how you were able to recover from those wounds. It's unnatural. It's safe to say you're not human since no human being can do those things."

Ravenous, Magni continued to dig into the food. The injuries to his body demanded he replenish himself with nutrients. "It's a good sign when you can accept what your eyes see. Some cannot." What he could not fathom was how she could have no knowledge of being Freya when clearly she was his beloved.

"So, I understand you've been alive for a very long time?"

"Are you familiar with Thor and Odin?" Magni asked.

Susanna nodded. "Yeah, well there was those movies they made of Thor before the sickness. They're characters of ancient mythology."

Magni chuckled. Dante told him about the movies the people of Midgard made about his father, and how he had become a superhero character. "The answer to your question is that I have been alive for over a thousand of your years."

Susanna whistled. She was picking at her food, her appetite not nearly as hearty as his. "That's a long time. And this Freya, the two of you were together for a while."

Magni nodded. "For over two hundred years."

"So, why are you convinced that I'm her? I don't want to say that you're delusional, but maybe the damage you sustained affected your mind."

"My mind is as clear as it could be. You are Freya. I am certain of it. In time you will come to realize that as well."

***

The following day Magni and Dante met with Hector Pedroza in his office. Hector sat behind his desk, which was barely able to conceal his girth.

Magni ran his fingers through his long, blond hair. "What happened yesterday changes everything. John Madison will know of my existence. He will know I am coming for him, but he won't wait. He will aggressively attack. He will want me dead and will take any steps necessary to do so. This area will be flooded with giants and soldiers before long."

"The war started yesterday," Dante said. "There's no time for half-measures. We need to be ready to fight him full force. We've made some strides in the past month, but we're still not there yet. Our intelligence suggests Madison's army is large and well-armed."

Hector Pedroza folded his thick arms. "I like what I saw out there yesterday. If we got you on our side, then we can win this thing. Yeah, I was okay with being under the government's thumb because it was the best deal in town, but this changes everything. Besides my people here in New York, I have other crews we can hook up with."

Dante shook Hector's hand. "Thanks. We're going to need support if we're going to expand our efforts nationwide and start a movement."

"No way, brother," Hector said. "What you really need is someone else like Magni there. He's a whole army unto himself. You got more of you out there in whatever place you come from?"

"My brother," Magni said. "He is my equal in combat. If only I could find him. He has to be in Midgard by now. But your world is vast, and I would not know how to locate him."

Dante narrowed his eyes. "I can help you with that. We can reach out to Modi using the internet."

Magni frowned. "Although I am not so familiar with your internet, my understanding is that the information would be public, in which case Loki is just as likely to find me as Modi would be if I make my whereabouts known."

"I'm not saying we're going to put a picture of you in front of the Statue of Liberty for the whole world to see," Dante said. "We could search for Modi using back channels; put the word out on specially encrypted anti-government forums that you're looking for him."

Magni nodded. "Then we shall try that."

Magni was more hopeful about finding Modi than he would have been a few days ago. After all, he had Freya back in his life. There was no reason he could not have his brother back as well.

Chapter XXX

Magni waited for Susanna to come out of surgery. She had been operating all morning on those who had been wounded in what Hector had dubbed The Battle for New York. She was dedicated in her job as a physician, which didn't surprise Magni at all. Freya was dedicated in all that she did.

When Susanna finally emerged, blood covered much of her scrubs, and her hair was disheveled. She looked perfect.

She smiled when she saw him. "You didn't have to wait here for me."

Magni shrugged. "After clearing the rubble from the streets, there was little else for me to do. I have been looking forward to seeing you all day."

Susanna sighed. "Well, I'm a mess. I need to clean up. There's a shower nearby. Can you give me twenty minutes?"

"Take as long as you wish."

While Susanna was cleaning up, a nurse drafted Magni into service. He held down a man whose leg needed to be amputated. It was gruesome business. Susanna and the two other physicians who worked with Hector Pedroza and his group here in New York had taken supplies from one of the nearby hospitals and set up their own makeshift hospital, but they did not have anywhere near the supplies, equipment, and medicine they once did in their modern facilities. They were doing the best they could under the circumstances, but apparently medical standards were not what they had been prior to the virus that had destroyed their world.

After Susanna returned, they walked to Central Park. Hector Pedroza currently controlled the Upper East Side of Manhattan. Although he fully expected Madison's forces to retaliate, Magni did not expect it would be so soon.

They passed the Guggenheim Museum, which once housed some of the most prized and valuable pieces of art in Midgard but was now in a state of disrepair. The museum had been looted and the exterior of the building had been vandalized.

They entered Central Park where they encountered three children running around playing some sort of game. It was a peaceful afternoon, almost giving the illusion that things were normal in this world. Magni carried a basket that held fresh fruit, cured meat and cheese, a bottle of wine, two glasses, and a blanket. Susanna appeared to be full of energy and in good spirits despite having gone through hours of surgery. He found a spot to lay the blanket, then set out the food and wine.

"I find it admirable that you tirelessly and selflessly dedicate yourself to helping the people here," Magni said. "But then you have always given of yourself in that manner."

"What, in the one day that you've known me?" Susanna asked.

Magni poured each of them a glass of wine. "You must be hungry."

"Ravenous. Thanks for packing this nice meal. Food has been easier to come by since we received that shipment your people sent to us on the truck."

Freedom for All had targeted two other food storage buildings after the first one in Philadelphia. It had been a well devised plan by Dante. There was no better way to gain the support of hungry people then by giving them food. Francois had been in charge of distributing the food to different communities. The effort had been tied to recruiting new members to join *Freedom for All.*

"Do you ever feel as if you are an outsider?" Magni asked.

"The people here need me," Susanna said. "And I'm glad to help."

Magni noted the defensiveness of her answer. "You did not answer the question. I'm not speaking of these people or even New York." Magni spread out his arms. "I mean here."

Susanna did not answer him.

"I know I feel as if I am an outsider."

"Of course. You're from some place called Asgard," Susanna said.

"Tell me how you would describe Asgard."

Susanna frowned. "How could I? I've never been there."

"Close your eyes and imagine. Picture what you think Asgard might be like and describe it to me."

"This is silly," Susanna said.

"Humor me."

Susanna closer her eyes. She sat in silence for a time. He could feel her resistance bend. Then it broke. It was as if she fell into a trance. "I see wide rolling hills with tall grasses. There is a forest with large trees, so tall they rival some of the buildings in New York. I can see a sea of deep azure with massive ships made of wood. And a majestic mountain off in the distance. Every so often, the rolling hills are broken apart by immense halls. I guess everything is big in Asgard."

Magni smiled. Truer words had never been spoken.

"And there's a rainbow. No. Not a rainbow. A bridge. A very colorful one."

Susanna opened her eyes. She vigorously shook her head.

"Sorry. It felt as if I was daydreaming. What did you ask?"

"I asked you to describe to me what you thought Asgard might be like," Magni said.

"How did I do?"

"You described it with uncanny accuracy."

Susanna shrugged. "Lucky guess. Maybe someday you can take me there."

"There is nothing I would rather do, but alas there is much to do here. We must take back this world from an evil authoritarian dictator. Someone who doesn't belong here."

They continued to eat their lunch. There was no more talk of Asgard or John Madison.

***

They spent another three days in New York. As bull-headed as Hector Pedroza was, even he concluded his people could no longer stay here.

One great development was that Freya, or Susanna as she now called herself, would accompany Magni. Even if Pedroza had not decided that his group would return with them to Philadelphia, Magni would have asked her to join him anyway. Despite her insistence that she was not Freya, they had gotten quite close over the last few days. They had spent whatever time they could together, and it was the happiest he had been since the eve of Ragnarok.

On the morning of their departure, he was helping her pack her medical supplies. As gently as he could, he placed IV bags in plastic tubs. They had already packed crates of medication into a truck for transport.

"I'm glad I'm coming with you," Susanna said. "You might just be the most interesting guy I've ever met."

"Might be?"

Susanna giggled. "Okay, you are the most interesting man I've ever met."

"Had the battle gone differently and Pedroza decided not to relocate to Philadelphia, would you return with me?" Magni asked.

Susanna looked up at him. She had golden hair, even lighter than his. Her eyes were bright blue, and her face unblemished. She was unusually tall for a human female, which made his own height not so imposing in comparison. "I would follow you anywhere you went. But just to make things clear, I'm not Freya."

"So, you continue to tell me," Magni said. "Are you trying to convince me or you?"

"That's silly."

"Is it?" Magni appraised her. It warmed his heart just to gaze at her. "Let me ask you this. What can you tell me about your upbringing, about your family?"

"I was raised in an orphanage. I never knew my parents or siblings if I have any."

"Very well. Where was this orphanage located?"

"In the South," Susanna replied.

"Can you be more specific?"

"Georgia?"

"Where in Georgia?" Magni asked.

"I don't… remember." Susanna flashed a look of irritation. "What difference does it make? It wasn't in Atlanta. It was somewhere more…rural."

It was as Magni suspected. The more he pressed for details, the more the façade of her memories deteriorated. It made sense for her to think she grew up in an orphanage. That would be less difficult of a falsehood to retain than having to create a family. Somewhere lurking in the depths of her mind was Freya. He just had to unlock her.

Susanna sighed. "Oh, Magni, you're so frustrating. I must be a fool for wanting to drop everything to be with you, but I can't help it. I'm drawn to you in an unnatural way. I can't stop thinking about you."

"There's nothing unnatural about it," Magni said. "You are drawn to me in the same way I'm drawn to you. We are meant to be together. Our love has endured for centuries. Just because we are no longer in Asgard, it should not end." Magni bent down and kissed her lips softly. She did not shrink back, but rather invited more.

Susanna closed her eyes. "I don't know if it's cosmic, fate, or whatever. I just know the way you make me feel is unlike how any man has ever made me feel before."

Magni kissed her more deeply this time. She even tasted like Freya. "If you follow me, there will be great danger."

"I've never shied away from danger," Susanna said.

"I know."

Susanna smiled. "I forgot. I'm your long lost lover." She drew him in closer. "I would like to be your lover once more."

***

John Madison could not stem his annoyance on this laborious trip. He had to travel to their stronghold for his meeting with the giants since it was difficult for them to travel far. They lacked the massive ships they used in Jotunheim and Muspelheim. The giants were currently constructing new ships for travel, but that would take time.

Through his agents, Mangor had sent word that they needed to meet urgently. It was unlike giants to make such a request. He still had an uneasy alliance with the frost giants. Their ambition matched his, and only time would tell if they were willing to be subservient to him. He tried to appease them whenever possible. He needed their muscle, but it was never far from his mind that they might decide to dethrone him and take Midgard for themselves.

What was working in his favor, both in the case of the frost and fire giants, was that they had no true leader to unite them. Surter and Thyrm fell at the Battle of Ragnarok. John had not been broken-hearted when he heard the news. As long as they lacked a uniting force, they were unlikely to challenge him.

It grated at John that he had to take time out of his busy schedule to meet Mangor, postponing the dedication of a statue erected in his likeness in the city formerly known as Moscow. He had been looking forward to the occasion. Yuri Uzelkov had assured him there would be a sizeable turnout with parades and festivals. As much as it pained him, he could not afford to cross the frost giants—not yet.

Getting to this section of the Appalachian Mountains proved to be a major headache. He took a private jet to New York City, followed by a helicopter ride, and a trek in an SUV to the giants' territory. They preferred to live in mountainous regions, which more closely resembled their old homes. Not the most civilized of creatures, they lacked the refinement to live in a proper society.

During the trip, he participated in three conference calls with his regional governors. His work never ended. Any mortal would have keeled over in exhaustion by now. Fortunately, he was a god, and not just any god, but the most powerful one alive.

The roads on his trip up the mountains were in need of serious repair. That was problem number seven hundred and fifty two he had to deal with. Being the ruler of Midgard was not always glorious. He had to tend to tedious problems, or at least assign them to other people to deal with. He concerned himself with big picture issues.

As he neared the frost giant stronghold in the Appalachian Mountains in the former state of New York, he had to put on his politician's face. In certain ways, he had always been a politician, using his charm to befriend Odin and the Aesir. Later, when he fell out of favor with them, he used the same charisma to befriend the giants, always maintaining a position of power.

Klaus accompanied him. Not much of a conversationalist, Klaus was here to provide muscle. Even among giants, he was an intimidating presence.

They had to hike the last mile to their destination, the air getting thinner. Klaus approached the journey with his typical stoicism.

"Perhaps the giants should invest in a smartphone. It would make life easier," John said.

Klaus grunted. "It would be too small for their hands."

John could not be sure, but he thought Klaus might have just made a joke. A sense of humor was not the German's best attribute.

The giants had built a handful of homes into the mountains, each huge in size as befitting their occupants. Other homes were under construction in anticipation of the arrival of more frost giants, but no giants had crossed recently, a cause of ongoing concern. He was still investigating the situation but had been tied up with other affairs.

They had transported truckloads of lumber, steel, and building materials for this massive construction project. John offered the use of human labor, but the giants preferred to do the construction themselves. Between clearing out the dead bodies and rubble, tearing down old buildings, new construction, maintaining electrical and utility facilities, there were hardly enough bodies to go around to do all the work.

A greeting party of frost giants welcomed them. John was surprised to find not only Mangor but Hrugnir as well. Hrugnir, who had settled in the former country of Canada, was gaining stature among the frost giants, which made John weary of him.

Since their arrival in Midgard, they had clashed on various issues.

"What a pleasant surprise, Hrugnir," John said. "To what do I owe the honor of your presence?"

Hrugnir glared at him. "Loki, you said they would all be dead. You lied. They are not all dead."

"Who is supposed to be dead?" John Madison asked.

Hrugnir growled at him. "The Aesir. They were all supposed to have died at Ragnarok. You guaranteed they would all be dead."

"It's freezing out here," John said. "Let us take this conversation inside. I would like some mead."

Hrugnir, who towered over John, stared down at him. "This better not be one of your tricks, Loki."

He had the overwhelming urge to knock Hrugnir down and teach him a lesson. He was not some schoolboy they could scold. Glancing at Klaus, the German seemed to have the same idea, his hand not far from his pistol.

John smiled. "We shall go inside and discuss these matters."

John and Klaus followed Hrugnir, Mangor, and a host of frost giants into a large barren hall. He took a seat on an oversized chair that was more like a throne. Based on the look Mangor gave him, it must have been his personal chair.

John refused to conduct business until they served him mead and food, which consisted of slabs of dried meat and cheese.

After John drank his fill, he turned to Hrugnir. "Now, what do you speak of? There are no Aesir in Midgard."

Hrugnir turned to Mangor. "Tell him what you saw."

Mangor grunted. "More than saw. I tangled with one of them."

"Who?" John could not fathom that so soon after the Battle of Ragnarok there would be Aesir here, even had they survived. They would be rebuilding Asgard after its annihilation.

"Thor's son," Mangor replied. "He killed five of my people."

John frowned. "Thor's son. Which one?"

"The strong one. He was wielding Mjolnir and killed five of my people. You promised us we would not have to deal with the Aesir any longer."

John waved his hand. "A minor nuisance that will be dealt with." Despite the cavalier attitude he portrayed, this new development deeply disturbed him. Magni was nobody to be trifled with. He was among the more powerful Aesir, especially if he had Mjolnir in his possession.

John successfully deflected the conversation to other giant business, but Magni never escaped his thoughts for long. That damned Aesir could destroy everything he had built since his return to Midgard five years ago in the guise of John Madison. He would do everything in his power to eliminate Magni.

Chapter XXXI

Magni felt truly alive for the first time since arriving in Midgard. His group had travelled for the past few weeks actively recruiting members, distributing food and other necessities, and getting into skirmishes with Loki's forces. Granted, some clashes had been brutal, and they had lost good people along the way, but they continued to make dents into Loki's empire. More importantly, Freya was at his side, even if she didn't believe she was Freya.

Although they had suffered their share of losses, their numbers continued to grow as they recruited new members. They became bolder in their defiance as they spread their message far and wide. Whenever they entered a new territory, people knew of them, even if they weren't always receptive to their message. The battle lines were becoming clearly drawn, and Magni no longer felt the need to conceal his identity.

Whenever they first arrived in a new area, Dante would meet with the leaders of local resistance groups and pitch them to join the group, but it was Magni they wanted to see. It was he who closed the deal, as Dante often said. He did his best to instill confidence in these people and restore their shattered dreams. In turn, they were drawn to him like a beacon of hope.

Magni held Susanna's hand as they walked along the Charles River just outside of Boston. Yesterday, it had been the scene of a battle in which they fought off a battalion of Loki's soldiers. The Trickster would soon be sending reinforcements. Magni and his people planned on leaving before they returned.

The blood on the streets was still fresh. They had spent much of the morning burying their dead and patching up the wounded. After a long couple of days, Susanna appeared fitful and restless, so Magni suggested she take a break and get fresh air.

"After all the dying, here we are still fighting each other," Susanna said. "It seems senseless."

Magni nodded. "I wish there was another way. I did not come here to fight humans, but Madison has assembled a fighting force and is using them to eradicate us. I don't see what else we can do but fight back."

"But what's the end game. Are we just going to keep fighting them until the end of time?"

"This will end when I kill Madison. My hope is to draw him out, to make him come to the realization that the only way he will get rid of me is to kill me himself."

Since that first battle on the streets of New York, Magni had managed to slay another ten giants in various skirmishes along the Atlantic coast. This had to be of great concern to Loki. If the giants couldn't manage to kill him, then what choice would the Trickster have but to openly engage Magni in battle? He would undoubtedly think he could defeat Magni, and at one point, Magni would not have disputed the claim, but he had proved his mettle at Ragnarok and on these blood-soaked streets.

"We lost eleven people yesterday. A boy, not even sixteen years old, I don't think he's going to make it either."

"You have done a remarkable job," Magni said. "You have saved many lives, but I think you can do more."

Susanna let go of his hand and took a step back. "Excuse me? I've been working nonstop day and night. I'm doing everything I possibly can with my limited resources to help these people."

"But you're not," Magni insisted.

"I can't believe you would say that."

Magni put his hand on her shoulder. "You misunderstand me. This is not a criticism of your effort. I have seen that firsthand. You have worked tirelessly at all hours, and I commend you for that. What you fail to realize or accept is that you have innate healing skills that no human physician could ever dream of. Yet you choose to confine yourself within the limitations of human medicine."

Susanna gave an exasperated sigh. "I'm not Freya. Quite frankly, I'm starting to get an inferiority complex. I know it's tough that you lost your lover, but we have something special here. Emerging from all the chaos and tragedy, I found for the first time in my life a man I truly care about. Don't do this to me."

"I can assure you I'm not delusional. I know who you are. I know you better than you know yourself. Give it a try. If I'm wrong, you have lost nothing, but if I'm right then you can save the boy's life. What his name?"

"Dean."

"I want you to try to heal him my way, the way you are capable of."

"I have no idea what you're talking about."

Magni looked into her eyes. "Will you at least try?"

"If this will get you off this ridiculous notion that I'm an Asgardian goddess, then sure, I'll try it. What do you want me to do?"

"Let's visit Dean."

Susanna showed clear apprehension as they walked along the Charles River. She seemed to have been enjoying their time prior to this conversation. As much as he hated to ruin the mood, it was necessary.

They arrived at the triage center she had set up for the wounded, which consisted of a series of beds at an old medical center that still had a fair amount of supplies left from the days when it had been operational. Dozens of people had donated blood in the last couple days. Although she had a few assistants, Susanna was the only physician.

They approached the young man who was barely clinging to life. He was hooked up to a machine that helped him breathe. He had a large bandage that covered the side of his face. He had been shot several times. Privately, Susanna gave Magni a grim prognosis that he would not last the night.

"So, what would you have me do?" Susanna asked.

"Use your innate magical, healing skills."

Susanna put her hands on her hips. "My innate magical skills? Really?"

Magni touched her shoulder. She was touchy about not knowing her own identity and remained in denial. "What do you have to lose? By your own admission, Dean will die."

Susanna blew out a deep breath. "Okay. What should I do?"

He could do little to guide her. His own attempts at magic were often clumsy and ineffective. Freya, on the other hand, had a grace and majesty to the way she used magic.

"Close your eyes," Magni said. "Lay your hands on him. The magic is within you. Let it flow through you."

With a resigned sigh, Susanna put her hands on Dean's chest. "Okay."

For a while, nothing happened. She looked up at him.

"Keep trying." Magni wished he had concrete instructions to give her, but this was something she would have to figure out on her own.

"Look, Magni, I know you mean well, but it's not going to happen. I don't have magical healing ability."

Magni spoke in a calm voice. "You're not trying hard enough. Fully commit yourself to this. Put your entire essence into healing this boy. His life is in your hands. If you do not find a way, he will surely die."

Once more, Susanna closed her eyes. This time he got the sense that she truly was trying and not just appeasing him based on the intense concentration on her face. He clenched his fist, willing her to succeed and discover who she truly was. He was focused so intently on Susanna that he did not notice Dean begin to stir, not until she gasped.

"Oh my God!" Susanna kept her hands on the boy's chest. A crowd gathered around them. They murmured their own surprise and disbelief.

Dean rose to a sitting position removing his breathing mask, his eyes cloudy. "Wha-what happened?"

Susanna took a few steps back, her hands to her face. "I can't believe it."

The others in the group helped Dean to his feet after unhooking him from his machine. He gingerly stood and walked, gaining confidence with each step. There was a great deal of commotion in the makeshift hospital wing. People were swarming around Dean, congratulating him, patting him on the shoulder.

Susanna, tears glistening in her eyes, mouthed to Magni, "Did I do that?"

Magni smiled and nodded.

Chapter XXXII

The intensity of the fighting between Loki's forces and Magni's new army increased daily. Much to Magni's chagrin, he seemed to always be on the run. They lacked the manpower and weaponry to face Loki's military might directly. They were losing good people in this senseless violence. If Magni did not do something soon, they would lose this war.

Thus far, Loki had not chosen to join the fray. If Loki would not come to him, then Magni would have to find the Trickster, something Dante was trying to do using contacts around the globe. Even if they found his location, there would be the difficult task of getting there. Transport across the ocean was difficult at best. Of course, Magni could fly there with Mjolnir, but he would be going alone against an army.

In the small hours of the morning, Magni found himself walking along the Chesapeake Bay, deep in thought. What he needed was a victory so devastating that Loki would have no choice but to meet him in battle. To this point, their victories were hardly decisive. It usually meant that the enemy retreated to lick their wounds.

Another ongoing source of frustration was Susanna's unwillingness to accept that she was Freya. After healing over a dozen people in the same way she had healed Dean, she now accepted that she had some unexplained natural healing ability but remained unconvinced about what was so maddeningly obvious to Magni.

The sound of a vehicle came in his direction. It was probably one of the patrols surveying the area. They now had a fleet of militarized vehicle confiscated from the opposing army. He spotted a Land Rover coming in his direction. François was in the back holding a machine pistol. He had a look of alarm on his face.

François jumped out when the vehicle came to a stop. The Frenchman had dramatically changed since Magni first met him. Physically, he looked different. His brown hair was now long and wavy. He had grown a beard and mustache and had several quality scars on his face and body. He was no longer a wide-eyed idealist. Fighting had hardened him. He had become a close friend and confidant.

According to Dante, he and François had gone to school together at Princeton, where they had been roommates. François had been very liberal in his political views and had been vehemently against the war efforts of the time. Now François was frequently on the front lines leading the charge. He had become adept in his fighting skills and his battle strategy. When Magni asked him why he had changed, François told him that he now had a cause worth fighting for.

"What is it?" Magni asked.

"A massive force is coming our way," François replied. "They've crossed the Maryland border, probably about a half hour away from us, maybe closer, coming in our direction."

"Then we will fight them."

François took a deep breath. "You don't understand. There are hundreds of them. They have giants. The scouts spotted seven or eight. They also have tanks."

"I take it these tanks are something we should be concerned about." Magni had seen photos of tanks before, but never witnessed one live. He had come to develop a healthy respect for the weapons of war used in Midgard.

"I'm going to get Dante," François said. "We need to get the hell out of here."

"We can't run forever," Magni said. "We have been on the run for over a week. The object of this conflict is to defeat them, not to be pests to John Madison's army. We haven't even been able to properly recruit new members lately."

Within a few minutes, they were at the building they had occupied since yesterday—an old hotel with a sufficient number of rooms to house their entire party.

They roused Dante from his sleep. The briefing was short. There was little time to waste.

"If they're less than a half hour away, we won't have enough time to gather our equipment and flee," Magni said. "They'll catch us."

"The tanks will level this entire place," François said. "Look, I want to crush Madison, but if they wipe us out here, it's game over. We need to be smart."

"Would I be able to destroy these tanks that concern François so much?" Magni asked.

Dante nodded. "I don't see why not. You can crush damn near anything with that hammer."

"In that case, I can meet our enemy in advance and engage them. This will give you time to prepare your defenses."

"Will those rocket launchers we picked up be able to take out tanks?" François asked.

"The hell if I know," Dante said. "I have as much formal military training as you do, which is zero. We can test them out. All right, Magni. Do as much damage as you can and buy us time. We'll try to ambush them. It's our best chance."

"I will." Magni had no fear. When he left Modi at Niflheim, he knew this quest would end one of two ways—he would either stop Loki or die trying. Today was as good a day to die as any.

François gave Magni the enemy's coordinates. Before he could leave, Susanna intercepted him. "What's going on? What's all the commotion about?"

Magni touched her long golden hair. "There is a large contingent coming in our direction, and they mean us harm. I intend to derail them before they get here."

Susanna had a look of horror on her face. "What? You're going alone? That's crazy."

"The others will be preparing our defenses and a counterattack," Magni said. "It's sound strategy."

"You're going up against an entire army and you call that sound strategy," Susanna said. "Are you trying to get killed? That doesn't sound like sound strategy."

Magni smiled. "My lady, we have already established that I am hard to kill. If Loki's forces could not kill me at Ragnarok, then these foes won't either."

Susanna covered her face with her palms. A face that pretty should never be covered. "I don't know if you're incredibly brave or foolhardy. Don't do this. I can't lose you. You mean too much to me."

Magni wanted to add levity to the situation, but the intensity and passion in her eyes gave him pause. "I lost you once. It tore me apart to see you die. I won't let you feel the same grief I felt. I will return. I promise you that."

Susanna lowered her gaze. "I guess that's the best I can hope for. Be safe."

"I shall. Make sure that you are not in the line of fire when the fighting starts."

She stood on her tip-toes, and he lowered himself to kiss her. That was all he needed to send himself off to battle.

He stepped out of the hotel building, raised Mjolnir, and flew into the sky. It was windy and cloudy with a great deal of turbulence as he soared above the blue water of the Chesapeake Bay. He could fly as fast as the airplanes of Midgard and had even done so once. Before the sickness, they had been commonplace. These days, they were quite rare, used only by Loki's people.

He encountered the opposing army far sooner than anticipated. He wasn't sure how they were doing it, but Loki seemed to be able to predict their movements. Perhaps he was using satellites or other technology. It was more than obvious that Loki had managed to confiscate the military assets from the former leaders of Midgard.

The giants were traveling on the back of large flatbed trucks. The convoy included tanks that had the appearance of behemoths of the underworld. Normally his first target was giants, but today, he would destroy the tanks. Covered in camouflage, they had single, oblong circular wheels on either side and a protruding gun attached to a turret.

He slowed to a stop in mid-air. Pointing Mjolnir downward, he shot lighting at the tank closest to him. Magni frowned. When the lightning struck the tank, it didn't damage it in any noticeable way.

Unfortunately, the lightning strike attracted the attention of his foes, who began to open fire on him. Magni's eyes went wide at the ferocity of the shells coming in his direction.

He flew out of the way of the incoming fire. The heat of the shells roasted the air around him. He fired more lightning. Although sparks shot off the armored vehicle, it stayed intact.

More incoming fire came his way. He retreated. He would have to get closer to do real damage, no easy task considering the enemy was trying to shoot him out of the sky. He took a deep breath and charged at one of the tanks with breathtaking speed.

He landed in front of the tank and took a huge swing, crushing the tank's gun cylinder. Machine gun fire was coming at him full force. He took several bullets before going on a hasty retreat into the sky.

Magni perched himself on a large rock and took assessment of his wounds. He had taken one shot in the leg, another in the shoulder, and one that grazed his forearm. In recent times, he had become no stranger to gunshot wounds. Fortunately, none were serious. That did little to lessen his pain. He roared, imagining the damage a shell from the tank would cause.

When the vehicles starting to move again, he left the rock on which he was perched. He flew at another tank, believing the first one he had attacked to be incapacitated. Before he could reach it, a fire giant jumped in front of him. They had become more common in recent days now that the weather was warmer. There were rumors of communities of fire giants in Florida and the Caribbean islands.

The one in front of him had fiery red hair and skin that was as dark as charcoal. They were taller and thinner than frost giants. The giant had a sword as long as Magni was tall. He wore a metal-plated shirt and a belt with the image of Fenris Wolf on the buckle.

"You should have died at Ragnarok," the fire giant said. "I will make sure that mistake is rectified."

Magni backed up a step so that he wasn't within range of the giant's sword. "And you were too cowardly to fight. You saved yourself from death—until today that is."

The fire giant swiped at him with his sword. Magni sidestepped the blow. He looked at the other vehicles driving off in the distance. He had to eliminate this fire giant before disabling the opposing army.

The giant went on the attack, taking long swipes at Magni that were getting perilously close. He would have to fight in close against his longer opponent. When the giant raised his sword, Magni stepped in and caught the hilt of the sword with Mjolnir. He kicked the giant's lower abdomen, causing him to double over. He leaped and kicked the giant's face, sending him falling backward.

Magni swung his hammer down at his fallen foe. The giant rolled to the side. Mjolnir hit the asphalt, cracking it open.

The giant swept Magni's legs out from underneath him, and he fell hard. He clubbed Magni with heavy fists. A bright light flashed before him, and his nose felt as is if it had been flattened.

After receiving more blows than he could count, Magni caught the giant's fist as he tried to strike him.

He rose to his feet, still clutching the giant's fist. With his free hand, he swung Mjolnir and connected solidly to the giant's ribs. The fire giant gasped for breath, clumsily swinging his sword. Magni easily stepped aside, and this time smashed the giant's head with Mjolnir, crushing his skull.

Magni stepped past his fallen foe. In the time that Magni had engaged his enemy, the rest of the caravan continued to move forward. He had barely slowed them. Raising his hammer, Magni flew into the air, trying to stop them before they reached his allies.

Chapter XXXIII

Before Magni could stave off the invaders, they reached his allies. There was nothing left to do but fight, even though his side was outnumbered and outgunned.

As he soared through the sky, his entire body throbbing in pain, he contemplated the best use of his power—to fight against the giants or to crush the tanks. Either option would leave his forces vulnerable, but he would take his chances against the tanks.

He reached the caravan just as the tanks began to open fire. Their initial volley of attack was intense as the tanks fired shells at the hotel in which they were staying. Dante had positioned troops at the tops of nearby buildings, and they were returning fire, but lacked the armament of the enemy.

He launched himself at a tank, certain that the one he battered earlier could do little damage. He had to disable the remaining two. As it was, they were blasting holes into the exterior of the hotel. Before long, they would level it.

A fire giant blocked his path. He tackled the giant off his feet. The collision sent him stumbling. Magni scraped his legs and face against the road before stopping near the tank.

He got up, ready to unleash damage on the tank, when he found himself staring at a wall of fire giants, three to be exact. It might as well have been an army. He couldn't take three of these ashen-faced monsters at once. He stepped backward, formulating a plan. He prided himself on his fighting prowess, but knew his limitations, and was not about to engage on a suicide mission.

He feigned an attack with Mjolnir and instead flew into the sky, where a barrage of machine gun fire greeted him. He ascended out of range of the bullets. Fire giants were surrounding the tank he targeted. Meanwhile, the tanks shelled the hotel as the opposing army continued to advance.

If he was going to get through the giants, he needed to create chaos. He began raining down lightning at the enemy in all directions, filling the sky with bolts. The roar of thunder combined with the gunfire was deafening.

Magni tore through the sky, too fast to be hit by the people shooting at him and landed in front of the fire giants blocking the tank. The one closest to him charged at him with a long sword. Putting Mjolnir in its holster, he removed his own sword from its scabbard and engaged the giant in a duel. The clash of swords rang loudly. He had the edge in speed and agility, landing a couple of shots against the giant.

When another giant joined the fray, he had to fight on two sides. Magni gritted his teeth as they drove him back. They did not even have to defeat him to be effective. All they had to do was keep him occupied.

Engaging in a sword fight with two giants at a time was pointless, even though he was holding his own. Putting away his sword in his scabbard, Magni charged at the closest giant and tackled him. They tumbled into the second giant. Magni quickly got to his feet, while his larger foes were still on the ground.

He brought out Mjolnir and smashed the giant in the abdomen. The giant gave a horrid, retching sound and began to convulse. Magni delivered a second blow and was prepared to give a third and hopefully final blow when he felt searing pain in his shoulder. Without having to turn to assess the damage, he already knew he had been stabbed by the fire giant's flaming sword.

Magni turned as the fire giant, Grumin, removed his sword from Magni's shoulder, flames crackling around his skin. Magni clutched his wound. The skin around it was burnt, and his blood flowed freely. Meanwhile, Grumin stayed on the attack, flashing his blade at Magni. Slowed by the sheer agony of the blow, Magni found himself on the receiving end of a slash of Grumin's flaming sword. As he stepped backward, he tripped over a fallen fire giant.

Grumin leapt toward him, trying to impale him with his sword, but Magni was quick enough to avoid the plunging sword. Magni crawled back to the sidewalk. On either side of the road were former business establishments. The opposing enemy surrounded him. The fighting between the two sides was fierce. Dante's forces spilled out into the street, using the nearby buildings for shelter. For the moment, he couldn't concern himself with them. He had to fight off these giants.

Grumin, with a mean snarl on his face, attacked him with his sword. Magni backed away, a store front only a few meters away. Grumin lunged at him, sword in hand. This time, Magni sidestepped him. His momentum driving him forward, Grumin crashed through the glass window of the shop.

Magni ran at an unsuspecting fire giant who had been avoiding bullets being fired his way. He smashed the giant's skull with Mjolnir, a loud crack echoing. His foe wavered, then crumpled in a heap. Two more took the place of the one that just fell. One had a long sword, the other an axe with a blade that spanned Magni's upper torso.

Using sound strategy, they put Magni between them. Magni tried to keep his distance but did not have much real estate with which to work. The first giant slashed at him with his sword. Magni stepped back only to find the axe coming at him from the other direction. Magni's quick reflexes prevented the axe from separating his head from his shoulders, but the blade had come perilously close.

Determined not to be on the defensive for long, Magni swung his hammer at the giant holding the sword. His blow came up short. Unfortunately, the fire giant wielding the axe had better accuracy with his next blow, taking advantage of Magni's unprotected rear. The blade clipped Magni's thigh. He yelped. His chain mail armor absorbed part of the blow, but the axe still penetrated his flesh.

In a fit of rage, Magni turned and blindly swung Mjolnir at the giant who had clipped him with his axe. The blow struck his foe in the chest, knocking him backward. This fire giant had a long, red mustache that matched his long, red hair. Hair and mustache flailed wildly as he tripped and landed on one of Madison's Jeeps, indenting its hood.

Magni jumped on top of the Jeep. He pinned the giant down and began to smash his head repeatedly against the hood. One of the men inside the Jeep stood and pointed his pistol at

Magni. Before he had a chance to fire his weapon, Magni grabbed his gun hand. He wrenched the man out of the Jeep and onto the ground, tossing the gun aside.

The fire giant with the long mustache reached up and grabbed Magni's throat. He raised himself, squeezing harder. Woozy, Magni brought his forehead down and smashed his foe on the bridge of his nose. He smashed the giant again with his forehead until he loosened his grip.

The Jeep began to move forward. Magni fought for balance. He steadied himself on the moving vehicle, lifted the giant, and threw him on top of the driver. As the Jeep spun out of control, Magni jumped off before it crashed into a pole.

The giant was leaning out the side of the Jeep, his head nearly touching the ground. He seemed dazed and out of it, completely vulnerable to an attack. Magni wanted to take advantage of his vulnerable state until he spotted a Madison soldier pointing a gun at him. Before he had a chance to fire, Magni launched Mjolnir at the human. The blow dismembered the man's gun hand. The soldier screamed in horror at his bloody stump while Mjolnir returned to Magni's hand.

This gave the fire giant enough time to escape the moving vehicle. As he was stumbling out, Magni launched himself and smashed the giant's face with Mjolnir, sending the fire giant crashing back into the Jeep. Magni followed this with two more blows from his hammer. His enemy's momentum flipped the Jeep on its side, the fire giant collapsing on top of it.

Fatigue, blood loss, and the wounds from the battle were settling in on Magni. He took a deep breath and tried to get a moment of rest. He always tried not to expend all of his energy at once if the battle was going to last a while. This was shaping up to be a long battle, and taking on giants was taxing work.

There was little time to rest, however, as Grumin exited the store. He hurled a spear at Magni. The spear was thrown with such velocity that Magni could not dodge the blow. It clipped his side. Magni cried out and fell to one knee. He wrenched out the spear, the pain excruciating as his skin tore from the removal of the spear head. He breathed hard as blood flowed freely from the wound.

Grumin advanced on him, a wicked smile on his face. Magni was leaning on Mjolnir, trying to catch a breath and rest. But there could be no respite. Before long, Grumin would finish him. If he did not get up now, he would stay on the ground forever. He had to find the inner strength to take the fight to the enemy. He could not die now—not while Loki still breathed.

He tensed, then lunged at Grumin's knees. He took the fire giant by surprise, knocking him over as if he were a tall tree being chopped down. Magni climbed on top of him, trying to pin him down, however Grumin was fresher and knocked him aside.

Grumin sprang to his feet with surprising agility. He grabbed Magni by the throat and squeezed. Still choking him, he lifted Magni off his feet and slammed him to the ground.

Magni's head was spinning. His body ached. He could hardly breathe. He crawled away, but Grumin would give him no reprieve. Grumin kicked him squarely in his ribs. Magni flipped over and landed on his back, undoubtedly breaking a few ribs. His healing power was far greater than that of a mortal, but that didn't mean he felt any less pain.

His lungs howled in agony. Grumin kicked him again. He used his large boot to step on Magni's neck. Magni could picture his foe thoroughly enjoying this. It was this rage and indignation that spurred Magni into grabbing the giant's foot and tripping him to the ground.

When Grumin landed flat on his posterior, Magni struggled to gain the advantage by pinning him to the ground, digging his knees into the giant's abdomen and thrusting his elbow into his chest. When he finally gained leverage, he used Mjolnir to hold him down. Grumin tried to thrust himself out from underneath Magni. When that didn't work, he used his long arms to punch Magni and rake his face with his fingers.

Magni got to his knees, lifted Mjolnir, and slammed it into Grumin's chest. He couldn't get as much leverage as he would have liked, but it was enough to knock the wind out of the giant. He was about to raise Mjolnir and smash Grumin—what he hoped would be a killing blow—when a massive fist smashed the side of his face.

Magni's legs gave out from underneath him. He wobbled and crashed to the ground. He tried to stand, got to one knee, before being caught with a massive kick to the face, which sent him falling backward. The back of his head smashed asphalt. The thudding pain reverberated through his skull and down his spine.

Magni looked up, his vision cloudy, his body racked with pain, to find a sword swiping down at him. Despite his clouded head, he moved in time to avoid being sliced.

Magni tried to clear his mind. He had to think straight if he wanted to make it out of this alive.

He stood on shaky legs, backing away. The fire giant, who had nearly decapitated him, was advancing toward him, sword in hand. Grumin was also on his feet. As if that wasn't bad enough, there was a third fire giant joining his comrades.

He grunted in frustration. His allies were clearly getting the worst of this battle. The opposing army continued to advance. Before long, Loki's soldiers would overrun them. Magni had been able to carry the preceding battles out of sheer will. His presence was often enough to overcome their deficit in numbers. Perhaps he had become complacent in thinking his presence alone would ensure victory. Perhaps he thought himself charmed. After all, he had helped the Aesir claim victory at the Battle of Ragnarok. Any such notions were foolish.

The giants began to attack him in a concerted effort. There was little he could do but back away from this multi-front attack. He was able to fend off their blows, but that did him little good. A decisive defeat could end their resistance movement. All of the work they had accomplished could be gone just like that. He had to do something to change the tide of the battle, but he had his hands full just fighting off these fire giants.

With a desperate sense of urgency, he began to swing Mjolnir at the giants with increased ferocity, but his hope was dwindling by the minute.

Chapter XXXIV

Magni could not find any way to gain an advantage. He landed several glancing blows, but they were hardly enough to do significant damage. To make matters worse, a fourth fire giant joined the fray. Magni felt a surge of desperation, and his attacks were more reckless. Whenever he wound up with Mjolnir for a kill shot against one of his foes, he left himself open for a counterattack. As a result, they had slashed and nicked him several times.

After overcommitting on a blow against Grumin, one of his foe's slashed the back of his legs with a sword. Searing pain ripped through his leg and thigh. Magni fell to his knees. He had been cut more times than he cared to count. His fatigue was wearing at him, and he was losing strength from his copious blood loss.

He looked up to find a wicked smile on Grumin's face. He raised his sword, preparing to give Magni a death blow. Magni tried to raise Mjolnir, but it felt incredibly heavy in his hands. Just as Grumin was about to bring his sword forward, a spear plunged into his back, piercing him and protruding through his chest.

Grumin fell forward, blood spilling from his mouth. His sword clanged harmlessly onto the ground.

A giant turned in the direction of the attacker, giving Magni the opening he needed. He got to his feet and swung Mjolnir, smashing the side of the giant's head. The fire giant flew forward, dead from the massive shot.

Magni did not need to look at who threw the spear. He already knew the answer, and this knowledge filled him with such overwhelming elation that he no longer felt fatigue or pain.

The tip of the spear indicated that it was Gungnir, and the person who wielded the spear was his brother. Modi was in Midgard and had found him.

When he looked up, he was not surprised to find Modi. He was, however, taken aback to see the red-headed, pale-skinned horde of people behind him. They looked like the Celts from long ago, bearing modern weapons of war and attacking Loki's army from the rear.

Modi ran forward, ducked a sword from a fire giant, kicked the giant in his chest, removed Gungnir from Grumin's carcass, and used it to stab his opponent in the neck.

Magni roughly patted his brother's shoulder. "It took you long enough to find me."

"I would say that I found you just in time. It comes as little surprise that you would be in trouble without me. I don't know how you managed to survive all these months."

They circled the remaining fire giant while maintaining their conversation. Modi jabbed at the giant with his spear. As the giant avoided the attack, Magni tried to time his attack with Mjolnir, but just missed.

"In trouble? I have been able to defeat Loki's army at every turn."

Modi eyed him skeptically. "Not this turn, apparently."

The fire giant turned from one side to another, trying to fend off attacks from both sides.

"Not true," Magni said. "We had them right where we wanted. The battle was about to turn in our favor when you arrived."

The fire giant overcommitted on his attack, and Modi swiped at him with his spear, knocking him down. Magni stepped forward and smashed his sternum with Mjolnir. The giant gasped before Modi ended his life with a thrust of his spear to his neck.

"I haven't had this much fun since Ragnarok," Modi said.

"The battle is hardly done." Magni surveyed the street. Now that Modi's clan of Celts joined the fray, the tide of the battle had clearly turned. Loki's forces were fighting on two fronts and getting the worst of it. The only reason they were still in this fight was the presence of the two functional tanks. "We must take care of the heavy artillery. Climb aboard."

Modi held onto his brother's waist. They flew toward the nearest tank, in the opposite direction from the tank's gun.

Modi released his grip from Magni's waist and landed on his feet. Magni swung Mjolnir at the turret, putting a severe dent into it. To ensure that this tank would do no further damage, Modi lifted it off the ground. Seeing his brother struggle, Magni joined him. Together, they flipped the tank. It landed on the asphalt with a solid thunk.

They ran to the next tank. Magni's eyes went wide when the gun turret turned in their direction. He launched Mjolnir at the tank, smashing its side and lifting it off the ground. Running at a full sprint, Modi lowered his shoulder and rammed the tank, knocking it onto its side. He went to the other side, and with brute strength tore open the hatch and lifted out a man who was inside. After tossing him aside like garbage, Modi proceeded to remove the other soldiers from inside the tank.

The outcome of the battle was no longer in doubt, something that became apparent to Loki's troops. Shortly after they disabled the tanks, the opposing army went into full retreat mode. However, Magni was not satisfied. He wanted complete and total victory.

To that end, there was nowhere for the enemy soldiers to go. They were blocked from any escape route with Dante's fighters on one side and the Celts on the other side. The opposing army surrendered quickly. Although he would have killed them all if it came to it, this was the preferred ending. The fewer people who had to die, the better off everyone would be.

Magni, Modi, Dante, and Sean O'Rourke, the leader of the Celts, accepted their surrender. This was the first time they had taken captives, over thirty in total. Magni had no idea what to do with these people. They did not even have a permanent location, let alone a prison. They had been constantly travelling since the Battle of New York. He would leave it to Dante and François to determine the prisoners' fate. His own preference was for them to join in the fight against Loki.

When the battle was over, Magni gave his brother a large bear hug, lifting him off his feet. When he first saw Modi, they had been in the heat of the battle, and he could not express his joy at seeing his brother again. Now, his tears flowed freely. This was the longest stretch of time they had ever spent apart. It felt like part of him had been missing.

"You came just in time, my brother. A moment later..."

Modi cut him off and put his hand on his shoulder. "You would have figured a way out."

"How did you find me?" Magni asked.

"It's a long story."

Magni smiled. "We have much to discuss. However, before we do that, there is someone you must meet. You will scarcely believe your eyes."

Chapter XXXV

Magni very much wanted to take part in the festivities that evening, but Susanna insisted he rest. He made a token appearance. Susanna was probably right. He had sustained serious injuries and needed rest in order to heal, but it was against his nature to not take part in victory celebrations.

The men and women who had fought gave him a hero's welcome. After a bottle of beer, he was nearly out on his feet. Modi had to practically carry him away. They abandoned the hotel they had been staying at since it took significant damage and were staying at a smaller place by the bay.

He slept through the night and well into the following day, waking up before dusk. When he finally awoke, he was annoyed because they let him sleep for so long. It was a great victory, but there was much work to be done.

He was sitting up in bed when Susanna came into the room. She had a terse look on her face. "You're going to give me a heart attack one of these days. Those wounds you took in that battle—if you were a human, you would have died ten times over."

"As we both know, I am hard to kill," Magni said.

Susanna gave an exasperated sigh. "It's like you have a death wish. One of these days, your luck is going to run out."

Magni swung his feet across the bed. They'd had this argument several times before. "As long as that day comes after I have killed Loki, then it will be well worth it."

Susanna softened her stance. She held his hand. "You can't do this to me. For the first time in my life, I've found someone I love. Now you want to take it away from me. You know, sometimes I feel as if I had been living in a fog before I met you. Everything was murky. I was going through life but not really living. But all that changed after that battle in New York."

Magni realized he should choose his words carefully. Of course, she cared for him, just as he did her. Their love was eternal, but his duty came first. He had been tasked with this mission by Odin, Thor, and the Norns, and he would see it through.

Magni touched her face. "I want to live and spend my life with you, but Midgard and its inhabitants will not be safe as long as Loki is around. Therefore, I must stop him. It is something I must do."

"I know. I just wish you could do it in a safer manner. Why do you have to put yourself out in the forefront so much?"

"It is the only way we can win," Magni said. "We have no choice."

"You need more rest."

Magni waved his hand. "I need food and wine, and I will be at peak strength in no time."

Susanna sighed. "It must be nice being a god."

"You would know." When Susanna did not respond, he asked, "Where is my brother? We must confer at once."

"The last I saw him, he was speaking with Dante."

"That is where I should be. Can you take me there?"

"At least get some food and drink before your go." Susanna took his hand. "Come on. I'll join you. I haven't eaten anything all day. They roasted a deer earlier. There should still be some left."

Magni's stomach grumbled. A meal would do him a world of good, but he was more than anxious to see Modi.

***

It was well into the evening before Magni finally had a chance to speak with his brother. They sat by a fire in the middle of the street. The celebration from the previous evening lasted to the following day. Before long, they would be on the move, but for now the weary travelers needed rest.

Although there were many people milling about, both Celts and Americans, Magni and Modi found a spot away from the others. In the background, the Celts were singing a song that had something to do with drinking and fighting. Although the Americans did not seem to know the words, they joined in the raucous celebration.

"How did you find me?" Magni asked.

Modi opened two bottles of beer and gave one to Magni. "It wasn't as difficult as you might think. You have been raising a ruckus here. Everybody on the other side of the sea has heard about you. The difficult thing was trying to determine your precise location. My friends and I arrived a week ago, and we found you through your Internet broadcasts and word of mouth."

Magni raised his bottle. "I'm glad you reached us when you did. The battle wasn't exactly going our way. How did you get here?"

"We used a large boat that my friends borrowed. It once belonged to the British navy, but seeing as how they no longer exist, my friends did not feel bad about taking it. Certainly better than Loki having it. Once we arrived on these eye-pleasing shores, we acquired some vehicles for ground transport. A wonder, these modern machines."

Magni nodded. "Indeed they are. A good thing you latched onto this group."

Modi smiled and drained the rest of his bottle. "They fight like demons. They drink like Viking hordes. They are loud, rude, and boisterous. My kind of people."

"They will be a good addition to the army we have been amassing. So, you had a chance to meet her. What do you think?"

"Susanna?"

Magni nodded.

"She's a fine woman. I take it the two of you are romantically entangled?"

"Yes," Magni said. "But that's not what I mean."

Modi didn't say anything for a while. He looked into Magni's eyes as if searching his soul. "I found it peculiar that you would seek someone who looks so much like Freya."

"You have it wrong. She is Freya."

"Magni, you know we always speak the truth with each other, so I shall not be dishonest with you. She is not Freya. Granted, she looks strikingly similar, but Freya died at Ragnarok. I saw it happen with my own eyes."

"She died in my arms. Don't you think I saw it as well?"

"That's why she cannot be Freya," Modi said. "Regardless of how much Susanna looks like her."

"What if I told you she has healing abilities?"

Modi shrugged. "Why should that surprise me? She is a physician of Midgard."

"No," Magni said, almost too forcefully. "She has magical healing abilities."

Modi raised his brows.

"An ability she had no knowledge of until I coaxed her into discovering it. She has now healed over a dozen humans with magic. She also does not believe that she is Freya, but I know she is with every fiber of my being."

"That's not possible. Freya died. How could she be reborn as a human of Midgard? Such a thing has never happened."

"Just because it has never happened does not make it impossible." Magni stood and began pacing. "The world as we knew it ended at Ragnarok and has been reborn, just as the Norns foretold. Midgard, Asgard, everything has changed. The rules as we knew them have changed as well."

"In the end, it won't matter whether I believe or not," Modi said. "It is clear you are convinced Susanna is Freya reborn, and nothing I say will change your mind."

***

Sean O'Rourke, the leader of the Celts, pointed forcefully at the image projected on the screen. "You're wasting your time with these insignificant strikes. You're like a gnat to Madison. We need to think bigger, act bolder."

Dante folded his arms. "Not true. We've caused serious damage to his operations. More importantly, we're steadily gaining supporters. We've also been able to gain weaponry and other resources needed to fight Madison. We haven't been strong enough to take him head on just yet."

O'Rourke threw up his hands. "Strong enough? We have the two most powerful beings in the universe on our side."

Dante's voice rose. "And we're in a much stronger position right now. But it still makes more sense to be strategic. Not to mention, it's not like Madison occupies a single country we can invade. He controls the entire globe. Even if we wanted to, there's the issue of how to draw him out, since this thing doesn't end until we kill Madison."

Magni spent the next two days recovering from his wounds while integrating Modi's forces from across the sea with his own. He was glad to have the extra manpower, but Dante seemed to be constantly butting heads with Sean O'Rourke. Fortunately, Sean heeded Modi's advice just as Dante heeded Magni's.

According to Modi, life in Europe was much the same as it was in North America. People had died by the millions. Those left were shattered, living under the thumb of Loki's rule. Some chose to not accept the laws he set forth under the guise of the benevolent John Madison.

During the brief time since Modi joined his newfound friends, they had been quite busy. After Sean O'Rourke informed him of a frost giant settlement in the hills of Scotland, they raided the village and killed the giants, seven in total. He did not see Loki, although rumors about him visiting London persisted, rumors that proved to be false.

***

On the day prior to the company's departure to Virginia, Magni found himself hiking through a wooded area with Modi and Susanna. The three of them together felt oddly familiar. He wondered if Modi had the same feeling.

Modi began asking Susanna questions about her background, and she immediately got defensive.

"Don't tell me that you think I'm this Freya as well."

"I don't think you are her," Modi said.

"Then tell that to your brother. No matter how hard I try, he won't believe me. I would think that if anybody knows who I am, it's me."

Modi nodded. "A proper supposition if I ever heard one. Unfortunately, Magni will not listen to me. He's hard-headed. He has always been that way, ever since we were godlings in Asgard."

Magni folded his arms. "Me, hard-headed? I'm not the one who wandered into the lair of Lanther Boda." He turned to Susanna. "She was a silver dragon with an extremely unpleasant disposition. Despite my many warnings that it was the lair of a dragon and that you were reading your map incorrectly, you failed to heed my advice and were nearly burnt to a crisp. Luckily, I was there to rescue you."

"That was when I was young and foolish. I was still a godling back then."

Magni rolled his eyes. "We were over two hundred years old at the time."

"Just as I said. I was young and foolish."

"And what of the time you nearly sparked a war with the Vanir after stealing an ancient relic from their temple and refusing to return it? If not for Odin's intervention, they would have had your head."

"I obtained it fairly in a wager," Modi said. "Anyway, it does not change the fact that you are stubborn. Am I correct, Susanna?"

She eyed Magni. "He's definitely head-strong and stubborn. Flying out to face an entire army, for instance. You're lucky you didn't get yourself killed."

Magni grinned. "I knew my brother would be leading a barbarian horde to rescue us."

Chapter XXXVI

Wanting to make this professional looking, Magni and crew commandeered a former local television studio that was still mostly intact. Dante had long since mastered the art of broadcasting videos over the Internet and making them go viral, all things that were a great mystery to Magni.

Modi, having just recently arrived from Asgard, was even more technologically challenged. Magni at least had some rudimentary knowledge of computers and the Internet.

He and Modi wore full battle regalia for the shoot, donning the same mail armor, tunic, and weaponry on their person as they had when they departed Ragnarok. Modi held his long shield by his side and Gungnir in his other hand.

Susanna wanted to make sure that Magni was well groomed for this occasion. She painstakingly brushed his long hair and trimmed his beard. Despite his protests, she even convinced him to put on light makeup, insisting it would look good on camera.

After looking at himself in a long mirror, he had to admit that he struck an imposing figure. Modi no less so. Although not as large as Magni, both in height and girth, he had an aura and intensity about him that Magni could not match.

The video package Dante was creating had footage of Magni flying and shooting lightning bolts from Mjolnir. It also had captured footage of Modi flipping over and destroying a tank from their battle at Chesapeake Bay. Dante insisted these were needed as proof that Magni and Modi were Asgardian gods.

Dante and François had written a script for them to recite in front of the camera, but Magni and his brother were not actors. Anything they said that came from the heart would have a greater impact than the eloquent words Dante composed.

When the camera started rolling, they stood in front of a blue screen. François was behind the camera filming them. Dante was the director of this film, although Magni had no real idea of what that entailed other than shouting instructions every few seconds. The only others in the room were Susanna and Sean O'Rourke, and two production assistants. The Celt had the temperament of an angry wolverine. When they first told him about the plan, O'Rourke was completely in favor of it, except that he wanted to be the one to fight Loki. Although brave, it would be foolhardy. Loki would destroy the young man, just as he would any mortal from Midgard. They weren't equipped to duel with someone who was both a master of weapons and a wizard of the highest caliber.

The Celts fascinated Magni to no end. After the arrival of the sickness and the institution of new rules by Loki, this band from across the sea had returned to their ancestral ways. They adopted customs and practices long dead, and even dressed like the Celts of old.

"Greetings, men and women of the planet Earth in the realm of Midgard. All of these months after the sickness, it is time that you learn the truth of your situation, how it came to be, and who is responsible. Many of you have seen me before, but a formal introduction is in order. My name is Magni."

"And I am Modi. We are the sons of Thor, the grandchildren of Odin. We hail from the realm of Asgard. Some among you may consider us characters of mythology. My people travelled to your realm over a thousand years ago and were worshiped by some as gods, but I assure you that we are real and not myths."

"Furthermore," Magni said, "Neither is the man you know as John Madison, who is known to us as Loki, the Trickster, the Deceiver. John Madison brought sickness to your world. He should have taken part in what was supposed to be the final battle that had been prophesied for centuries, but instead chose to infest you with an incurable disease, transport giants, and rule your world with an iron first despite his claims of benevolence. Any claim he makes of caring about you is false. The only one he has ever cared about is himself."

Modi continued, "Since we arrived here, we have been fighting back against John Madison and have slain many of his giants. We are here to liberate you from the oppression you face. That is why we challenge you, Loki, to a fight to the death. You may have escaped your fate at Ragnarok, but your inevitable death has only been delayed. You will die, Loki. That much I promise you. The only thing you have to decide is whether you will perish with dignity in the field of battle or die like a coward as we hunt you down from one end of this world to the other."

"To all of the people watching this broadcast, this is an open call to defy John Madison." Magni's voice rose. He had managed to control himself, but his composure was waning. "He can only control you if you let him. John Madison may have annihilated your world and killed billions. Despite that, he and his giants are grossly outnumbered by your kind. No more giants can arrive in your realm. My brother and I have destroyed the portal that allowed them passage. It is time to join us and rise against Madison."

Magni stepped back as Modi spoke. "Loki, you escaped your fate once, but you won't escape it again. Should you choose to accept this challenge, meet us one week from today at the town of Valley Forge in the state of Pennsylvania in the United States of America where once an army waited for a cataclysmic battle. We will be there. Unless you would like to commit the ultimate act of cowardice, you will meet us there."

Dante signaled for François to stop filming. The camera he held was smaller than the size of Magni's hand. The last time Magni had been in Midgard, those devices had been massive.

Susanna stared into Magni's eyes. "That was pretty powerful."

Dante clasped hands with Modi and then Magni. "That was good work, both of you. The only question is, will he accept the challenge?"

"Nothing can ever be certain with Loki," Magni said. "He plays by his own rules. The situation will not be without complications, even if he does accept, but we will be ready for him."

***

John Madison had been in a foul mood for the better part of a week now. His inner circle was finding reasons to avoid him. He realized he was unpleasant to be around but couldn't help it. Ever since he seized power in Midgard, the road had been filled with obstacles. As a being of supreme intelligence, talent, and skills, he could overcome them, but it was becoming increasingly laborious.

He didn't like the person he had become. John always tried to keep the atmosphere light and morale high among his followers. He was fully aware that despite being superior in almost every way to the mortals of Midgard, he needed them. He couldn't do this alone. Midgard was a large place, and his reach could go only so far.

His despondency started with a crippling defeat against Magni's forces. Satellite photographs indicated that Modi had arrived on the battle with forces to aid his brother in the fight. By that time, it had been too late to mobilize additional troops. Instead, he received reports of a complete and total defeat. It was both humiliating and devastating. Those damned sons of Thor had caused so much damage, depleting his assets. He couldn't sustain more losses.

Even before they challenged him, he knew he would have to dispose of the brothers himself. It had been different when they were separated. Now that they were reunited, they would be that much more difficult to defeat.

He had been hoping the giants would handle these two troublemakers. They were his muscle. They enforced his rules and intimated those who opposed him, but they failed him. It was beneath him to fight, but he would have to destroy these two pretenders. He would have defeated Thor, had his Asgardian rival ever challenged him. Thor, who was the most feared of all the Aesir, was not his match, let alone his sons.

"So, what will it be?" Klaus asked.

John had forgotten he was standing there, waiting for an answer, so that he could disseminate it to the others in his inner circle.

John took a deep breath. "Yes. Yes, I will accept their challenge. They are foolish to challenge me and will face my wrath. Let the others know that I will meet them in the town of Valley Forge, and that we are to prepare for battle."

Chapter XXXVII

Loki's response came one day later. Magni saw and heard it in its various incarnations: first broadcast on the government television station—the only station that was currently operational—then on Internet broadcasts, and finally on the radio. Loki sent his message loud and clear. He would meet them at Valley Forge, where he would execute them for crimes against humanity. Well, Loki was always good at hyperbole.

While Dante, François, and the Celts who had accompanied Modi across the sea went to gather their forces to prepare for battle, Magni and Modi spent the time much the same way they did preparing for the Battle of Ragnarok—by nonstop drilling each other with combat techniques and going over battle strategy. In many ways, Valley Forge was proving to be more difficult to prepare for than Ragnarok. They had no idea what to expect. At Ragnarok, they knew their foes and how they would fight. At Valley Forge, the only thing that was certain was that Loki would be unpredictable. Who knew if he would even appear?

Day bled into night as they started at dawn's early light and continued until the evening, singularly focused on their upcoming battle.

After the others left, Susanna stayed behind. Magni did not argue with her when she told him she would be staying. She would be safer with them than with the caravan heading north. Magni was not sure how she kept herself busy during the day.

She would disappear for long stretches and then return, bringing them food and beverage, and offering encouragement.

He was glad to have her. She had a calming influence on him and helped him stay focused. Modi did not even argue about her presence here, even though he had expressed misgivings about Magni spending so much time with Freya prior to the Battle of Ragnarok.

At the end of the second night, the brothers were unwinding with two bottles of beer. As was her custom in Asgard when she was Freya, Susanna was consuming a glass of wine. They retrieved these beverages from the hotel that had nearly been destroyed in the fight against Loki's forces. For food, they roasted two rabbits over an open fire.

Holding up a piece of meat in his fork, Modi said, "Our time did not come at Ragnarok. We were foretold the battle would usher in a new day for humanity, and it has. Whether or not it will be one in which Loki rules Midgard is yet to be determined. However, win or lose, this is our time, our moment. We were spared from death at Ragnarok to play another part in the fate of all worlds. The fight against Loki will truly be our final battle."

Susanna put down her glass. "How can you say that? You can't take that attitude into such an important battle. You're condemning yourself to lose."

Magni looked up at his brother. "You are not usually so fatalistic."

"I have been thinking about this since the end of Ragnarok," Modi said. "It makes little sense that warriors far more accomplished than either of us: Tyr, Odin, our father among them who were not able to survive, yet we did survive."

"I like to think our skill in combat had something to do with it," Magni said.

"Undoubtedly it did, but the bigger component is fate. One way or another, we have played our role. The world has changed not just in Asgard and in Midgard, but in all worlds. The prophecy has been fulfilled."

Susanna folded her arms and glared at him. "That doesn't even make sense. I might not know as much about this prophecy as you, but it would stand to reason for it to come true, you would have to defeat John Madison."

Modi took a swallow of beer. "Not so. It only stated that the world would start anew with us at the forefront. There was no mention of the quality of life in this new world or who would lead it."

Susanna wouldn't relent. He fondly recalled some of their verbal sparring matches. It was usually hard to tell who got the best of whom. They were friendly, but they enjoyed needling each other.

"You're what, over a thousand years old?"

Modi nodded.

"How did you get to be so old by having that kind of attitude? You're defeating yourself before you start."

"I know my role in the world. It's the sort of thing that comes with being so old. I also know that Loki did not get to his current position by being easy to defeat."

They went on like that for a few more minutes until Modi turned to his brother. "I am starting to think you may be right about her being Freya, after all. She sounds just like her."

Susanna punched his shoulder. "Hey, I thought you were on my side about that?"

Modi shrugged. "Well, the evidence in this case is hard to refute."

***

Two days prior to the scheduled battle, they returned to Philadelphia in a large Jeep. Susanna drove since neither Magni nor his brother had figured out the art of operating a motor vehicle. It was on Magni's to do list, but there were many other things he needed to accomplish first.

It had been Magni's idea to stay behind and focus on the battle ahead while Dante coordinated their forces and prepared to mobilize their weaponry, although Dante had misgivings about being separated during this crucial time. Magni was looking forward to seeing his mortal friend. From the beginning, he knew he couldn't enter Midgard and depose of the Trickster alone. He needed human allies since Loki would have his own human army at his command, not to mention this was their fight as much as it was his. He couldn't have picked better allies than those he first met upon his entry into Midgard. It wasn't a coincidence that he landed in Philadelphia and encountered Sheila. The hand of fate was evident.

Their former dwelling place that had very much been conspicuous and in the shadows now looked like a military outpost complete with checkpoints and patrols. The guards let them in without argument. He couldn't imagine he needed identification.

There were many new faces in camp, undoubtedly the result of Dante's recruitment efforts. The first familiar face he saw belonged to Sheila. She had been speaking with a guard—arguing was more like it—when she spotted them. She immediately ran toward them.

She wrapped her arms around Magni's waist. "It's been a month full of Sundays since I've seen you. Let me tell you, this place has become a war zone, and I don't like it one little bit. I liked it more when we were quiet, and nobody knew we were here. Now you got all these people actin' like they're in the marines. I asked Dante about it, and he told me 'Aunt Sheila, what do you expect? We *are* in a war.' That may be so, but it don't make me like it anymore. How you doin', Magni? This young lady treating you well?"

Magni separated himself from her embrace. "I am doing well, and Susanna and I have been getting along just fine."

"Well, that's good. Someone's got to take care of you. You might be an Asgardian god and all that, but you're still a stranger in these parts. And you always put yourself in danger. I heard all about your challenge to John Madison. You sure that's a good idea?"

"Whether it proves to be a good idea remains to be seen," Magni said. "However, it is the only move we can make. I came here to destroy Madison. There is no room for half-measures."

"I know," Sheila said. "But I worry about you. You and Dante both. You're all I have left."

Magni felt touched that this woman thought of him as a family member. She who had lost so much now was concerned about his well-being. He hardly knew what to say.

Modi approached and put a hand on her shoulder. "You must be the Sheila that Magni has told me so much about."

Sheila's eyes went wide. "You're another big one, aren't you?"

"This is my brother, Modi. He has joined me from the realm of Asgard."

"Well, well, well. They sure grow you boys big in Asgard. Welcome aboard. Any brother of Magni's is fine with me."

"Is Dante around?" Magni asked.

"Sure is. Somewhere, at any rate. Dante's not easy to get ahold of these days. Let me call him on the radio." Sheila removed a radio from her pocket and signaled Dante.

She gave them a tour of the camp. They had fenced in an area about a kilometer in radius. Inside of the camp numerous military vehicles including tanks roamed about. Dante and Sean O'Rourke joined them a few minutes into the tour and explained that this was Hector Pedroza's work. He had raided military bases in the area, which were minimally defended, and had stolen the heavy armament.

"He's been a good asset to our group," Dante said.

"I would say so," O'Rourke added. "He's a thief, a crook, and a swindler. Just the sort we need."

The last time Magni had seen Dante and O'Rourke together, they had been butting heads and nearly came to blows. They seemed to be getting along now.

"I had my misgivings about Pedroza," Magni said. "I am glad that you are a stronger judge of character than I."

Dante smirked. "That's because you're not from the neighborhood. The biggest challenge is finding people who know how to operate this equipment and training others on their usage. We've lined up people who have had military experience before the virus turned the world. Hopefully, it will be enough."

"And this will be ready to move in two days?" Magni asked.

"Some of it hasn't been used in a while," Dante said. "So, we can't be sure how functional the equipment will be, but we don't have a lot of time for field drills. We'll do the best we can to mobilize."

"Good," Magni said. "We will need all of the help we can muster. We may not have a great deal of time to prepare, but neither will Loki."

Chapter XXXVIII

The days leading up to the Battle of Valley Forge were cold and rainy. Magni and his brother did their best to help coordinate the machinery of war and assist in crafting the battle plans, but there was little he could do other than provide his presence, which seemed to have a great effect on the men and women. He knew little of how to fight with guns, rocket launchers, and grenades. His role in the battle was simple. Find the biggest threats and neutralize them. Find Loki and kill him.

He did not envy those charged with creating the battle plans. They'd had their share of skirmishes with Loki's army but had no way of telling what the Trickster would resort to. Loki had greater military resources. To make matters worse, he had no moral fiber and would not hesitate to kill civilians if it furthered his cause. He also had frost and fire giants, not to mention his own considerable magic to employ. This was what they were least prepared to deal with. His wizardry was as powerful as Magni had ever seen.

Telling them about Loki's battle prowess would do no good. It would just frighten them, and they had enough to worry about. It did not matter anyway. Magni and his brother would ultimately have to defeat Loki. They just needed to draw their nemesis into combat.

On the eve of the battle, Magni attended a war meeting. There had been many such meetings, but Magni had only made it to a couple of them. Dante produced charts and maps, and had numerous computer simulations of how the battle might go.

It was all quite impressive. Afterward, François and Dante approached him.

"What gives, man?" Dante asked. "You've always been front and center helping out with battle plans, leading the troops, and so forth. Now, you're just kind of staying in the background. I expected you to have a lot to say tonight."

"We need you," François said.

Magni smiled. "You are doing a fine job. There is little I can add. If I thought there were flaws in the plan, I would indicate it. But these plans are well devised. Where you need me is out in the battle field. All of this ends when I kill Loki. That is my role in this conflict. If I fail, then my brother must succeed. All that I ask is that you give me the opportunity fight Loki. Keep the opposing forces on edge and on the defensive."

Based on their reactions, this did not seem to satisfy them.

"You have proven yourselves to be more than capable field generals, strategists, and leaders of men. I am convinced that fate and destiny brought me in contact with you. I need you to restore Midgard as much as you need my help to gain victory. That is why the two of you along with Sean and the Celts must lead. I am and will always be an outsider in this world. My place resides in Asgard"

Dante nodded. "Okay. We'll do what we can to keep the enemy on their heels. I know that you'll come through for us."

Magni appreciated his optimism. He could only hope he would justify it.

**

When he encountered Susanna, she folded her arms as she approached him. "I already know that you're going to want me to stay behind, but I've made up my mind, and there's nothing you can say to change it. I'm going with you tomorrow."

Magni stared into her eyes, enjoying her defiance. It only made her all the more irresistible. "I would not dream of doing such a thing. In fact, I insist that you come."

Susanna eyed him warily. "What? That doesn't make sense. You've always wanted me to stay behind enemy lines. Now you want me to be with you? Are you trying to employ reverse psychology? Because it won't work on me!"

Magni gently touched her face. "I would never employ tricks of the mind on you. You are far too intelligent to succumb to such a thing. I need you to accompany us tomorrow, and not because of your skill as a healer or simply for moral support. I need you there to affect the outcome of the battle."

Susanna pursed her lips. "Wait. You want me there to help you in battle?"

"Indeed I do."

"Now you really have me confused. I don't know anything about fighting. What good would I do out there?"

"You have always been a capable and fearsome warrior."

Susanna took a deep breath. "I'm no warrior. And why the sudden change of heart?"

"I have tried to protect and keep you away from the battle lines since you did not believe in yourself. But the final battle is near, and whether you believe in who you are no longer matters. I need your help. Loki is a dangerous enemy."

"You're serious. You actually want me to be with you when the fighting starts?"

"I couldn't be more serious. We need every possible asset. Of course, I won't force you to do anything. This is entirely up to you. If you choose not to participate, then I will understand."

Susanna kissed him softly. "I told you before that I will follow you to the ends of the Earth. If you think there's some way that I can help you against John Madison, then I'll be there."

Chapter XXXIX

Magni felt little emotion on the cool October morning as he stepped onto Valley Forge National Park. After Ragnarok, no other fight could contain the emotional turmoil of that fateful day on the plains of Asgard. He knew most of the people he cherished would die that day. Part of him perished as well. Now, he felt calm, knowing he had prevailed before and could do so again.

Susanna stood beside him brandishing no weapons. He questioned repeatedly the wisdom of asking her to be here. His instincts told him this was the right thing to do. Behind him, Modi walked in full battle regalia and had the same countenance that made him a deadly force at Ragnarok.

Dante would command the troops. They had an impressive array of military vehicles and weapons. No doubt, the enemy would have an even more impressive arsenal. Regardless, Magni was certain that modern weaponry would not decide the outcome of today's battle. In the end, what mattered was whether he or Modi could make it through the obstacles leading to Loki and kill him.

It was early in the morning, and the skies threatened rain. Although chilly, it was not cold enough for snow. As they waited for the enemy to arrive, Magni could hear people in their company questioning whether John Madison would be bringing his forces to meet them or if he would back out. Loki would be here today. Magni could feel it in his bones.

He turned to Modi. "Should I fly out to scout the enemy?"

Modi shook his head. "They're coming."

Moments later, he heard the sounds of the approaching army, including engines roaring and the rotors of helicopters.

He glanced at Susanna beside him. She showed no fear.

"Are you ready for this?" Magni asked.

Susanna shook her head. "How can I possibly be ready for something like this?"

"You don't appear nervous."

"Of course I am. This may be the last time we're together. I would rather be by your side than wait to find out if you lived or died, whether we won or lost. Having said that, I don't see what value I'm going to be to you out here."

"Don't underestimate yourself," Magni said. "Stay by my side as much as you can."

"I'll try."

"Are you ready, brother?" Modi asked.

Magni nodded slowly. "As I was at Ragnarok."

"Maybe so," Modi said. "But this will be entirely different from Ragnarok."

Two fighter planes roared through the sky. Magni gritted his teeth. This would give the opposition a significant advantage since they had no such planes on their side. He would have to ensure they would not be a factor in this fight. He raised Mjolnir and roared into the sky straight at them.

A missile flew at him with blazing velocity. He stopped in midair and flung Mjolnir at the missile. The result was a massive explosion. Still in the pull of Mjolnir, Magni was suspended in the air as his hammer returned to him. He then flew at the jet and smashed into its side.

Magni's entire body throbbed as he collided with the metal hull. The jet went end over end, flying sideways. Magni watched as it went into the path of the other jet. The second jet made an evasive maneuver but still clipped the meandering plane.

The first jet lost altitude quickly. It caught fire on its way to the ground. When it crashed onto the earth, it caused a massive explosion. The reverberations sent him flying backward. Much like the jet that crashed, he flipped over several times in the air.

When he finally gained his balance, he searched for the remaining jet. It was not hard to find it since a stream of dark smoke trailed in its wake. It was coming toward him. He couldn't imagine this plane would be able to fly for much longer in its current condition.

The jet shot two missiles at Magni. He could smash one out of the sky, but how would he deflect two of them? Perhaps he could evade them. He flew away from the missiles. Much to his chagrin, the missiles continued their pursuit.

Magni shifted and turned as he streaked through the sky. No matter where he went the missiles followed, which gave him an idea. He changed his trajectory so that he was going toward the jet. He wasn't sure if the jet was unaware of his location or if it was too late for the pilot to react. With the missiles right behind him, he dove downward just before reaching the jet. A massive explosion formed as the missiles blew the jet out of the sky.

The shockwaves only accelerated Magni's fall. He found himself hurtling down to the ground and crashed onto the grass, splitting the surface of the field underneath him. Darkness surrounded him as his face planted into the earth.

Muffled sounds came from above, and the ground shook. He tried to pull himself out but was unable to. His arms, like the rest of his body, were wedged into the ground. He felt tugging on his feet. Somebody was wrenching his body from the ground. He wanted to let the person know they could stand being a touch more gentle, but he knew who was pulling him out, and gentle wasn't part of his nature.

Before long, he was standing. His feet decided they did not want to hold him upright, and he collapsed onto the dirt.

Modi's strong hand once more pulled him to his feet. Magni's entire body ached with a pain that would not subside and encompassed his entire body.

Susanna stood in front of him, examining him, her eyes filled with concern. "Are you okay?"

Modi brushed dirt off his brother. Every time Modi patted him down, Magni's body shouted out in agony.

Magni grabbed his brother's hand. "Enough." He turned to Susanna, who was taking a close look at his bloody forearm. "I will be fine."

"There is little time to rest," Modi said. "The enemy is fast approaching."

Susanna turned on Modi. "Are you crazy? He can't fight like this. He just plummeted to the ground like a shooting star."

Magni took a deep breath. "My brother is right. There is no time to heal my injuries. I will fight."

"You can't," Susanna said.

"I can and will. This is our last stand. The only thing that will stop me is my death."

"You take another blow like that and you will die," Susanna said.

Magni couldn't argue with her logic. He was surprised he was still standing. Slowly and gingerly, he moved forward.

Modi supported his weight as they walked. "That was quite a feat. Are you going to manage? I can finish Loki on my own."

"Perhaps you could, but that would deprive me of all the fun. Not to mention a healthy dose of revenge. There were many good Aesir who died at Ragnarok, and Loki was responsible for that. I want him to die at my hands."

The ground shook from the approaching vehicles. The jets were merely a warmup, perhaps a reconnaissance effort. He wondered how many more of those vessels Loki had. Dante told him earlier that although Loki had most of the military assets left in the world, he would not have many people capable of operating them since much of the population had died during the initial onset of the virus. Furthermore, Magni and his group had dealt them significant blows over the past few months, taking out machinery and weapons along the way as well as soldiers.

A park stood on the site of where once had been an encampment a few centuries earlier during the American Revolutionary War. Some of the old buildings were still standing. The park had paved trails and picnic areas. More importantly it had open fields. They wanted to minimize collateral damage, and Dante had thought this an ideal location.

A host of frost and fire giants approached on flat beds of trucks. It must have taken Loki serious negotiation to have fire giants travel to what certainly had to be an inhospitable climate for them. Magni stared into their dark faces and red eyes. They had to know he killed their leader, Surter, during the Battle of Ragnarok. Undoubtedly, they would seek revenge.

They were welcome to try to gain revenge. The only good fire giant was a dead one, and he would see to it that Mjolnir would take many of their numbers before the day was through.

Frost giants were also present in abundance. He couldn't imagine that there were many left after he and his brother had killed so many already. Perhaps this represented the last of the frost giants.

The tanks on the other side opened fire. Magni's forces responded with their own barrage. The fight was on in earnest.

Modi turned to Magni. "Let's kill some giants."

Chapter XL

The battlefield erupted in a deafening, cacophonous roar as both sides unleashed their modern weapons of war upon each other. Magni's first job was to get Susanna out of the line of fire. He grabbed her waist and launched into the sky. He glanced at Susanna, whose face had lost its color as they flew.

From mid-air, he shot bolts of lightning at all angles. His attack had the desired effect as the enemy ran for cover. Mjolnir shot bolt after bolt of lightning, targeting vehicles, especially those with visible weapons.

This attack did not go unnoticed, as the enemy volleyed artillery fire and missiles at him. He flew out of their path and hovered in the air. Looking down upon Valley Forge Park, he found that Modi had already made it to the front line, equipped with a shield he brought from Asgard, one that served him well at Ragnarok.

Now that Magni was able to get a view from behind enemy lines, he became disheartened. His side was badly outnumbered. Loki had to be sending the full extent of his forces because wave after wave of soldiers flooded the area. There were also a fair number of giants, but no Loki, at least nowhere Magni could see. He couldn't believe Loki would not show up this time. He couldn't be that much of a coward.

Loki's forces were pounding his army with their heavy armament. Magni gritted his teeth. He and Modi would have to be the difference in this battle.

He also had to consider Susanna. All of his instincts told him he was doing the right thing by having her here, but how was he going to fight if he had to worry about protecting her?

There was no time for second thoughts. They each had made a decision they would have to live with. The best tactical move was to land near his brother. The two of them together were more than the sum of parts. They multiplied their skill level when in close proximity to each other.

With that in mind, he descended toward Modi, who was battling two fire giants. He landed on a run and released Susanna. Without looking back, he ran forward and gave a massive uppercut swing with his hammer. Mjolnir gave a thudding sound as it connected with the jaw of the nearest fire giant. The giant's head rocked backward, and he flew upward, landing several meters away. Magni pursued his foe and smashed his sternum with a blow from his hammer.

As he turned to find Modi, a half-dozen fire giants appeared between them. Susanna stood in front of the giants, a wild-eyed look on her face. A fire giant threw a spear in her direction. Magni felt his heart sink, but Susanna dropped and avoided the flying spear. Magni ran past her and engaged the fire giants in front of them.

The next few minutes were a whirlwind as Magni moved with great agility, avoiding spears and swords from the fire giants while landing his own shots with Mjolnir. Knowing how the previous battles had gone, he had to avoid heavy damage early. This had the makings of a long skirmish and he could not afford to get weakened, especially since he already sustained heavy damage after his free-fall from the sky. With the giants wanting to separate his head from his shoulders, that would not be an easy task.

The fire giants were taller and thinner than their frost giant counterparts. They were generally between one and two meters taller than him. Their arms and shoulders were thick, but their legs were spindly. Although not as strong as frost giants, their long arms made them challenging to fight.

He shattered the knees of a fire giant and was going in for the kill when Susanna screamed, "Magni, watch out."

He turned in time to see a sword coming in his direction. He did the only thing he could—drop on top of the giant whose knees he shattered. He flipped onto his back to find the same fire giant ramming the sword at him. He rolled over to avoid the blow. The fire giant beneath Magni grabbed his legs so he could not evade another blow. This time the sword thrust into Magni's ribs.

He gave an agonized gasp for breath as the fire giant removed the sword from his ribs. He stood above Magni and was going to strike again until Susanna launched herself at the giant.

The giant had a stunned look on his face. He raised his hands to defend himself. That was enough for Magni to get to his knees and attack with Mjolnir, but the giant anticipated his move and stepped backward to avoid the blow.

In the background, Modi was hacking through a line of frost and fire giants, effectively spinning in between and away from his foes. Gungnir seemed to be an extension of him as he dealt blow after piercing blow to the enemy.

Susanna gasped as the fire giant who she assaulted now had his hands around her neck. Leaving himself open to attack from the fire giant he faced, Magni spun and launched Mjolnir against the back of the giant choking her. Mjolnir struck his back, but in the process, he fell on top of Susanna, crushing her under his bulk.

He caught Mjolnir in its return flight and spun around, anticipating a fire giant sword from behind. He was quick enough to block the attack. Much to his relief, Modi made his way to them and distracted the giant enough to allow him to reach Susanna.

He grabbed the fire giant on top of her and realized it was a female. In simpler times, the males of their species did the fighting, but their numbers in Midgard had to be diminished. He was hardly comforted by this knowledge.

Magni wrenched away the female fire giant. Susanna's face had turned blue. Seeing her in this state filled Magni with rage. He spun and swung Mjolnir, caving in the head of the fire giant who had been strangling her.

"Are you okay?" Magni asked.

Susanna nodded, but her eyes were glassy, her body trembling.

Magni gritted his teeth. What had he been thinking bringing her to the front lines of this battle? Even if she was Freya, she no longer had the same combat skills she once possessed. In the middle of this apocalyptic battle, she was going to get killed.

A half-dozen frost giants joined the fight. Others advanced on Magni's allies. One picked up a Land Rover and flipped it over, crushing the men inside.

Magni and his brother were not having the effect on the battle they had hoped for. Loki's foes continued to advance. Even though they had killed about a dozen giants, there were still many more. He couldn't imagine he and his brother would be able to defeat them all. And there was still Loki to contend with, if he was even here in Valley Forge.

There was little Magni could do at this point to help his army. He and Modi had their hands full with the giants, each engaging with three or four at a time.

He attacked with Mjolnir using wide swings, trying to connect with more than one target on a single blow. This tactic at first proved effective. He was able to inflict several blows on his foes, even killing a fire giant, but they soon became wise to his tactics and would get out of range of his hammer before launching their counter-attack. This left Magni vulnerable, and his opponents slashed him repeatedly with swords and axes. Meanwhile, he kept glancing back at Susanna. They were focused on attacking him and, for now, were leaving her alone. She was doing her best to avoid any nearby giants.

A loud grunt came from behind him. A backward glance revealed Modi in desperate trouble. He was on one knee, a fire giant poised above him ready to strike with his sword. There was nothing that Magni could do to help his brother. He kept fighting while keeping one eye on Modi.

His brother must have been feigning injury, for the next thing Magni saw was Modi thrusting Gungnir into the belly of the fire giant that was close to decapitating him. With that, Magni fully focused on his own fight. The wave of giants kept him off balance. There were too many for him, and they kept inflicting blows. None were serious, but he was losing a great deal of blood and before long, his strength would wane.

Magni was constantly on the retreat. He preferred to dictate the pace of the fight, attacking and not relying on counter-attacks. Being on the defensive made him feel vulnerable. Even though he had slayed a few giants, there were always more ready to fight. He was so thick into the battle that he completely lost track of the combat between the opposing armies.

He continued to swing Mjolnir, sometimes connecting against the giants in front of him, sometimes missing. He was growing weary and losing ground. All the while, he was conscious of Susanna's presence behind him, until she was no longer there.

A scream came from a short distance away. He turned to find her pinned to the ground after having been struck in the side by a fire giant spear. Blood seeped through her clothes.

Magni ran toward her but three fire giants blocked his path. He snarled and swung furiously with Mjolnir, striking one of them dead.

Before he knew what happened, a frost giant axe clipped him from behind. The searing pain drove him to his knees. He tried to rise, desperate to save Susanna, but the blow had been severe, and he could barely stand.

Susanna was trying to crawl away, her face covered with agony. A frost giant stood above her, making sure Magni could see what he was about to do.

He roared in frustration. He wouldn't be able to get to her in time. The frost giant was going to kill her. He had been so sure that she was Freya. He wanted so badly to believe, but in the end, he had been a fool. He was convinced that if she was in this extreme life and death situation, that Freya would break through Susanna's shell, but that clearly was not going to happen. Because of his hubris, she would die, and he had nobody to blame but himself.

Chapter XLI

Susanna felt pain unlike anything she had ever felt in her life. She looked down at the blood spilling from her abdominal wound. She was going to die. She would not be with Magni ever again.

It had been a wild ride, having met and fallen in love with him, even if he believed her to be an Asgardian goddess. She cherished their fleeting time together. For a while, she thought maybe he was right. After all, he knew she would be able to heal people when she considered that to be impossible. But in the end, she was no Asgardian goddess.

She remembered vividly that fantastic moment when she had been able to heal the boy who had been gravely injured. Magni told her to reach deep within her and find her magic. She did exactly as he instructed. She reached deep inside and found the magic. Now she could heal people at will.

She retraced those steps that first time Magni had shown her the way and reached deep within herself.

She remembered.

It all came back to her in a flood of memories that was like a tidal wave breaking on the shore. In an instant, her reality became crystal clear as the brightest burst of light she had ever seen exploded from her.

***

Magni couldn't look, couldn't bear to watch her die a second time. The first time at Ragnarok, seeing Freya fall at the hands of Surter had been utterly devastating.

As he was about to strike his next foe, everything disappeared. A blinding light covered the area. He could not see in front of him. He turned, disoriented, not sure what was going on or what he should do. The only solace was that the enemy was facing the same problem.

Slowly, the light faded, at least to the point where he could now see. He turned, trying to find the source of light. It was almost as if the sun had lowered itself to the earth's surface.

Then he saw it, a sight that nearly made him fall to his knees in wonderment. Standing tall, immaculate, and radiant was Freya, looking just as she had at Ragnarok. Her blonde hair flowed in the wind. Her bright, blue eyes sparkled with intensity. She raised her palms, and bolts of blinding light erupted from her hands. She blasted the giants in her path, knocking them senseless. They scattered away from her, and she continued her pursuit, destroying frost and fire giant alike with impunity.

With renewed vigor, Magni attacked the giants in his path. He hurled Mjolnir at a fleeing fire giant and sent the giant flying forward, her head crushed by his hammer. As Mjolnir returned to him, he glanced at Freya, who appeared dazzling and destructive in a way he had never seen before.

She worked her way toward him. They had reduced the giants in half in a matter of minutes. They were either dead, incapacitated from wounds, or had fled.

Magni engaged with a female frost giant, who was attacking him fiercely with her sword. Magni repelled her blows, but before he could mount a counterattack, Freya cut her down from behind, setting her on fire with a blast of flames. Magni kicked the giant aside as she writhed in pain, the flames quickly consuming her.

"Magni." Her eyes were filled with power as she regarded him, something that had been missing since she had been in Midgard. "I remember all of it now. I remember Ragnarok, my death, and our old life together. I remember who I am. I am Freya of Asgard."

Magni grinned. "What took you so long?"

He desperately wanted to take her in his arms, but there was no time to reacquaint themselves with a battle raging around them.

Magni turned in time to see his brother hurl Gungnir. The spear sailed through the air past them and pierced the chest of a fire giant. Magni ran to the fallen giant, who was choking on its own blood, and tore out the spear. He tossed it to Modi, who caught it on a run.

Modi turned toward Freya and gave a slight bow. "Welcome back. We've missed you, especially your combat skills. Now, if you don't mind, we have a battle to win."

"It's time to find Loki," Magni said. "With the tide shifting in this fight, he is sure to make his presence felt."

As if answering the call, the sky darkened, and lighting ripped through the heavens. Thunder boomed in the background. This felt too unnatural to be a storm.

A shrill piercing voice came from above. Magni looked up to find the image of Loki filling the sky. Even though he was already familiar with Loki's magical prowess, he was nonetheless impressed by this trick. He scanned the area. Most of the fighting has stopped. The participants in this battle had awestruck looks.

"How dare you traitors oppose me," Loki's voice shouted. "I have given you a new life. I have rescued you from darkness. If you are not with me, then you will die."

The earth rumbled and wide crevices opened. Magni grabbed Freya by the waist and took a running leap, avoiding an opening in the ground next to them.

Loki's attack was blunt and crude. The gaps in the earth were swallowing up as many of his soldiers as they were Magni's people. More lightning crashed down around them.

Magni turned to Freya and Modi. "I have to find Loki before he creates unmitigated disaster."

Without further discussion, he raised Mjolnir and ascended into the sky, straight at Loki's image. As he suspected, there was no substance to the image. It was just mist that had a thicker consistency than the surrounding air.

He turned around in mid-air, looking for the Trickster. The fighting had mostly stopped. The soldiers on both sides were trying to survive Loki's maniacal onslaught. Magni flew in the air, still searching. He spotted a tall building nearby. Inside, he found the shadow of a figure standing by a window. The figure's movements and gestures mimicked the projection in the sky.

He flew toward the building and spotted Loki. They stared at each other for a long moment. He didn't want to go at Loki alone since the Trickster would undoubtedly have backup. Magni would bring Freya and Modi with him, but before he did, he sent Loki a message to remember him by. He shot a lightning bolt from Mjolnir that shattered the window Loki was standing next to, causing the Trickster to duck for cover.

He flew back to the battlefield at Valley Forge. Now that Loki's image had disappeared, the fighting started again, but not with the same fervor. Both sides were still trying to retrieve their people from the fractured earth that had swallowed not just soldiers but also many of the tanks and vehicles on the battlefield.

Magni flew toward Modi, who engaged two frost giants in combat. Meanwhile, Freya was using her magic to levitate people on both sides of the fight that were stuck in the crevices. Magni assisted his brother by flinging his hammer at one of the fire giants. The hammer struck the giant in the rib cage, causing him to crumple to the ground in a heap. Modi finished the other giant, piercing his chest with his spear.

"I found him," Magni said. "Off in a building. We need to finish him before he does more damage."

Modi nodded, trying to catch his breath. "Let us end this now."

Magni ran to Freya and tugged her arm. "I know you are trying to save these people, but it's more important to go after Loki. That will save more lives than rescuing those who are stuck."

Freya took a deep breath and nodded. "Very well. Let's finish Loki and end this. How do we get there?"

"Since there are no first class flights available, I will have to provide you transport," Magni said. "I'm afraid this will be a full flight. My brother will be joining you."

Freya rolled her eyes. "Are you finished with the airplane metaphors?"

Magni tilted his head, as if contemplating the question. "I believe I am."

"Good." Modi grabbed his left arm. "Do you know how long I have been waiting to kill Loki? For centuries now."

Freya held onto his waist. There was no hesitation in her movements and actions as there had been when she thought she was Susanna. Magni would miss Susanna. He had grown to love her, but it was Freya who he cherished. It was Freya who was his soulmate.

They flew to the building where he had seen Loki earlier. When they arrived, a host of uniformed soldiers awaited their arrival. As soon as they touched the ground, the humans opened fire on them with a variety of weapons, including the machine pistols that Magni detested. It was bad enough to get hit by one bullet, let alone a spray of them.

In a whirlwind of motion, Modi charged forward with his spear and shield. Freya used her magic to repel the bullets and counterattack, and Magni smashed the soldiers with his hammer. He felt guilty for having to do this. These humans were not his enemy, but he had to clear the men standing in his path in order to get to Loki.

The battle continued in their favor. They had to step past a trail of broken bodies on their way to the building.

Chapter XLII

John Madison paced back and forth in the penthouse suite of the office building he had commandeered for this battle. Klaus and Yuri Uzelkov stood by his side. He debated throughout the morning both internally and with his two advisors about whether or not he should join the fray. Victory seemed all but certain until Freya returned from the dead to turn the tide of the battle. His intelligence told him she had died at Ragnarok, but his eyes did not deceive him. She was here ruining things for him.

At the onset of the battle, his soldiers had been beating down the enemy with their superior weaponry and training. The giants had pinned the sons of Thor and had them all but defeated. Loki was about to swoop in and finish them, delivering a glorious victory. Then, out of nowhere, Freya entered the fray. *That bitch.*

Uzelkov put his hand on John's shoulder and spoke in Russian. "We must retreat. Our forces have sustained heavy losses, and the Asgardians know your location. They will be here any minute."

John glared at the former KGB director. "Let them come. Do you think I'm afraid of them?"

Uzelkov raised his hands. "Of course not. I would never suggest such a thing. You have smashed your enemies repeatedly and will do so again. Perhaps this is not the proper venue. You accepted an engagement on their terms. We should do so on our terms."

Klaus got off the phone with a field commander. "The time for fleeing has past. They have arrived."

In the background, machine gun fire rattled. John hustled toward the window and saw the three Asgardians doing battle with his people—his last line of defense. He knew he had to eventually vanquish his enemies, but he figured it would only be Magni and Modi—if they even made it through the giants. Freya's presence complicated matters.

John armed himself with a sword and his staff. His staff allowed him to channel his magic in a deadly form. "It is time to crush these intruders." He wanted to take them by surprise while they were engaged with his soldiers.

John left the conference room followed by Klaus and Uzelkov and entered the elevator. He was not the least bit nervous. He had been in many difficult situations over the last few thousand years. He had stared death in the face countless times and always prevailed. Today, he would kill the last of the Asgardians, and there would be nobody left to stop him.

***

As soon as the soldiers opened fire on them, Freya created a shield invisible to the naked eye to deflect the bullets. Round after round bounced harmlessly away from them. As soon as they stopped shooting, Magni yelled, "Drop the shield."

Magni flung Mjolnir while Modi hurled Gungnir at the soldiers. Both weapons found their mark. While Magni waited for his hammer to return, Modi charged into the fray with his sword and shield wreaking havoc on the enemy. Freya threw a series of fiery blasts, scorching the soldiers and sending them fleeing.

Magni charged forward, ready to strike down a man armed with a machine gun. He was glad to see the man turn and run. He searched for more enemy combatants, but Modi finished off the last one who decided to stay and fight.

He was ready to enter the building when a fresh batch of soldiers stormed out of the building and opened fire. They went on the defensive once more as Freya put up a shield. The assault was furious, and he could not find an opening.

Magni stared in disbelief at Loki, flanked by his large German bodyguard and the man Dante identified as the former president of Russia. Loki was wearing a sleek black tunic with gold-plated armor, nothing like the clothing typically found in Midgard. He had a sword sheathed by his side and carried his staff.

At long last.

Loki slammed his staff into the ground, splitting it down the middle. Magni jumped for cover to avoid being swallowed by the opening. He was now separated from Modi and Freya, who stood on the other side. Loki opened fire, shooting beams of golden light at Magni. Meanwhile, led by the German, the ground troops opened heavy fire on Modi and Freya.

He hurled Mjolnir at Loki. His aim was true, but Loki reacted quickly, eluding his war hammer. As he was waiting for his hammer to return, Loki blasted shots of light at him from his staff. Magni ducked for cover, nearly falling into the chasm. He was on all fours when he caught Mjolnir on its return flight.

Focused on Loki, he did not notice the giant coming from behind him until Magni was enwrapped in his massive arms. The frost giant was squeezing the life out of him, creating intense pressure on Magni's chest and sternum. Gasping for breath, he could not move. He needed to get his arms free.

Magni was out of breath. The world around him was getting hazy. He had one move left to play. He dropped to his knees, feigning unconsciousness. The giant let him drop, and in the process, he rammed Mjolnir onto the giant's foot.

The giant screamed and released him. Magni collapsed to the floor. His insides felt as if they had gone through a meat grinder. He wanted to get back to his feet to resume the fight, but he lacked the strength. The frost giant was on top of him before he had a chance to recover. He grabbed Magni by the neck and lifted him.

Magni raised his knees and put them between himself and the frost giant. He then wrapped his left leg around his adversary's neck. He clamped his right leg over his left foot, trapping the giant's neck in between his triangulated legs. He squeezed as hard as he could. The giant let go of his neck and tried to pull Magni's legs apart, but he clamped harder, choking the life out of the giant. His opponent fell to one knee as his resistance waned.

After the giant fell unconscious, he let go of the choke hold, since the giant was no longer a threat to him. When he got to his feet, he watched in horror as Freya was lying on the ground. Meanwhile, Modi staggered back, stunned from a blow by Loki. The Trickster drove his sword through Modi's chest. Modi fell to his knees, blood spilling from his mouth.

"No!" Magni shouted.

When the giant had attacked him from behind, Magni assumed Loki would use that as an opportunity to strike him while he was engaged with another foe. Instead, he attacked Modi and Freya, who had their hands full with the assault squad.

In a fit of violent rage, Magni threw Mjolnir full force at Loki. The hammer clipped the top of his head, knocking him to the ground. Had he aimed more carefully, he could have delivered a killing blow, but he had been blinded by anger. By the time his hammer returned to him, the German and the Russian were dragging Loki into the building from which they had come.

Magni caught Mjolnir on a run, leaped over the chasm, and landed next to Freya and Modi. Freya, with a dazed look, slowly got to her knees. She gasped as she stared at Modi.

Magni took his brother in his arms. Modi was spilling blood as he let out a low, wailing moan.

Modi winced and raised himself up slightly. He struggled for breath. "You have to finish this, brother. Kill Loki."

Magni knew he had to kill the bastard, but how could he leave his brother to die?

"Do it," Modi said. "Kill him. It has to be you."

Magni nodded as he fought back tears. "I will." He turned to Freya. "Will you manage here without me?"

Freya nodded. "I will protect Modi and do what I can to heal his wounds." Her eyes betrayed the lack of confidence in that last statement. "You must be the one to kill Loki."

Magni let out a roar. The Trickster had killed his father and grandfather, had destroyed Asgard and Midgard, and had mortally wounded his brother. Humanity was on the brink of collapse. If only he could make Loki suffer a thousand deaths, but one would do.

When the soldiers opened fire again, Freya created a protective shield. She stared up with him, her blue eyes intense and fiery. "Go now. This must end here."

Magni raced into the building with a single focused intent.

***

Backed into a corner, there was nothing left for John Madison to do but fight. Yes, he had avoided the Battle of Ragnarok. Despite what the sons of Thor asserted, that was not an act of cowardice. It was part of his master plan. It had been an inspired move, a master stroke. He was damned good at fighting as evidenced by his slaying of Modi. Too bad he hadn't had enough time to dispose of Freya as well. He wanted to watch her die. It would have to wait until after he disposed of Magni like refuse.

He called Uzelkov on the radio. "Where is he?"

"Coming your way," the Russian responded.

"I'll handle him. Incapacitate the woman. Don't let her join the fight."

"Understood."

He was on the fourth floor of the building. He debated whether or not to go to higher ground.

Klaus said, "I have an idea."

***

Magni had no way of knowing where Loki was hiding. He would have to search this building until he found him. The first three floors revealed nothing. When he climbed the stairs to the fourth floor, he heard movement and conversation. At the top of the stairs, the German was waiting for him, a big smile on his face. Magni saw something in his hand but did not recognize the grenade until the German tossed it in his direction.

Magni jumped down the stairs he had come from, stumbling in the process. The concussive force reverberated through the walls. The sound of the blast was deafening. Cracks opened in the roof above him, and debris fell to the floor.

He waited to make sure that another grenade would not be coming toward him. When he was reasonably confident it was safe to proceed, he stalked up the crumbled steps. At the top of the stairs, he turned the corner and found the German at the end of the hallway. He hurled Mjolnir at him. The German turned the corner and ran. Mjolnir missed his target but smashed the wall.

The building shook. Debris fell from the ceiling, but it still stood.

He ran toward Mjolnir and caught it on the run. With his henchman nearby, Loki could not be far behind. He followed the German's trail but could not find him. He ran to the end of the hallway, turned the corner, and came face to face with Loki. His heart pounded in his chest. This was his chance to finish the Trickster. He raised his hammer and swung at his foe, but

Mjolnir only caught air. He gritted his teeth. It had only been an apparition.

The German stepped out of a room and fired his handgun at Magni. The bullet caught him in the chest. Magni cried out in pain and fell to his knees. The German once more fired at him. Magni hurled his hammer just before another bullet caught him in the shoulder.

Blood dripped from the wound on Magni's shoulder. His armor absorbed most of the impact from the bullet to the chest, but the shot to the shoulder pierced his flesh and exited through the other side. His only solace was that he had struck the German dead. Magni caught his hammer with his good arm. He struggled to his feet, fighting the pain not only from the bullets, but from the myriad of injuries he sustained today.

Loki strode down the hall, a wide grin covering his face. "You have been nothing but a royal pain. I should have killed you long ago, but I will be glad to remedy the situation."

Chapter XLIII

Loki walked with the confidence borne of an assured victory. Granted, he wished he had not had to go through with this challenge to his authority, but killing Magni and Modi—hopefully the last two remaining Aesir—gave him an unrivaled pleasure that was worth the hassle and headache they caused. That still left Freya, and he would deal with her soon enough.

He stood over Magni. "You may play at being the hero, but you're not your father. Thor, well he would have caused me great concern, but my son, Jormangandr, killed him at Ragnarok. With him dead, and Odin laid to waste at the hands of Fenris Wolf, there is no one left to stop me. Certainly not you or your brother. You're both pretenders. You are boys playing a man's game."

Magni reached for Mjolnir, but before he could get his father's hammer, Loki shot a frozen blast from his staff at his hand, causing Magni to scream. It was a gratifying sound.

It was time to finish this pretender. Summoning the magic that resided deep within him, he shot out fireballs from his staff. The blasts scorched the decorated walls of the office building. The glass of a picture frame shattered from the intense heat. Magni summoned Mjolnir, and it reached his hands before the fireball hit him. He swung his hammer in what had to be an act of desperation, but regardless of the intention, his strategy worked as Mjolnir's magic absorbed the fire.

Loki cursed under his breath. That damned hammer. He shouldn't even be able to wield it. Mjolnir belonged to Thor and

Thor alone. Loki had thought about stealing it on occasion in the past, but it would do him no good since he wouldn't be able to wield it. Nobody else but Thor could...until now. Nonetheless, Magni was wounded and even with Mjolnir, he was no match for Loki.

Loki used his staff to shoot out a series of green bolts of energy. Magni got to his knees and once more bounced the blasts off his hammer.

Loki snarled. It would be one thing if Thor came down from Asgard to smite him, but his two sons were insignificant. Yet somehow, they survived the Battle of Ragnarok and found him here in Midgard. They were not even worthy of facing him, yet here Magni was fending off his best attacks.

This time Loki used his magic to generate icy blasts that were sharp as daggers. He sent dozens of them at his foe, trying to overwhelm him, but Magni repelled blast after blast.

Loki screamed in frustration. *Enough of this.* He drew his sword. He would pierce the pretend god's heart with it. He advanced forward, slicing through the air.

Out of nowhere, Magni leapt to his feet, making Loki wonder if he had been feigning injury all along. Loki was the Trickster, not Magni. To be played by him was maddening.

Loki hesitated, but for only a moment. He slashed at Magni with his sword, but Magni moved away in time. Loki slashed at him again, but Magni stepped backward. Before he could take another swipe, Magni tried to smash him with Mjolnir in a clumsy attack that Loki saw coming before his foe even thought about it.

Loki stepped to the right to avoid Mjolnir, then thrust his sword into Magni's exposed rib cage. The Asgardian blade penetrated Magni's armor, and Loki felt the blade ripping through his opponent's flesh. When he pulled back his sword, it was covered in blood.

Loki savored the sight of Magni wincing in pain. He had seen the damage Magni had suffered earlier on the battlefield. A few more well-placed thrusts would end this pretender.

Loki stepped forward only to receive an upward thrust kick that caught him in the jaw. Apparently Magni still had some fight left in him. No matter. Loki was about to give him a killing blow, possibly decapitate him, when a voice from behind startled him.

"Loki!"

He turned. It was Modi, standing in full battle armor. That was impossible.

Loki pulled out his staff, rage building inside of him. He blasted Modi with an icy blast, which went right through him. Loki cursed under his breath. Of course, it had been impossible for Modi to be here, something he realized a little too late.

***

Magni readily admitted he was not much of a sorcerer, but that didn't mean he was completely inept. Most of the time Freya spent teaching him magic in Asgard had been in vain. There was, however, one small piece of magic he had become fairly adept at using. In the most crucial battle of his life, it served him well.

He had projected his brother's image and voice behind Loki. He used this spell to play pranks on his fellow Asgardians from time to time. It was one of a few incantations he had mastered. However, he never thought he would use it in a combat situation.

Loki, who undoubtedly did not think him capable of wielding magic, fell for his trick, giving Magni a few moments respite. He gritted his teeth, got to his feet, twirled Mjolnir, and let his hammer fly.

Loki's eyes went wide as Mjolnir turned end over end as it hurtled toward him. There was no time to react. Loki tried to jump to the side but could not avoid the weapon. Mjolnir smashed him full force in the chest. He folded in half and crumpled to the floor.

Loki let out a low groan. He tried to get to his feet and made it to one knee before collapsing to the floor. Magni slowly walked toward him after catching Mjolnir in its return flight. He felt like a locomotive had run him over, but at this moment, Loki probably felt worse. Loki crawled forward, but Magni's large boot stopped him as he stepped on Loki.

"Please spare me," Loki begged.

Magni shook his head. "You have committed untold crimes against the Aesir. For that alone you deserve to die, but what you have done to the people of Midgard, killing billions of people, is beyond unforgivable. I left Asgard when I should have been grieving for my brothers and sisters, my father, my grandfather, and trying to rebuild our world, but I travelled here instead. I did that for one reason—to stop you.

"You tried to avoid your fate by not showing up to the Battle of Ragnarok, but the funny thing about fate is that it has a habit of catching up to you. You have been living on borrowed time. Goodbye, Loki. You won't be missed." Magni crushed Loki's sternum with Mjolnir and did not stop until Loki was dead.

Chapter XLIV

Magni lifted Loki's dead body and carried it with him. It wasn't enough to claim to have killed Loki. He needed proof. At least for the giants. Prior to exiting the building, he wasn't sure he would make it. He felt drained both physically and mentally, and just wanted this ordeal to be over. He wanted to be back in the plains of Asgard. Before any of that could happen, he had to end this war and begin the process of healing that was desperately needed in Midgard.

Outside the building, the fighting had stopped. The cries of the wounded broke the eerie silence. Modi was still on the ground. Freya hovered over him, working her magic.

He knelt next to the two of them after laying down Loki's corpse. "How is he doing?"

As if in response, Modi opened his eyes. "Did you do it, brother?"

"I did. Loki is dead."

Modi smiled. "I knew you would. It had to be you. Odin was the leader of the Aesir, but father was his warrior. You are more like him than I." Modi closed his eyes.

He turned toward Freya, her face calm and still. "How is he? Will he live?"

Freya hesitated before nodding. "He has stabilized. Your brother is strong."

"It looks like we are both hard to kill."

"What are you going to do now?" Freya asked.

"I need to stop this war. Where is Loki's Russian lackey?"

Freya pointed to the wooded area. "He and his men fled. After I killed a few of them, they decided that fighting me would not be wise for their long-term health. I had to take care of Modi, so I did not give chase."

"Then I will." Still carrying Loki, Magni took to the air above the trees in search of Yuri Uzelkov. With Loki dead, he would be the de facto head of the government forces. He would have to convince Uzelkov that it was no longer worth fighting, that the battle was over. He soared overhead and caught up with a band of humans travelling on foot. In the middle of the group was Yuri Uzelkov.

He swooped down and dropped in front of the group. Before the first soldier drew his gun, Magni took out his knees with a swing from Mjolnir.

He dropped Loki's body in front of them and spoke in Russian. "Your leader is dead." He raised Mjolnir in front of Uzelkov. "You will join him if you do not tell your men to stop fighting immediately. Do we have an understanding?"

Uzelkov looked around before turning back to Magni. He nodded, dropped his rifle, and fell to one knee to accentuate the point. He then yelled out to the other soldiers to drop their weapons.

"Good," Magni said. "I have killed enough of your people already and do not wish to shed more blood. Come with me. You will need to convince the others that they must end this fighting."

Magni did not give any further explanations of his intentions. Instead, he grabbed Uzelkov by the waist. He draped Loki over his shoulder. They flew back to the battlefield where the bloody battle was still raging, although with significantly less intensity. It was hard to tell who was winning the combat, but Magni estimated the losses to be high on both sides.

In an effort to get their attention, Magni began raining lightning across the sky away from the combatants. Dozens of lightning bolts streamed from Mjolnir in a variety of directions, and, before long, the fighting stopped. He landed on an open spot on high ground that would make him visible to most of the combatants. He dropped Uzelkov next to him. He wished he had a vocal projection spell in his arsenal that he could use so everybody could hear him, but he would have to settle on speaking loudly.

The air was filled with the smell of gunpowder, artillery fire, and blood. Limbs and bodies were strewn across the ground. He tossed Loki's body to the ground next to the other corpses. He was no better than the least of them. "John Madison is dead. To the frost and fire giants, the promises he made to you were empty. You were nothing more than a tool to further his goals. His never intended to share wealth and power with you. His aim was to use you as a weapon. Without Madison to tell them otherwise, the humans of Midgard will never abide by you. This isn't your land. If you agree to surrender, I will guarantee your safe return to Muspelheim and Jotunheim where you belong.

"To those who followed John Madison, my fight was never with you. John Madison brought the disease that wiped out most of your population. There is no reason to continue this fight. Madison did nothing but deceive you. He can no longer lie to you. He can no longer hurt you. The only thing left to do is rebuild your world. So many have died already. Why should any more have to? Join me and my brethren in restoring and rebuilding this great land. If you once followed John Madison, we will not hold it against you."

Magni shoved Yuri Uzelkov forward. "Now is your opportunity to convince Madison's forces to stop fighting. I would suggest that you do so as if your life depends upon it, because it does."

Uzelkov glanced back nervously. He scanned the soldiers gathered before them. His English wasn't great but it was passable. "We all made mistakes in this bloody conflict. The biggest one is fight each other to death. We must stop that and come together. Magni speaks truth. Lay down your weapons and embrace your brothers and sisters on other side because there is no other side. We in this together."

Unexpectedly, Uzelkov turned toward Magni to shake his hand. Magni accepted the handshake. Even more surprisingly, the handshake turned into an embrace. He had to give the former Russian president credit; he certainly was making a hard sell on this truce and new partnership. After releasing the embrace, Uzelkov raised Magni's right hand. The men and women on both sides cheered. For better or worse, he had entered into a binding partnership with this duplicitous, murdering bastard. Dante and his mortal friends would have to keep a close eye on him.

Magni pulled him close and spoke in a low tone in his ear. "Well done. Don't even think about turning back on your word. It will not result in a good outcome for you."

"I would never dream of doing such thing. We are partners now. We are friends. We will do great things together."

Magni was not so sure about that last part. Perhaps the Russian would surprise him. He certainly had his doubts about Hector Pedroza, and the reformed gangster turned into a valuable asset.

Dante was making his way toward the hill in which Magni was perched. There were many in between them, so, Magni raised Mjolnir and flew toward him.

The combatants left a space for Magni to land in front of Dante. Magni's friend was bleeding from his forehead. His shirt was torn, and he was covered in dirt.

They embraced. "Is it over, man? I mean, really over?"

Magni nodded. "That was why I had to kill Loki. Without him, what reason would the others have to fight? Midgard will once more belong to the inhabitants of your world."

"I can't possibly thank you enough," Dante said. "And I'm sorry you had to go through all of this, that you had to lose all of those people that you were close with."

Magni nodded. "We all suffered loss, but I made many good friends along the way. At least I have Freya back."

Dante frowned. "What are you talking about?"

"Freya has truly returned. She now knows who she is. You shall see."

"That's fantastic. I can't wait to meet the real Freya," Dante said.

"You will have your opportunity, but I must go. My brother was gravely wounded."

"Then go to him."

Without another word, Magni left the battlefield and flew off to see Modi. He was hopeful since Modi had been conscious and alert when he left. If anyone was capable of healing him, it was Freya. He could only hope Modi would be returning with him to Asgard.

Epilogue

"I realize that we must return to Asgard," Modi said. "I just wish it did not have to be so soon."

Magni could not hold back his laughter. Even though Modi would never admit to it, Magni knew precisely why his brother did not want to leave Midgard. His recovery from the injuries he suffered at Loki's hands had taken a substantial amount of time. Freya had recruited a human physician to assist her with Modi's recovery. She was a physician named Victoria Andrade. Victoria had been born in Brazil and had moved to the United States after graduating from college and medical school. Modi and Victoria had spent a great deal of time together and had gotten quite close.

"There is no reason we can't return to Midgard. That was a mistake we made in the past. We ignored what was happening here, so concerned were we with our own affairs. There are many good people here, and I am sure they will need our help to rebuild."

Modi smiled. "Yes. Our home is Asgard, but we will need to return. These are our people, and we must be their guardians."

"And we have many dear friends here," Magni said.

"Yes, we do."

They walked toward the old United Nations building in New York. Dante chose this building as a command center since they had great communications infrastructure that could be suited to their purpose. From there, they kept in contact with communities from around the globe. They could assess their needs and deploy resources to help them. Much of this would not be possible without Yuri Uzelkov's assistance. He had given them access to the network Loki had created after taking control of Midgard. Thus far, he was fully cooperating. Of course, Magni was still in Midgard, and the threat he posed may be the only thing keeping Uzelkov in line.

Freya met them inside. Magni was not sure how she would feel about leaving Midgard. She undoubtedly had a much different experience here than either he or his brother had since she had been in some mental fugue when she was under the illusion that she was Susanna of Midgard. She could recall little of that time, only vague flashes of memory.

Freya greeted Magni with a long embrace. "What took you so long? The television producers are waiting for you."

"We had many goodbyes to say," Modi replied. "Some took longer than others."

Magni smiled. "I thought Sheila was never going to let go of me."

"I long to return to Asgard," Freya said. "Yet, I am frightened of what is waiting for us there. I have no recollection of what took place after my death. What are things like there?"

Magni sighed. "It will be much different than how you remembered. There weren't many of us left after Ragnarok."

"And so much had been destroyed during the battle," Modi said. "Just like Midgard will have to be remade, so will Asgard, but we Asgardians are a resilient people and we will recover."

It was going to be difficult for Magni to return to Valhalla and see its great halls empty. Freya would not be the only who would have a difficult time adjusting.

Security guards escorted them though the United Nations building. They met Dante, François, and Yuri Uzelkov in the Security Council Chamber. Magni had hardly spoken to Dante since the Battle of Valley Forge. Dante had been so consumed with taking the leadership mantle and fixing all of Midgard's problems that he hardly ate or slept these days. His suit barely hung on his skinny frame.

Magni clasped hands and hugged Dante and François, while he gave Uzelkov a firm handshake.

"I really wish you guys didn't have to go," Dante said. "I could use your help. What you three could accomplish here is amazing."

"I appreciate the sentiment," Magni said. "But we don't belong in Midgard."

"And just as you have much work to do," Modi said, "We also have work to do. Rest assured, we will be back and we will assist you in any way we can. Not to mention that there is a certain female physician who would miss me terribly if I did not return."

"You're always welcome here," Dante said. "There will always be a place for you. We have a debt to you that we can never repay."

"Let us not speak of debts. Make Midgard a place that we will look forward to returning to," Magni said.

"And thanks for agreeing to speak to the people of the world," Dante said. "There's so much strife and problems around the globe, I think it will do people a lot of good to hear from you."

"Yes," Magni said. "But I will not be speaking. My brother will be delivering a speech of hope and peace. He is a far better orator than I."

Dante patted Modi in the back. "In this case, I thank you for doing this. It's important to the people. Across the globe, everybody knows who you are. They know what you've done for us."

The show would be seen live on television and the Internet. The producers prepared Modi for his appearance. Magni enjoyed watching the preparation. A woman was attempting to apply powder on his cheeks, but Modi kept pulling away from her.

She raised her hands. "But you need this to show up better on the screen. Trust me. I've been working on television broadcasts for twenty years."

Magni laughed. Better Modi than him.

He held Freya's hand as they watched Modi give his speech.

"People of Midgard, you have looked into the face of death and destruction, and you have survived," Modi began. "The tragedies that you have experienced are unprecedented in your history. You have been tested time and time again, and you have shown remarkable resiliency. For that I commend you. I stand here in admiration of the inner strength and courage your people have demonstrated. You have persevered and will emerge stronger than when you started.

"The tyrant is dead. No longer will you be subjugated by a wicked oppressor. You will be able to direct your own future.

But let this be a lesson for this world and all worlds. I think of all the blood that has been shed, all the lives lost." Modi paused. "This must stop. I have been bred as a warrior since I was a godling on the plains of Asgard, but I wish for nothing more than to put away my sword and spear and never have to use them again. That is what we must all strive for. And that is the challenge I pose for each of you listening to me today. Rebuild society with fairness and care for human life without resorting to the violence that has plagued us in the past. It is that same spirit and attitude that my brother, Freya, and I will use when we return to our home."

Freya turned to Magni, a tear in her eye. "I don't know if I will be able to handle returning to Asgard. My brother. I'll never see him again. So much has been lost."

Magni held her hand. "I know. The toll you have paid is a great one."

Tears streamed down Freya's face. "What happened to me? I died at Ragnarok. How am I here?"

Magni shook his head. "It is as much a mystery to me as it is to you. Perhaps one day we will visit the Norns, and they could provide us insight. All I know is one thing—you are the reason I am still alive and we are here today. We were all but defeated at the Battle of Valley Forge until you rose like a phoenix from the ashes in a beautiful and blinding display of power unlike anything I have ever witnessed. It was a glorious site to behold. I don't know how it happened, but in the time of humanity's greatest need, you were there for them, just as you have always been there for me."

He wiped the tears from her eyes. "And I will need you again as we rebuild Asgard. Modi will assume Odin's role as the leader of the Aesir."

"He will?" Freya asked.

"We had already decided this before leaving Asgard. He is more suited for the role, and I will be his warrior just as Thor was to Odin. Hopefully, I will not have to fight to defend our world. But I can only assume this type of great responsibility with you at my side. Will you be with me?"

"Of course I will."

Magni put an arm around her shoulder. She had yet to have the opportunity to fully grieve, but she would in time just as he would. "Ragnarok isn't about destruction. It's about renewal. The restart of life, and we'll be there to forge it together."

Beyond the Shadow
By Carl Alves

Beyond the Shadow is a terrifying journey into a world where reality and what lay beyond is blurred.

All around ten year old Jared, people are dying at the hands of a killer that nobody can see. Only he is spared. No matter where he goes, people are massacred. Nobody is safe. There is no sanctuary. As the lines between our world and those beyond converge, Jared learns more about the father he has never known, who died before he was born. Jared's mom and Detective Chaney will do anything to protect him and stop the killer, but Jared knows that he is the only one that could stop this spectral murderer. Mirrors lead from our world to the next and are the key to ending this madness. But can anyone stop a psychotic fiend who doesn't obey the rules of the natural world?

The Invocation
By Carl Alves

The Invocation is a thrilling combination of Stranger Things and The Exorcist.

When Kenna Trigg plays with an Ouija board, little does she know that she is about to unleash a malevolent spirit upon the world, leaving her and her older brother, Jake, to stop the spirit as it leaves a trail of dead bodies in its wake.

In The Invocation, a supernatural thriller, Kenna Trigg and three of her friends from the fourth grade manage to befriend a spirit named Mia, who died in her late teens in a drowning accident, using of an Ouija board. Cotter, a malevolent spirit who had been a con-man and criminal in life, tricks Kenna and her friends into releasing him into our world by posing as Mia. Cotter has the ability to take control and possess people he comes across. With this new power, he begins a vicious crime spree. Kenna turns to her older brother, Jake, a professional mixed-martial artist who has recently been released from prison. Now, Kenna and Jake must stop Cotter from unleashing havoc in our world.

Battle of the Soul
By Carl Alves

Andy Lorenzo has no family, few friends, poor social skills, and drinks and gambles far too much. But in a time when demons are becoming increasingly more brazen and powerful, he has one skill that makes demons cower in fear from him—he is the greatest exorcist the world has ever known.

In *Battle of the Soul*, a supernatural thriller that is a combination of Constantin and The Exorcist, since graduating high school Andy has left a long trail of demons in his wake while priests are dying while performing traditional rites of exorcism. Andy is the Church and society's ultimate weapon in combating this growing epidemic. He needs no bibles, prayers, or rituals. Andy is capable of going inside the person's soul where he engages in hand-to-hand combat using his superhuman abilities that only reside when he is in a person's soul. When eight-year-old Kate becomes possessed, Andy finds an elaborate trap waiting for him. He will do whatever it takes to win the most important fight of his life—the battle for Kate's soul.

"Ready for a lighthearted Battle of the Soul? Andy Lorenzo's got the requisite exorcism skills, but he's no single-minded zealot nor cynical bleak arts practitioner. He gets the biz done with a deft touch and a wink and a nod to family values. It's not John

Constantine here but try Cary Grant in Monkey Business. Battle of the Soul is a fine, fun supernatural read! — Mort Castle, Bram Stoker Award Winning Author of The Strangers

About the Author

Carl is the author of eight published novels which span the horror, fantasy, and science fiction genres in no particular order. He lives in Central Pennsylvania with his wife and the two most awesome boys you have ever met. When not feverishly conjuring stories about monsters, aliens, and things that go bump in the night, he works as a quality manager for a medical device company. Find out more about him by visiting his website at www.carlalves.com.

Printed in Great Britain
by Amazon